ALL WHO WANDER

A NOVEL

JOE CLIFFORD

SQUARE tire books

Square Tire Books, Austin, TX.
Book cover by Christian Storm

Author contact: joe@joeclifford.com

First Edition 2023

This book is dedicated to Erik Zalkin,
the best civil engineer (and most mediocre golfer) I know.

CHAPTER ONE

January 8, 1998, 1:24 a.m.
The Morning of the Disappearance

Sitting in a bitter and desolate roadside motel parking lot in Briarboro, Vermont, just over the border from Massachusetts, Brooke Mulcahy used the flickering motel sign to read the tattered gas station map. Oil stains, creases, and Native American etymology wasn't making it easy. Snow slanted through lamplight splashing down from tall poles. The winds picked up. The late hour meant all the rooms were silent. Judging by the lack of cars in the parking lot, there weren't many guests registered. Then the motel sign flickered once more and went dark for good. Brooke had never felt more alone.

The motel billboard advertised cheap rates. Given the time, she considered calling it a night. Get a room and some rest, resume her journey in the morning. If she gave into the fatigue now, she might change her mind later. It had taken too long to decide to leave. Clearheaded rest might impede the inspiration. She had to keep going.

The weather report projected a furious swath passing through the Berkshires en route to Cape Cod, where a low-pressure system and rapid drop in atmospheric pressure predicted a bomb cyclone. A Nor'easter on steroids. The front wasn't supposed to be this high up, targeting Eastern Mass, Boston, and Rocky Cove, her hometown, the shoreline, coasts, and beaches. The weather report got it wrong.

She thought she'd gotten out ahead of it. Brooke hadn't been on the road long before heavy snow started to fall. Not enough time had passed to put sufficient distance behind her. Brooke didn't want to be driving blind in a snowstorm without any idea where she was going. Each minute she waited was another minute wasted.

Pick a destination.

Smoothing the wrinkled map on the dash, Brooke zeroed in on Niagara Falls and the greater Buffalo area. She remembered vacationing there with her mother and father before everything fell apart. The trip was one of the few pleasant memories she held onto. She wasn't wedded to the region, and was also considering Chittenden, Winooski, and the tinier, insignificant dots on the map like Ashton, New Hampshire. She didn't give a shit. *North.* That's what the little voice in her head kept repeating. She'd venture into Canada if she had to. Brooke hadn't brought any documentation with her. Did she need paperwork to cross the border? No, Canada didn't require passports, did they? She was pretty sure they didn't. Brooke hadn't thought this through. Not really. Not well. For months—and these last few weeks in particular—the desire to get out of Rocky Cove had been weighing on her. The *need* to leave, however, had come on fast and undeniable, the culmination of a crushing defeat on the heels of a lifetime of disappointment, a final push past the tipping point and over the edge. Then again, it hadn't taken much. Brooke believed in signs, in fate. Be open and receive the call. She got it last night. So she packed a few clothes, important medications like birth control pills and antidepressants, sentimental belongings—necklace, old letters from her mom. She made one last stop to see the only person who mattered, her best friend Aaron, promising that she'd be back. It's not a lie if you believe it.

Near the motel walkway, Brooke spied a pay phone. She considered calling Aaron once more. By now Mike had to be on the hunt, raging and out of control, and sooner or later he'd go to Aaron. Which was why she couldn't tell him where she was going. If he didn't know, then he didn't have to lie. Mike hated Aaron. It didn't matter what she said, how she and Aaron were just friends (Brooke *wished* she thought of Aaron that way). Mike was jealous of their relationship. If he thought Aaron knew something, he'd beat the shit out of him first, ask questions later. Mike could already be at Aaron's, waiting for her to call. She couldn't risk it.

There's no such thing as a quick fix. Geographical cures don't work—Brooke had picked up that much in her classes and training. At least you give yourself a fighting chance. Rocky Cove, Massachusetts, wasn't the mean streets. She'd grown up in a stolid middle-class neighborhood. That didn't mean she had it easy. Everyone has a story. And Brooke didn't want hers ending with another used-up girl, clutching her fading beauty like smoke, getting nailed against dumpsters behind townie bars.

There was a span, right around graduation, where Brooke felt genuine hope. She'd be going to college. The first one in her family. No Mulcahy had ever gone to college. Generations of Mulcahys were born to toil in factories and die unfulfilled. She didn't care that it was a state school, or that she wasn't sure what degree she wanted (nursing seemed as good a guess as any). Brooke was breaking the cycle. And that felt like progress. She had a direction, and by moving forward, she'd be leaving something behind. There was nothing left worth holding onto in Rocky Cove.

Brooke's problems didn't begin when her mother left. But they got worse when Connie returned. Brooke was sixteen when Connie came back, out of the blue, brand new baby brother Bobby in tow, as if ten minutes had passed and not ten years. Of course, Paul wasn't turning her away—her father never loved anyone else. And that was before Connie told them she was sick. Eleven months later, she'd be gone again, this time for good, the cancer finally delivering Connie to Jesus and that eternal life she craved. All Brooke got out of the deal was Bobby, a cross-eyed interloper who'd been nothing but a pain in her ass since day one.

Brooke knew she couldn't pin everything wrong on her bastard half-brother. She'd been going down a bad path for a while, too many drugs, bad guys and worse decisions digging a deeper hole. Now she was so low down, covered in dirt, suffocating—recovery was a pipe dream. There was no one person to blame. Not Mike. Not Bobby. Not Connie or Paul, not her married basketball coach, Rod Collins. This moment, this snowy night, presented a bona fide crossroads—a head-on collision in the ongoing war between the two distinct parts of Brooke Mulcahy: the one that was screwing up, and the one that knew she could do better.

Brooke was tired of thinking about where it all went wrong. Who cares about the exact order of events? Born under a bad sign, rotten luck, shit circumstance, this guy or that, sex turning the male species into lunatics. She was still stuck outside a low-rent roadside motel at close to two in the morning, one state over, and not feeling any safer. Stasis equaled surrender.

It doesn't matter where the time goes. So long as it's gone.

The map showed Route 23 was a quicker shot than Interstate 91. The rural road should be clear of traffic this time of night. Ice started mixing with the frigid rain, joining the snowy slop dumping buckets of muck, slicking the streets and speeding up the clock. Brooke pulled off the shoulder and back onto the road.

With each mile, Brooke felt as though she were being lifted from the earth, unburied, dirt washed off and sprayed clean, rebirthed. Ascending, she felt her throat open, passageways unblocked. Even though it was a blizzard, Brooke unrolled the window, stuck out her head, and inhaled deep. The icy air tasted sweet.

Rescued from the grave, she could breathe again.

CHAPTER TWO

NOW

The radiator clanks, water in old pipes gurgles, and the heater thrums back to life. Fake ficus leaves tremble beneath the soft billow of tepid air. I stare off into space trying to both remember and forget. I'm so sick of talking about where it all went wrong.

"Robert?" Dr. Amy says, as if I've been slacking.

I've run out of things to say. Twenty-plus years of the same routine, rehashing tragic upbringings and paying a stranger to listen to you complain. You can't reinvent the wheel, and no one needs another origin story. My stepsister—my half-sister Brooke—disappeared one snowy night over two decades ago. Talking about her fifty minutes each week isn't bringing her back. I'll never know what happened, how badly it ended for her. The only thing state troopers found: Brooke's abandoned, cracked-up car on the side of a snowy rural road. No tracks. No body. Nothing. The blizzard that sent her car careening in a ditch was the worst in years. After this long without a single lead, I've given up on closure.

I catch Dr. Amy glancing at the tiny clock on her table, a tip-off our time is up. She turns over her notepad, purses lips, and furrows brow. I can't help but feel I've let her down. Like all my mental health practitioners, Dr. Amy focuses with such intent, trying to coax the words out of me, as if she can crack the deepest reaches of my subconscious through will alone. I wish it were that easy.

"We need to stop," she says, before passing along a folded piece of paper, a tally for the past month and a half of attempting to locate the underlying source of my discontent.

I write the check, tear away the two-hundred-dollar co-pay, and nod a terse goodbye. I step into the blustery parking lot. The January winds stir, threatening the worst is yet to come. Upstate New York this time of year is nothing but one storm after another. Where I live, in the valley of Diemen, cold rain breaks up the spurts of snowstorms. Miserable. My cell buzzes. My wife Stephanie has my schedule down to the minute.

"Hey, hon," I say, sliding on the iPhone, tapping the remote to unlock my Porsche, a recent purchase and the nicest thing I've ever splurged on, celebrating what's been a great year.

"There's a write-up about the awards dinner in the *Times Union*." She says this lacking enthusiasm. I don't let the apathy hurt my feelings. There is a natural competition in any marriage. When one shines, it's difficult for the other not to feel overshadowed. Stephanie brought her own money into the marriage—she's never lacked. But inheriting wealth and securing professional success are different beasts. Not that being a civil engineering professor is the mountaintop.

Since our son Peter was born, the precipitating event that cemented a lifelong partnership, Stephanie has been a stay-at-home mom. Now that Peter is almost thirteen, she could go back to work if she wanted to. She also doesn't need to.

Before I feel guilty about the grant, I remind myself I've earned it.

I settle into the stiff leather bucket seat, fire up the car, and wait for the butt warmers to work their magic. There is a lag before the call switches over to the sound system, downtime I use to plan the order of errands I must complete before tonight's ceremony.

"Did you hear me?" My wife's voice booms over the car's speakers.

I turn down the volume, forgetting having been engrossed by NPR and *All Things Considered.* "I'm leaving the doctor's," I say. She, of course, knows this. I allow the engine to idle, calmed by the purr of pristine, finely tuned German craftmanship. Regardless of a lifetime in therapy, I know I can be knocked off my axis without much effort— that raging little boy still lurks in there somewhere. "I'll be home—"

"I don't know how smart it is for them to keep broadcasting something like that."

"Like what?" I pat my pockets, seized by panic when I can't find my phone. Only to realize it's in my hand, which makes me chuckle to myself over both how absentminded I can be, and how dependent we've become on these damn things. A car backfires up the street, and even though Dr. Amy's office is in a nice section of town, I flinch. One of the unfortunate hallmarks of the type A personality: being wound tighter than a drum.

"How much money you are receiving," my wife says.

"It's an NEH award, Steph. We're not talking MacArthur." I try not to groan having to defend the obvious. I know my wife is playing devil's advocate. Academia can be a prickly place, with so many hungry mouths to feed fighting for limited morsels. Even at an upscale university like Uniondale, these awards are few and far between and hard fought to secure. The amount of money is rare for a scholarly venture; however, that is not the real allure. The prize comes with a sabbatical, granting that rarest of commodities: time.

I switch on the wipers to clear away the raindrops and fat snowflakes that have already begun to melt. "Civil engineering lands a long way from rock star," I say, attempting levity, shifting into reverse, centering the camera. "This is dull, pedagogical research."

Stephanie sighs and tells me to drive safely. I hang up, steering down slick side streets, as I make my way to the office. Even though Uniondale is on winter break, I don't deviate from my daily schedule. I'd planned to get a start on the book but find my mind circling back to this morning.

As always, I woke before Stephanie, who likes to remain in a warm, toasty bed with thick comforters and high thread counts for as long as humanly possible. I prepared as quietly as I could, slinking downstairs and into the kitchen. There I found the boy, loading up his backpack for the day. Peter bobbed his head, the teenage version of hello, which is all I can expect from his age. Recent outbursts notwithstanding, Peter is far more self-assured than I was at thirteen. Of course, I didn't grow up with the stability we've given him. This has been one of my life's greatest achievements: breaking the cycle. Peter will never have to wonder where he will be sleeping tonight, if there will be enough to eat; he will never have to live in a house with one parent absent, questioning whether the other loves him.

As I made my coffee, we were aware of one another's presence but did not speak, two separate entities moving about this shared space, alone but together. This silent awareness comforted but also filled me with a pervasive sadness—the inevitable extraction, the father losing his son who was once dependent on him for everything; the son who, like all boys, once viewed his father as the strongest man in the world. Now that he is older, Peter can see I am just another man. We watched *Die Hard* together before Christmas. Just he and I. A special treat, since he's underage and it's rated R. He seemed to enjoy it. So, it's not like we don't have our moments.

Before he left this morning, our eyes met. That was our entire exchange, surrounded by ticking clocks, percolating coffee, and knives scraping across toasted bread, wordless. I don't know why I am reviewing the interaction through such a melancholic lens. We are still father and son. We remain close in our own way—we have dinner together most nights—but he is on his way to being his own man, going the route I once did, where he will have to face difficult situations and make hard choices, some that have dire, life-altering consequences; and that is a hard concept for a father to accept. Because it works the other way too, that dependency.

By the time I head up the stairwell to my office, I'm gripped in the throes of despondency. Time has coalesced these worrisome, fretful thoughts.

Work is the great distractor. Pulling up a folder on the computer, I prepare to dive into the project the NEH is paying me handsomely for. I have several ideas for where to start—I've researched the project for months, compiling extensive outlines, motifs, and conceits that will show how cities, ancient and modern, are living, breathing entities. That's my thesis: the reciprocal relationship between man and his creation. The possibilities are endless. I am so excited; I can't contain my enthusiasm.

Before I get a word on the page, I realize someone is watching me.

A young woman stands in my doorway. She possesses a vague familiarity, though I know she is not a student. It's the raven-black hair and penetrating green eyes, the way they seem to be able to stare through me. Also, how tall she is—thin, sinewy. Like Lori Singer in that old Kevin Bacon film from the 1980s, *Footloose*. She must be at least five foot ten. Déjà vu. That's what I will say later, when I look back and reflect on a moment no longer defined by the present, because time isn't always linear. It can loop back on itself, reshaping moments, altering our perceptions, until we, quite literally, rewrite our own history.

"Bobby?" she says. "Er, um, Mr. Kirby?"

I take off my glasses, blink, a pointless delay of the inevitable. A part of me knows what is coming next. Because I have replayed this by now, returned to the moment, processed what she is about to say, her having already said it; it's been sorted and slotted into its appropriate mental file.

"Yes," I reply with professional decorum. "I am Dr. Kirby." There is no one else on the department floor. The university is still on winter recess. It is doubtful anyone else is in Willard Hall. We are not a commuter school, Uniondale a ghost town over the long breaks. "How can I help you?"

The girl shuffles, bites her lip, checks down the hallway as if listening for footsteps that will not come. I feel like I am looking at a ghost.

"My name is Lily," she says, stilted. "I'm your—I'm your sister Brooke's daughter."

CHAPTER THREE

December 12, 1997, 5:03 p.m.
Twenty-Eight Days Before the Disappearance

Brooke sat by the window in her bedroom upstairs. Pristine flurries floated through streetlamp halos, fighting against a day's dying light. Bundled boys and girls hurled snowballs at vehicles returning home to two-car driveways. Joyous voices squealed. To most, Rocky Cove represented the American Dream. Not Brooke.

The suburb outside Boston was a fine place to grow up; a regular town where regular folks worked their butts off all week. Weekends packed with beer, football games, and grilled meats. It was also stifling. Every few blocks sported a different Catholic Church, multiplate variations of brownstone. Inside, stiff Parson Brown sermons urged you to accept less than you want, forget about desire, and be grateful for the opportunity too. Humility. Piety. Take your hits in this life—your suffering will be rewarded in the next. For now, it was factories, mills, and warehouses. Mortgages, utility bills, and health insurance. During your spare time, you work on that project in the garage, popping pills each morning like her father, praying your back held up. These were the subjects Springsteen could make sound romantic. The working-class hero who'd one day walk in the sun. Maybe. But until then life sucked.

Brooke could hear Bobby downstairs in the kitchen, stuffing his face as usual. She had no clue how he paid for the Doritos, Cheetos, and other junk food he bought at the corner market, stashing packages throughout the house like a chubby, neurotic squirrel. At fourteen, the kid didn't have a job, and her dad, Paul, wasn't generous with cash. Spare change scavenged from the couch? What did she care what the kid ate? Let him swell up to the size of a whale.

When Bobby first came to live with them, Brooke tried to be excited. An only child her entire life, she suddenly had a sibling. An actual brother, another human being who shared the same blood and genetic material. They'd share thoughts and feelings and have to bond, right? She couldn't stand the kid.

The circumstances that delivered Bobby into their lives were as strange as Bobby himself. After ten years of nothing but the occasional letter or postcard, her mother Connie was back, standing on their porch with her new son. Brooke never got the chance at resentment or reconciliation, her mother's body already riddled with the cancer.

The end came quick. Less than a year. Then it was just Bobby, the brother she didn't know and who, no matter how hard she tried, couldn't connect with. The more time Brooke spent with Bobby, the more she wondered if something was wrong with him. Like mentally, when your mother drinks or uses throughout a pregnancy. The kid wouldn't meet your eyes when you talked to him, gazing everywhere but. Like Tom Cruise's brother in that movie *Rain Man*. Bobby wasn't stupid. He could do weird shit well, like fix broken stereos or other electronics. He'd spend hours constructing intricate LEGO configurations, *Star Wars* and wizards, nerd stuff, mammoth undertakings with tens of thousands of tiny pieces. Boys that age were supposed to be staring at pictures of naked girls and whacking it in the bathroom, not erecting elaborate spaceships and castles. There must be an official diagnosis for whatever was wrong with him. Before dropping out of Midfield State—"dropping out" was melodramatic, more like she stopped going—Brooke had been enjoying her studies, in particular all the ways the human brain could break. Around Thanksgiving, Brooke started to get depressed. Maybe she was broken too.

Brooke headed into the kitchen, reminding herself to be kind. *Don't be a bitch.* Soon as her bare feet touched cold linoleum and she saw the chunky thing shoveling cereal into his piehole, milk dribbling down his chin, coke bottle glasses crooked, Brooke knew she'd break that promise. Every time she saw his face, Brooke remembered her dead mother and the years stolen from her. That wasn't Bobby's fault. He was the only one left to blame.

"Hey, fecto," she said, rounding the corner. That was her nickname for Bobby, short for "defective." Brooke knew it was mean. Sometimes she felt bad calling him that. She never settled on a better nickname, and bad habits are hard to break.

Bobby pushed the glasses on his nose, peering through unruly tangles of hair, fidgeting. The wooden kitchen chair creaked beneath his hefty frame. The house was cold—her father griped about higher bills in the winter. Bobby's soft flesh was clammy, dampened with flop sweat. From ten feet away, she could see flesh glistening.

Outside, snow fell. Brooke leaned against the counter, stretching taller. Golden light shimmered in small, distant squares, happy families seated around the dinner table. Brooke didn't know where she inherited her height. Not from Connie, who was five-five in heels—and her super religious mother never wore heels. At five feet ten, Brooke was nearly as tall as Paul, whose height was impossible to determine—her dad had abysmal posture, shoulders and spine rounded, contorting him

hunched over, a tormented James Dean minus the cool. His mainte-
nance job at Logan Airport tore his spine to shreds. For a while, Brooke
played basketball. She was good. For a while, she thought it was her
ticket out of here. Until she fucked that up, too.

Stretching, Brooke could almost reach the ceiling. She felt vertebra
crack. And Bobby's lingering stare. Brooke doubted the boy ever saw a
real woman up close.

Brooke made for the liquor cabinet, plucking the key from the
teacup on the windowsill—an obvious hiding spot. She poured vodka
into a tall glass, splashing orange juice. Brooke paid as many bills as
Paul—anything in this house was hers too. Still, she winked at her
baby brother, finger to mouth. Their secret.

"I need you to do me a favor," Brooke said sweetly, coming up
behind Bobby and tucking an unruly lock of hair, feigning an attempt
at sisterly affection.

Bobby peered up through his thick glasses.

"If Mike calls tonight, tell him I wasn't feeling well and went to bed
early."

"Why?"

"None of your business." It was a simple request. "Jesus, Bobby. Can
you do this for me or not?" Brooke gave her best fake pout. "Please,
baby brother?"

Brooke adored Aaron Reardon. As a friend. And they'd been *best*
friends since they shared a cubby in kindergarten, when Aaron used to
bring Brooke extra Oreos. He was the first person she called with good
news, and the one she leaned on most when it was bad. Aaron came
from a good family. The guy was wicked smart too, enrolled at Tufts,
majoring in finance. He made no secret he was crazy about Brooke. But
the heart wants what the heart wants.

Tonight, they'd made plans to hang out at the Fun Zone, the low-rent amusement park on the outskirts of town, which featured go-karts, batting cages, putt-putt golf, and an arcade. Something was *always* out of service at the Fun Zone. Off the causeway, the amusement park sat on the edge of a sludgy pond. In the winter, go-kart operation was suspended. No one used the batting cages, and it was too cold outside to play miniature golf. Aaron ordered a large pizza and exchanged cash for quarters.

Most of the arcade games were knock-offs from the '80s—*Lock 'n' Chase* instead of *Pac-Man*, *Alien Attack* not *Space Invaders*. When parts broke, they didn't get replaced, the carcasses of these old games carted off to electronic graveyards. People from Rocky Cove seldom went to the Fun Zone, unless it was poorer families that didn't know better. Which was half the appeal, having the run of the place, not getting recognized by anyone from school.

It was supposed to be kitschy laughs for Brooke and Aaron, even if they were the only ones in on the joke. Except tonight, Brooke wasn't having much fun.

"What's wrong?" Aaron asked as they strolled, arm in arm, bellies full of pizza but still sharing a box of popcorn, Brooke's head on his shoulder. Inside the musty old arcade, lingering diesel from turnpike traffic failed to evoke holiday spirit.

Brooke didn't want to discuss her depression. Aaron would ask what she was depressed *about*. And it wasn't like that. Though Brooke had plenty of reasons. Post-graduation life wasn't going as planned. In high school, she told everyone how she'd leave Rocky Cove. A college dropout working part time at the nursing home didn't constitute living well.

Unwilling to give up on the night, Brooke led Aaron by the hand to *Street Fighter II*, the Fun Zone's sole concession to anything modern, forcing a big smile on her face, as if Aaron had misunderstood her mood. Usually, she'd show off in the batting cages, Brooke's natural athleticism allowing her to hit the fastest pitches. With the cages out of commission, she'd have to settle for kicking his ass digitally.

After Aaron coasted to three easy victories, he stopped punching buttons, grabbing his oldest friend by the shoulders, and forcing her to meet his eyes. "What's up?"

"Nothing."

"You look upset."

"I'm not upset."

"Is it Mike?"

"Everything isn't about Mike Rakowski." Brooke wasn't lying. The Fun Zone was *their* spot—she would *never* come here with Mike. In fact, Brooke hadn't thought of getting high or drunk all night, which was how she suffered Mike's company. "I broke up with him."

"How many times does this make?" Aaron rolled his eyes, nudging her ribs. The playful jab failed to land.

Aaron wasn't wrong. Brooke had broken up with Mike dozens of times. They never made a conscious decision to get back together. It just … happened. Maybe that's what Aaron read on her face. Resignation. Defeat. The inevitability of it all.

"No," she said, firm. "This time it's over, for good."

Brooke slapped the joystick and headed outside.

Traffic on the causeway zipped past, people in transit, moving onto better things. At the chain link, Brooke clasped fingers to cold steel, staring through the cage over the snowy embankment, counting the cars, trucks, and buses. Aaron came up beside her.

"Talk to me," he said.

Brooke studied the racing streaks of red, white, and yellow, one long tracer light. How easy it would be to climb over this fence and step in front of one of those barreling tractor-trailers. She wasn't suicidal. Death didn't have to be morbid. More like she could turn out a light, go to sleep, and not wake up. The thought was comforting.

They stood in silence. Brooke could feel Aaron trying to extract a response.

"I don't know what I'm doing with my life," she said.

"No one does."

"You had your major picked out in seventh grade."

"I like finance."

"What am I going to do?"

"Is that what you're worried about?" Aaron threw his arm around her. "I'm going into *finance*. I'll take care of you."

Brooke smiled at the joke. Aaron wasn't joking. It wasn't a bad offer. She *did* love Aaron. They'd made a pledge that if neither of them was married by thirty, they'd marry each other. There were worse things than being married to your best friend. Maybe she could learn to be attracted to him? Except ... the heart wants what the heart wants.

After that, the night was beyond salvaging.

Aaron dropped her off, the house dark, no lights on, inside or out. Flurries drifted as they sat in the front seat of his car. Already hopeless, Brooke felt worse, like she'd let down her friend. She made to open the door when Aaron said hold up. He slipped in a disc and "Mambo No. 5" came over the stereo. The Lou Bega song was her cure-all. Of course, Aaron knew that, which helped fuel the smile—he knew her so well. They started singing along, making silly faces, fingers waggling in the air, which cracked them both up—Aaron could be such a goofball. When the song ended, "Un-Break My Heart" by Toni Braxton slipped on. Brooke realized it was a mix CD for her. Brooke seamlessly switched from jaunty mambo to a slow, sexy lip sync serenade, which made Aaron laugh harder.

Out the windshield, Brooke caught Bobby upstairs watching. Though it was dark, she could make out his plump shadow. Peeping Tom pervert.

Brooke didn't get a chance to be angry before the truck skidded into the driveway, brakes screeching to a halt.

Mike Rakowski exited his Ford, storming toward them, baseball bat by his side. He ripped open the driver's side door, hand wrapped around Aaron's coat collar. Mike tried dragging him out of the driver's seat, but the seat belt tangled and twisted, restraining Aaron. Frustrated, Mike flung the baseball bat, using both hands to yank harder.

"Stop, Mike!"

Mike didn't stop. He also couldn't figure out how to get Aaron out of the seat. With Aaron hanging half upside down, Mike proceeded to punch and kick his kidneys, ribs, sternum, and face, any exposed body part. Shrieking, Aaron didn't put up a fight, covering up, crying, taking it.

"Mike!" Brooke shouted, leaning across Aaron's lap, which didn't help.

Aaron's inability to defend himself only pissed off Mike more. By now Brooke had gotten out of the car, running over, punching Mike in the back. Aaron's unwillingness to engage sucked up all the fun. Mike hoisted the bloodied and bruised mess back in the driver's seat.

"Get the fuck out of here!" Mike hollered as a battered and humiliated Aaron managed to shut the door, get his hands on the wheel, and flee, fishtailing into the black night. A few neighbors' lights switched on.

Mike directed his anger at Brooke. "Have fun being a whore?"

"We're just friends! And you don't own me!" She turned up the walkway to go inside. Brooke was so sick of Mike and his possessive bullshit—they weren't even dating! She'd made it to the stairs before Mike ran up behind her, snaring her jacket, causing Brooke to lose her footing. Slipping on the ice, she smacked her head on the hard ground.

Brooke and Mike had gotten in plenty of fights over the years. Their relationship was defined by drunken shouting matches and bottles thrown. This was the first time Mike had put his hands on her, physically assaulted her.

Brooke lay on the frozen floor, feeling split in two. Brooke prided herself on her toughness. She'd never backed down from Mike, never felt the need to acquiesce. For the first time since she knew Mike, Brooke feared for her safety.

The screen door nudged open. Mike spun around and kicked it shut, catching Bobby's fingers in the door, causing him to wail.

Her little brother's intervention, however feeble, snapped Mike out of his rage.

Mike stalked down the walkway, grabbed his bat, and broke for his truck, fleeing like Aaron had moments earlier.

As long as she stayed in Rocky Cove, Brooke knew she would never be free of Mike.

CHAPTER FOUR

NOW

"Well," I say, "this is a surprise." Which is understating the obvious. Last thing I expected when I left the house this morning was meeting a girl claiming to be my dead sister's daughter. I can't be having this conversation. Not now, not ever.

I jump up from my seat and gather my belongings—laptop case, winter coat, patting pockets for the keys I already hold in my hand. I glance around the office for other possessions that don't exist.

The girl looks understandably baffled.

"I would love to catch up," I say, glancing at the clock, its oversized black hands dragging. "Unfortunately," I add, laughing at an incomplete joke, "the thing is ..."

"Lily."

"Lily," I repeat. Saying her name aloud sounds inauthentic, like when a non-Latino forces the Spanish accent. "I have somewhere to be." Then to bolster the validity of my claim, I add, "I am receiving an award tonight. I need to stop at the dry cleaners before they close." That is not a lie. Those details are true. I need my suit.

The young lady pulls the letter from her purse.

"It's from your sister," she says, passing it along.

I recognize the handwriting, which is Brooke's. Or made to *look* like it. No salutation. First clue. It's addressed to no one in particular. It's short, a day in the life. Casual—too casual. Second clue. I read the letter, which contains references to specific, major events that took place *after* Brooke went missing—9/11 and the 2004 tsunami—pop culture moments shoehorned in to timestamp the missive as proof Brooke didn't die that night in 1998. Third clue. Like when a film wants to establish an era, showing a newspaper headline, alluding to that year's winning World Series team. The insistence to do so is clumsy and heavy-handed. For instance, the line about the tsunami: Brooke feels overwhelmed because "such is life in a post-9/11 world." Brooke would *never* say that. And no one writes or speaks in such metaphors. These allusions are too rehearsed, too focus group tested. I get it. The letter was penned *after* Brooke disappeared.

"I found that letter when I was cleaning out her belongings." Lily pauses, forlorn and lachrymose. "After she passed away."

Died? Convenient. Fourth clue this girl is full of it.

I have a part to play. There is no way around it. I can't call her a liar, not yet. I'm not up for a confrontation, and since I can't dismiss my sister's death, I must say, "I'm sorry." And, "When did she pass?"

"Two years ago. She was first diagnosed back in twenty-ten. She was in remission."

"Cancer?" I ask, already knowing the answer. This is what our mother died of. Anyone doing their homework would pick a genetic disease. Cancer, both fatal and common, fits the bill.

Lily nods.

"Tell you what," I say, accepting getting rid of her won't be so easy. "Why don't you give me your number? We can get together for coffee." I grab a pen and pad from my desk, passing it along.

"I'm not in town long—"

"How's tomorrow morning?" I point through the brick. "Hallowed Grounds. Coffee shop next door. They open at nine." I shrug, nonchalant. Take it or leave it, Lily, best offer.

Lily scribbles down her number. I snatch back the pad and usher her out the door, locking up my office. I wince a grin as I beeline for the exit. I don't wait for her to catch up. I can't make the stairs fast enough. Heavy doors slam shut. I fall against the wall. It's all I can do to breathe.

Sitting in the faculty parking lot, I blast the defroster. Freezing rain has hardened my windshield into a skating rink. I can't shift to drive.

My stepsister Brooke's disappearance was big news up here twenty years ago. The internet explosion of the late '90s and subsequent social media wave only increased interest. We used to get calls and letters all the time, weirdoes claiming they'd seen my sister. Burlington. Albany. Lake Champlain. Canada. She was working as a waitress, a cashier, traveling with the circus, whatever. No different than campfire ghost stories. A black-veiled passenger on a train, the bus rider who never makes any stop, an apparition whispering foul play across the moors at midnight. It was all bullshit. Didn't make a difference *where* they'd seen her, whether she was living with a new family, under an assumed identity, or camped alone in the mountains. These callers did not lack for creativity. Although this is a new one: a daughter. Frankly, I'm shocked it's taken this long. One of the enduring rumors—unsubstantiated and un-true—was that Brooke was pregnant when she fled Rocky Cove, leaving no note, informing no one, including her friends and family.

It's easy to understand why such a mystery would titillate. A pretty, young, and troubled twenty-year-old girl from a nice town goes missing, vanishes without a trace. It screamed true-crime podcast. Brooke's browser history showed she *had* researched the long-term effects of alcohol on a fetus. Big deal. My stepsister partied. She drank, did drugs.

The press skipped the part where Brooke had been taking nursing classes at the time and could've been working on a term paper. No one followed up with the school. Because Brooke flunked out. My stepsister wasn't what one would call an "overachiever."

Technically, Brooke was my half-sister. But our relationship was hard to define. When she disappeared, I was fourteen years old. I wasn't a kid. I wasn't a man. It was a strange time for me, coming on the heels of a life on the run with Connie, my unstable, über-religious mother. I'd be shoved in schools halfway through a semester, only to be yanked out a couple weeks later, redeposited in whatever new town we called home. More than a few wretched winter nights were spent huddled in a car, buried beneath mounds of dirty laundry so we didn't freeze to death. We seldom spent a night outdoors—there were always motels and shelters, a stranger's spare room—but we were, in effect, homeless.

Living that way would mess up *any* child. Until we moved in with Brooke and her father Paul, I didn't know the meaning of the word stability. We hadn't been settled long before Connie announced the coup de grâce: she was sick. Cancer. Terminal.

With my mother dead, Paul, my new de facto stepdad, couldn't kick a little boy to the streets. I was angry and confused, unable to express emotions in a healthy, constructive manner. I could go months without talking to anyone, retreating into a ball before the slightest affront would trigger me and I'd lash out.

I can't say Paul and I got to know each other well. He kept a roof over my head. For that I will always be grateful. But he wasn't nurturing. Rail thin with a perpetual wet cough, the guy smoked and drank too much. Despite the nice house—which he inherited from his parents—the guy always lacked money. He and Brooke fought like hell. He mostly ignored me.

I won't speak ill of the man. Paul worked a steady job, kept me clothed and fed, which is why I pay for his nursing home now; why I pay for his medical care; why I drive the two hours back to Rocky Cove to visit.

As for Brooke and me, we were more strangers than siblings. Though she had reason to ostracize. Given facts, I'd have been resentful too.

I learned the details piecemeal. How my mother married too young, got pregnant, though that order might've been reversed. Six years later, one cold January night, my mother, suffocated by premature responsibilities, packed up and left behind her husband—and child. Brooke. Didn't leave a note. Like mother, like daughter. Shortly afterwards, Connie met a man in church or at the bar. Then I was born.

When we went to live with Brooke and Paul, I didn't consider how that might've affected my new stepsister—Connie's abandoning her but keeping me—I was a kid, reeling from a life on the road, entering puberty; I had problems of my own. I didn't have the wherewithal to understand these nuances in such mature terms. We were all hurting in that house.

After Brooke vanished, there was so much media attention. Soon TV cameras noticed a teenager living alone with a man like Paul, who wasn't even a blood relative. The state intervened and I was shipped off. Which was when doctors got involved, patched me up, fixed my broken brain.

It wasn't an easy road. I hadn't been dealt the greatest cards, but I made the most of a lousy hand. Through years of therapy and hard work, I've learned to reconcile my mistakes and heal. Twenty years is a long time. We hadn't received one of these calls in years. I thought it was over.

Until today.

CHAPTER FIVE

NOW

The university dinner is not solely on my behalf. There are a number of awards being handed out tonight, for lecturers and students alike. But, yes, the sizable National Endowment for the Humanities grant I am receiving is the highlight. This year's final entries came down to, as expected, me and Ortho Warsh, who at fifty-whatever is a relic at Uniondale. I'm sure Ortho, a creative writer, feels he should've been this year's beneficiary. Judges felt otherwise.

The appeal of my endeavor—and why the NEH chose my project—lies in its literary bent, its creativity, the melding of two distinct worlds in a wholly original way. I will be treating civil engineering in poetic terms, drawing comparisons between natural biology and artificial creation, e.g., veins and arteries as highways; electrical substations, the nervous system; wastewater, digestive tracts, and so on. From Roman Empire aqueducts to contemporary city sewage, I propose to show how cities and towns are, in effect, living, breathing entities. Of course, it's more complicated than that. Because I am using such a novel approach, one that broaches Ortho's area of expertise, i.e., language, I know my victory has rankled some. Few things in academia raises hackles like not staying in one's lane.

We arrive. The valet hands me a ticket and takes away my Porsche. I tell him to be careful, and Stephanie chides me for being overprotective about a car. The admonishment comes with a playful poke. Yes, I chose to buy a Porsche, which is admittedly clichéd. It's the source of endless ribbing. To which I'll often respond, as far as mid-life crises go, a sports car beats sleeping with one of my students, a joke that receives a deadpanned stare more often than it does a courtesy chuckle.

Stephanie, as always, looks radiant. She's wearing the same red dress as the afternoon we met. Which is a delightful story I will retell, perhaps as many as three times tonight. A crowd-pleaser, it's stood the test of time. An oft-rehearsed performance, I present the boy-meets-girl tale with great affectation and aplomb, gesticulating with appropriate facial expressions while calling requisite attention to my beautiful wife. In situations such as these, where anecdotes carry more weight, one needs heartwarming, crowd-pleasing cocktail fodder.

I should be feeling on top of the world. I've waited a long time for this evening, and here I am, surrounded by peers, allies and adversaries alike, ready to reap what I've sown. Instead of basking, however, I can't shake my last-minute visitor from this afternoon. Lily. My dead stepsister's *alleged* offspring. I keep assuring myself it's a con. Anyone can find the details online. The "why" is always tougher to deduce. Or maybe not. People are lonely, desperate to matter, feel relevant—who cares why they do what they do?

"What's wrong?" Stephanie asks as we enter Founder's Hall, which is lined with elegant, gold-gilded paintings of university deans, past and present. Colleagues stream in. We lock eyes. I acknowledge their terse, congratulatory nods with equally wordless response.

"Peter," I say, turning to my wife, choosing the path of partial truth. I don't need to add more. While Lily impacts my moodiness, I am not lying. I have been concerned about our son. To be more specific, the rift I feel growing between us.

"He's fine," my wife says.

At thirteen, our only child Peter has been having difficulties at school. On one hand, his problems are indicative of that age. An introvert, Peter has difficulty making friends. To expand horizons, I told my son, who enjoys hockey, he should try out for the team. He was reticent. To sweeten the pot, I said I would compensate him. Four hundred dollars, the exact amount I was aware he needed to purchase a new video game console. Though I deplore the virtual world he's retreated into, I knew he was desperate for money, and I used that desire to foster more physical activity and real-life interactions. Still, I had a tough time getting him to step outside of his shell. But he did it. He tried out for the team and earned a spot, if as an alternate. The problems began when Peter confided in one of his teammates about the monetary incentive. Without benefit of context, his teammates, these children, couldn't understand the intricacies. Some of the older players took exception, chiding Peter's not being there for the "right" reasons. Whatever that means. Peter has a temper. For the past few weeks, he's been getting into altercations. The most recent includes my son punching the team captain on the travel bus. He was disciplined by the coaching staff. Peter can still practice but hasn't been allowed to dress for games. Which isn't an issue, since Peter is second team. But the ordeal has ostracized him from his teammates, causing him to want to quit, which I will not allow.

Right now, the situation explains my outward distress. Which is easier than telling Stephanie about a girl who walked in off the street claiming to be my dead sister's long-lost daughter.

"This is your night," my wife says, squeezing my hand.

She is right. I must eschew negativity. Earning a doctorate is hard enough. Under the trying circumstances of my youth? The feat is more impressive. As someone with a propensity for self-loathing, I must, like Dr. Amy says, find a way to embrace the good in my life. Many couldn't have survived my upbringing. I not only survived, but I found a way to thrive.

"Enjoy it," my wife adds, pecking my cheek.

I squeeze her hand and tell her I love her. Without Stephanie, none of this would be possible. My life and career took off when I met her. She is my rock and inspiration to be the best man I can be.

We find our tables, prime position in front of the podium. The ornate table settings of lace and origami are splendid. So too the touch of fresh winter flowers. Before sitting, I read the name cards of who will be joining us this evening. David Cappella. Mary Anne Nunn. Christine Doyle. All fine. Then I see Ortho Warsh's name and I am seething.

I'd been explicit in my discussions with the department chair that I not be seated next to Ortho. I explained that while I understood seating finalists together is standard operating procedure, I requested an exception. On good grounds. Since receiving official notification I won, I have heard, through the academic grapevine, Ortho's grousing and complaining that I, a non-literato, bested such a renowned and internationally acclaimed poet. (As if *anyone* cares about poetry besides other poets.) My suggestion that they break with tradition and seat me apart from Ortho did not feel like overstepping bounds. I'm not the new guy in town. I've been at Uniondale since the day I graduated Cornell. Not honoring that simple request feels like a deliberate slight, an old boys' club favoring one of their own.

My instinct, while churlish, is to leave. Let them hand out the award to an empty seat. See how that goes over with boosters and donors. I am trying to regulate my emotions when Ortho approaches, offering a magnanimous hand.

"Congratulations, Robert," he says loud enough for the whole table to turn and appreciate how gracious he is being in defeat. Pompous ass.

"Thank you, Ortho," I respond. "I am only sorry they weren't able to award two grants this year." I try to chuckle.

"You know what they say. It's an honor just to be nominated." He smiles kindly beneath his pretentious gray goatee. "And," he adds in a casual aside, "I can tell you, firsthand, having served on a number of boards that make these sorts of decisions? When you get to the finalists, you're basically throwing darts in the dark." He laughs. The rest of the table joins in. Ortho and I meet eyes, and I let him know the backhanded slight didn't go unnoticed.

I wince appreciation, for company's sake, making sure to maintain my grin as I silently judge him for his stupid facial hair choices and that ridiculous bowtie.

It's taking too long for waitstaff to come around with wine. While I get a drink, Stephanie takes the opportunity to use the ladies' room. The line for wine isn't long, the selection not requiring great deliberation. When I return to the table with my pinot, I can tell by their faces—David, Christine, Mary Anne, and their partners—Ortho has been talking about me. You'd think academia, which champions intellect, would be immune to such petty antics and gossip. Hand out any award of significance and you'll never find a bigger bunch of petty bastards and sore losers. Last year when Franz Weinberger won the National Book Prize, the *moment* he left our company, the effusive praise and gladhanding gave way to charges of nepotism and sexual misconduct. Made me sick.

I am not blaming alcohol for what happens next, though I am drinking more than my share. Despite the hardships I've overcome in my life, I have never been comfortable with attention called to it. I'd prefer my accomplishments speak for themselves. The tense situation with Ortho doesn't help.

As the awards wrap up, saving the best for last, I now have the bottle of wine at the table. Dean Druthers takes the stage, starting with a brief history of the National Endowment for the Humanities award, Uniondale's place in the professorial pantheon, padding rich tradition with personal involvement. Which is all fine. Except when he gets to my bio. Instead of listing my professional accomplishments, as requested, he evokes the same old, played-out story of the little orphaned boy who went from being a ward of the State of Massachusetts to earning his place at this esteemed table tonight. It's a great story. They all love that angle. Every time a news outlet interviews me, that is the story they want to talk about. It's easy, lazy. I don't know why it's necessary to have overcome adversity for one's work to resonate. Yet, with each interview, no matter how big or small, they all draw on that catastrophic start—the loss of a parent, the familial upheaval, and of course the disappearance of a stepsister I barely knew.

I am summoned to the lectern to give my acceptance speech, which I've spent considerable time crafting. But I no longer feel inspired, my big moment eclipsed. I mutter half-hearted thank yous, and can't get off the stage fast enough.

Bustling staff now brings food, pressed starch collars and swirling synchronization that makes me queasy. My head swimming, I pour another glass of wine and see most of the bottle is gone. No one else's glasses are filled. I pretend I don't feel the eyes on me, and make sure my expression doesn't turn dour, forcing myself to fake cheer. I know I'm feeling sorry for myself. This is supposed to be a celebration. I can't get out of my own head.

I don't touch my steak. Stephanie sees I'm upset and can discern it's about more than our son. There's no *one* thing upsetting me. I am being trite but can't stop, my head unable to reverse course in the wake of too much wine. This is more than Dean Druthers' unoriginal introduction; more than sons and apples and how far they fall from trees; more than Ortho and the pack mentality that attacks those who dare to dream. Even in my impaired, inebriated sate, I understand that I'm being chided by a specter. Lily's preposterous claim of being my dead stepsister's daughter has stoked the embers of memories I believe I'd stomped out. I feel my temperature rising. That frustrated little boy, the one they called "Bobby," who used to get picked on, teased, bullied is back and ready to lash out.

Over the din of silverware clanging and nauseating sounds of animals masticating, I am searching for opportunity to leave. Stephanie stares. I can't convey what is happening inside my head. Perfunctory conversation grates more than usual. I sense someone calling my attention. I try to steady my eyes, hoping it's a simple yes-or-no question.

"So," Christine Doyle's husband—a man I've never met and whose name I do not know—asks, gesturing at Stephanie, "how did you two meet?"

Stephanie turns to me with a smile, because I am the one to tell this story. I am very good at it. It's a delightful tale of true love. It begins when I was renting a room in graduate school, and she, Stephanie, lived next door in the house she owned. Stephanie is five years older than I. Back then, Stephanie had a brood of hens she was raising in the backyard. This summer's day, she'd come outside in the same elegant red dress she wears now (I may have mentioned that part). I was watching from the back porch. Not spying or lurking. Nothing inappropriate. Just observing. Stephanie was—and is—a beautiful woman. I'd be lying if I said I hadn't had my eye on her since I'd moved in, too intimidated to say hello. Stephanie was out of my league, and even on my best days now I can't shake the feeling she could do better. And, to go back to the story of how we met, she'd started singing to her chickens. This little made-up, nonsensical, adorable song, which she belted, warbling off-key with great enthusiasm. It made me fall more in love with her. I will never forget seeing her that afternoon, the way the sun seemed to shine on her and her alone, a spotlight fixed, my dream girl singing bare-footed among the chickens... I approached afterward, and for reasons I'll never understand, she agreed to go out with me. We were married the following summer after I earned my degree. An unexpected pregnancy helped speed along that process. I have no regrets, then or now. Like I said, Stephanie is the best thing to happen to me.

While all eyes fix on me, I can't escape Ortho's lascivious glare. And now I do not want to tell that story about Stephanie and the chickens. Everyone at this table has heard that story. I am not a monkey, summoned to perform. Perhaps Christine Doyle prepped her husband beforehand, urging him that should there be a lull in conversation, he was to ask me how I met my wife. Like I'm this evening's entertainment, here to amuse them.

When I wave off the pestering requests to share the chicken story, Ortho chimes in. "Come on, Robert. We all love that joke."

"Joke?" I repeat. "You think how I met the love of my life is a joke?"

Ortho raises a dramatic recant. "No offense. I meant because the way you tell the story is so funny."

Ortho is not with his wife. As far as I know, the man has never married, which has led to all sorts of rumors and innuendo, given his fussiness and peculiar exactitude. I have never partaken, regardless of his pettiness, never stoked the flames of bigotry. And what is my reward for taking the high road? Suffering his insults.

When Stephanie grabs my hand, she does so in a loving, supportive gesture. She is trying to reassure me. Out of pure instinct, I yank away. And when I do, the back of my hand smacks the glass full of red wine I have just poured, its contents splashing on Ortho.

The table gasps. It feels as if the entire room stops breathing.

Like a benevolent king, Ortho raises a hand, the lord presiding over his court. "Okay, Robert," he says with good humor. "You're cut off."

And they all laugh at me. Even Stephanie.

CHAPTER SIX

December 13, 1997, 10:48 a.m.

Twenty-Seven Days Before the Disappearance

Fuck Mike and his macho, knuckle-dragging bullshit. Abusive asshole. He's lucky the goddamn cops didn't show up. Even if the screaming and bat above his head was mostly theatrics. Even if Mike didn't mean for Brooke to slip on the ice and crack her skull. He still grabbed her. No man puts his hands on her. If her dad had been home… Then again, what would Paul have done? Her father came from the same school. No, he never hit Connie or any woman, far as she knew. But, like Mike, her dad believed in a man's world, don't take no lip or aggravation, whatever guys say in a barroom when women aren't listening. Maybe her dad didn't say it, but it was evident in the way Paul talked, walked, and acted, he believed it. Men are like that. Maybe not a guy like Aaron. Or a boy like Bobby. Then again Brooke had never been attracted to guys like Aaron. And Bobby? Who knew what was wrong with that freak?

Brooke didn't like asking these questions, sitting in her bedroom, cold sunlight refracting off the icy parts outside and making the back of her head throb even more. All the men Brooke had been with were bad news, and if they weren't, they bored her shitless. The men Brooke *wanted*—the Mike Rakowskis and Rod Collinses—were the ones who hurt her most. Mike was a violent, temperamental asshole. Rod was married, emotionally distant, and closed off. There was a thrill in being with men like that. Brooke knew it was wrong; that's what made it feel so good. Did that make her as fucked up as they were? All her romantic relationships sucked. And there was only one constant variable in each of them: her.

Brooke hadn't been doing well. Everyone could see it. She'd quit attending classes and was mailing it in at her part-time job at the nursing home. Who knew how much longer she'd hold onto that one? Brooke had plenty of reasons to be upset, but she couldn't articulate them. The few times she tried talking to friends, they missed the point. Like Aaron, who couldn't understand why Brooke wasn't more pissed at her mother. Brooke *was* pissed at Connie—her mother abandoned them for ten years—but when she came back, a part of Brooke understood. Brooke was her daughter, cut from the same cloth, or formed from the same mold, however that saying went. Despite not knowing her mother well—Connie danced to her own drummer—Brooke understood her motivation for wanting to run away and leave it all behind. Plus, the woman was dead. Four years. What good did it do to hate a dead woman? As her mother lay in hospice, Brooke allowed Connie to make amends. Brooke was proud of that. She'd thought forgiving her mother would make closure possible. It hadn't. Some days Brooke hated Connie more than ever. Others…

Reaching into her closet, Brooke pulled down the shoebox, which contained letters from her mother over the years. These came infrequently, and yes, at the time, that infuriated Brooke. Rereading them after Connie's death, Brooke found the words impacting her differently. Her mother ceased being a complete selfish asshole. Connie had been twenty years old when Brooke was born, the same age Brooke was now.

Brooke struggled taking care of herself. She couldn't imagine being saddled with a child.

Connie wasn't a victim in Brooke's eyes—and her decision to keep Bobby and dump him on their doorstep wasn't cool—but it was possible for Brooke to feel cheated and wronged, *and* still have empathy for her mother.

Such moments didn't come often. Calm, serene, chill. Sitting cross-legged on her bed, shoebox on lap, she unfolded the handwritten notes. Like re-reading a favorite poem for the tenth time, new passages popped out. Brooke slipped Fleetwood Mac into her CD player. While Stevie gypsyied about gold dust dreams, Brooke could read between the lines. A young mother in Rocky Cove, stuck in a loveless marriage—and there her mom pulled no punches. Paul was a good man, a decent man—an … okay … man. But if Connie hadn't gotten pregnant, no way she stays with him. And from that very first letter, her mother lamented how hard it was leaving her daughter behind. Brooke missed this the first time, not interested in understanding or ready for forgiveness. Paul had a support system. His parents, though elderly, lived in town and had the resources to help. And when they passed, which they did shortly after Connie left, they'd leave him this house. Paul had the job, the means to offer a stable life. Money would be tight for a while, but a house this big, this close to Boston—someday it would be worth millions. Connie could offer nothing but embittered regrets.

The phone rang. Brooke let it go to voicemail. Mike. Apologizing for last night, swearing it would never happen again, professing his undying love. Like every other time, begging forgiveness for some stupid shit he'd done. Mike had been calling all morning. He wouldn't stop until Brooke picked up.

Mike's voice came over the speaker, pleading, remorseful, before he got pissed at being ignored, calling her a "bitch" and worse.

Brooke almost picked up the phone, let him have what's what.

Then a line in one of her mother's old letters caught her eye, made her stop, forced her to re-read what she didn't recall.

You get one *life, Brooke. Don't sell it out to anyone or anything.*

Generic, soccer mom advice. Stay true to yourself, don't be fake. Basic, ordinary. Nothing breached insightful. Except when Brooke returned to those two lines, they hit someplace deeper, resonated. Gave her chills.

You can hear clichés all day—nothing ventured, nothing gained; takes one to know one; those who don't remember history, etc.—then one day, for whatever reason, you get it. You *understand.*

This was what had been plaguing Brooke, the gnawing inside her skull, the voices that wouldn't shut up. Her mom wasn't talking about any one mistake. It wasn't getting married too soon or having a child before you are ready. It was bigger than that. The lesson reverberated loud and clear: *One life. Don't give it away.*

Brooke glanced around her room at the posters she'd tacked up. Mostly bands she didn't even like. The room had no style or substance, no personality. It was an impermanent shelter, a stopover that didn't speak to who she was. Because Brooke didn't *know* the answer yet.

There were a few movies she liked, a bunch of songs, even a book or two she'd been forced to read in school that left an impression. Brooke had seen paintings that stood out. She enjoyed making her own pottery that one summer at camp. There had been conversations, random and unconnected, which had stuck with her. Apart, these were nothing. A spattering of experiences and individual preference. But placed *together*… A clearer picture emerged. She was glad no one could see her now, half laughing, half crying, because they couldn't understand what was happening. She couldn't understand it herself. But if pressed, gun to head, goddamn it, she felt alive. Brooke could be something *more.*

Hearing the engine outside, she felt her heart seize up. No, she wasn't scared of Mike. He snuck up behind her last night, surprised her, and that wouldn't happen again. Still, she didn't want to deal with another confrontation on the front lawn.

Rushing to the window, Brooke didn't see Mike's battered Ford truck, relieved to find Aaron's reliable Honda instead. Exiting the car, her better dressed best friend sulked toward the front door wrapped in a plush North Face winter coat.

"Been calling all morning," he said, hands deep in pockets, face hidden, words twisting in another cold, windy day.

"I figured it was Mike." Brooke hugged herself, descending the front porch steps, getting a closer look.

Aaron kept his face tucked in the down collar, but he couldn't hide the purple shiner.

She reached out to touch his face, which was puffy, swollen, uneven. He turned away, mumbling, fat lip as much to blame for his garbled speech as the wind.

"I'm sorry," she said.

"I should be saying that to you." Aaron nodded up the block, in the direction of Sandy Anderson's house. The old woman was the neighborhood gossip. "Called me this morning. She said Mike hit you?"

Brooke shook her head. "I was walking up the stairs. He tried to grab me. I slipped on the ice." Brooke tried to shrug it off like it was no big deal, though they both knew that wasn't true.

"I shouldn't have left you alone with him."

"It's not your responsibility. You pay enough of a price for being my friend." She reached out to touch his face, and this time he let her.

"I'm fine." Aaron covered his hand over hers, squeezing it. "He's going to kill you one of these days."

"Mike gets worked up. Sometimes he can't get out of his own way."

She extracted her hand and gestured for Aaron to follow her back into the warmer house. "I'm not scared of him."

When they were inside, Brooke closed the door and slid the chain. "You broke up with him how long ago?"

"I still see him around." Brooke reached past Aaron's shoulder and turned the deadbolt too. Saying it aloud forced Brooke to accept her part in all this. She'd never cut ties with Mike, not all the way. "We run in the same circle, have a lot of the same friends. I can't *avoid* him."

"He's a bad person. I know you think he'll learn his lesson someday, and maybe he will, but not like you think." Aaron gestured around the house. "You can't have *any* relationship with a guy like that."

"I know," Brooke said, flustered. "He calls or comes around, and I should tell him to fuck off, but I don't."

"Stay with me," Aaron said. "You'll be safe there."

Brooke knew Aaron's concern was authentic, his offer genuine. Aaron's apartment, closer to Boston where he went to school, was big enough for two. She liked the idea of being near the city. Brooke also knew living with Aaron wouldn't solve her problems. She couldn't hide from them. Mike could find her there, too, and Aaron, good heart and intentions aside, would pay the price. Some problems you have to take care of yourself.

A sudden wave of nausea hit, cramps crippling, and Brooke doubled over.

Aaron put his hand on her back. "You okay?"

"I'm not feeling so hot." Brooke fought the urge to vomit.

"Do you need to go to the doctor?"

Aaron thought this was due to last night's fight. He was wrong.

This was something different.

This was something much worse.

CHAPTER SEVEN

NOW

By the time Stephanie and I return from the gala, Peter has been dropped off from hockey practice and is already upstairs, sequestered in his room with his video games and make-believe worlds. I know he is awake because I hear the occasional patter of feet and general bustling. He made dinner for himself, a collection of leftovers—various meats, starches and breads, some Chinese we had delivered. As is typical of that age, Peter didn't pick up after himself, plates caked with sticky, sweet General Tso's and egg roll sauces, gelatinous globs shimmering across smooth surfaces.

My wife and I tidy up, no one talking about what happened at the awards dinner. We didn't speak about it on the drive home, the sole acknowledgment, her taking the car keys from me in the faculty parking lot because I was too drunk to drive. After she pours herself a glass of white wine, Stephanie leaves to catch up on whatever Netflix series has her attention these days, and I trundle off to my home office intending to work on the new project. There was a time when I found solace in words. Tonight, all joy stripped is away, the creative process sloughing the youthful, foolish optimism that such expression can be fun. Once something becomes a job, the mystery and sense of wonder are rendered secondary, if not outright obsolete. To master craft, one must exchange the mystery to understand the machinery.

Ensconced upstairs, I don't feel like working. I can't locate the gear to kickstart collecting notes, gathering thoughts to put down on paper, never mind arranging those thoughts coherently enough to import into a Word document. The blank page taunts, its emptiness daunting.

Instead, I poke around the internet, checking missed emails and scrolling social media feeds, reading updates on people I couldn't care less about. At some point I trade cyber-stalking for the night Brooke disappeared.

Though I am more than acquainted with the story, I reread the official version, which can be found anywhere—all the major online trades and journals carry it—hoping that maybe *this* time I will discover the one curious detail I've missed the other two hundred times. All I have to do is put "Brooke Mulcahy" in a search engine, and I have countless sites to choose from. I pick one from *Medium*, 2017, two years old.

Why my half-sister, my stepsister for all intents and purposes, decided to leave Rocky Cove is subject to speculation. The "when" is not. Wednesday afternoon, January 7, 1998. This much has been proven, irrefutable, a timeline etched in paper trails, ATM receipts, and toll road cameras, which showed her alone, no one else in the car. There's never been any indication she was pressured, or that she didn't choose to leave of her own volition.

That January afternoon, around two p.m., Brooke visited her bank, where she all but cleaned out her account, which wasn't much—two thousand dollars—leaving behind a few hundred. Then, an hour later, she visited an ATM and withdrew that too.

The rest of her day leading up to the disappearance? No one knows where she went. She hadn't been staying at the house since her latest fight with Mike Rakowski, her on-again, off-again, violent, belligerent, asshole boyfriend. At some point, Brooke returned home, packed a small bag of clothes, "enough for a few days," and fled in the dead of night. She brought along medications, including her birth control pills. Paul "thought" some trinkets were missing—personal items, letters our mother may've written during the years they were estranged. Then again, the police asked leading questions. She called no one that day. At least there was no record from our phone. Despite her reputation as a screw-up, my stepsister wasn't entirely lazy. Brooke played college basketball, or she did until she gave up and dropped out. Brooke had been working at a hospice. Or maybe it was a nursing home? Something to do with the old and infirmed. I remember that she kept working there after she quit college. Until she was fired for stealing medications. There had been an arrest, an investigation, and she was looking at possible jail time. Many speculated this was her motivation for skipping town. I'd agree except the charges were dropped a few months later. Brooke may not have known that then, but she would've found out if she were still alive, which wouldn't explain why she wouldn't at least send a "wish you were here" postcard, something, *anything* to let friends and family know she was okay. There was no way Brooke didn't know people were looking for her.

While checking our phone records, the police *did* discover some … irregularities. In the weeks preceding her decision to leave Rocky Cove, there were several calls to motels up north. The police were adamant about that. *Weeks*, they said, not days. My stepsister had been inquiring about lodging while telling no one about taking a vacation. The move wasn't totally impulsive; some planning had been involved. Paul said, long ago, before my mother left, they'd spent a week together vacationing at Lake Champlain. Brooke might've been five? He didn't recall its having been a good or bad vacation. Just a vacation. The police scoured the Lake Champlain region, every accommodation scoped, hotels, motels, bed and breakfasts, Airbnbs, which weren't even a thing back then. Nothing. Given the notoriety of the case, it's hard to imagine someone like Brooke being able to escape detection for almost a quarter of a century.

Which is why most agree Brooke died that night. Theories about how vary. It's hard to retrace timelines to the minute. We do know that sometime after midnight, Brooke ended up on Route 23, just over the border into Vermont's foothills, no man's land. There was a snowstorm, which got worse the farther north she drove. And in the mountains, higher altitudes meant slicker roads. Without ample streetlight, Brooke took a corner too fast, sliding off the rural route, slamming into a guardrail, smashing her front fender, crumpling the engine, and leaving her car undriveable.

We know Brooke was okay after the accident. At least its immediate aftermath. Multiple witnesses saw her walking around, coherent and relatively unharmed.

Nathanial Jones, a sixty-one-year-old local resident, was returning home following his second shift job in Greenfield (and maybe several drinks at a roadside bar, a detail police used to undermine his testimony). Observing the wreck, Jones stopped to see if Brooke was okay. He told police my stepsister had been rattled by the crash but was otherwise lucid. He asked if she wanted to go back to his house and wait for rescue workers—he lived a couple miles up the hill, and temperatures were in the single digits. She said no thank you, that someone had already phoned roadside assistance. Which struck Jones as odd since the closest house was across a snowy pasture. Remember, this was before cell phones became popular. It turned out the woman who lived there, Hope Washington, a sixty-eight-year-old retiree, *did* hear the crash and had, in fact, called 911. But this part of Vermont is the cuts, everything spread out, houses separated by hundreds of yards, so it's not like the old woman could've rushed out to offer an update. Brooke didn't want to get in a car with a strange man, especially one who stank of booze.

Washington confirmed the interaction with Jones, having witnessed the two converse from her window. Afterwards, the old woman went to get dressed—this was the middle of the night. She estimated this process took five, ten minutes tops. When Hope Washington returned to the window, snow fell harder, storm in full force. She saw no sign of Brooke.

Fifteen minutes later, police and EMT workers arrived. They found my stepsister's car but no sign of Brooke. No one else had seen a thing. My stepsister had vanished into the night.

In the coming months, theories concerning her fate only grew weirder and wilder. Rumors swirled, and, yes, one of them had Brooke pregnant. Brooke was a wild child. She drank, partied, did her share of drugs. And there's no way to say this without sounding like I am disparaging the dead—and after twenty years, she most certainly is dead—Brooke was promiscuous.

For a long time, on-again, off-again boyfriend Mike Rakowski was looked at, hard. I can't say I got along with Mike, who was a bad guy on his best days. Police *wanted* to pin this on him, and if they could have, they would have. They couldn't. I don't know what happened to Mike. My best guess is he's dead or in prison.

There were other men, romantic partners, lovers. Each one had been investigated and exonerated. One of these men, Brooke's married college basketball coach, Rod Collins, with whom she'd purportedly had an affair, had been considered a strong possibility, his alibi dubious. According to authorities he and Brooke hadn't spoken since she quit college. If allegations of an inappropriate relationship between Collins and Brooke *were* true, no one could prove anything—this was before email was so prevalent, with Collins the only one left to confirm or deny. He denied.

Like most, my stepfather Paul blamed Mike. I was on Paul's side, rooting for Mike to be guilty. Brooke ran around on him, cheating on him with friends, and when they found her car abandoned on Route 23, all evidence pointed to Brooke's planning a new life, far away from Mike, far away from here. This theory juxtaposed in stark contrast to Mike's insistence they were in love, with plans to one day leave Rocky Cove together. You couldn't believe a word Mike Rakowski said. The guy was a born liar.

I type "Lily Mulcahy" in a search engine but find nothing applicable. Then again, if Brooke had a child, it's doubtful she'd be using her real name. Plus, Brooke would never name a child that, Lily as pretentious as Brooke. Brooke always hated her own name. I remember overhearing my stepsister on the phone, complaining, wishing she had a regular name like Jill or Jennifer, something equally benign. Lily is too trendy, too niche, chic; it screams glossy magazine populism, a townie desperate for relevance.

I close all browsers and pull up a Word doc. It's after midnight and I've wasted hours on this nonsense. I've researched the project for months—my proposal alone is eighty-six pages. I convince myself I am excited. I will show the city is alive.

I can't get out a goddamn word.

Deny it all you want, Bobby, but you'll never find peace until you know for sure...

When Brooke first disappeared, the specifics of her vanishing were ripe for media speculation. At one point, I even received a call from the producers of *Unsolved Mysteries*, the television show. By then, my stepfather's health was failing, and he needed in-patient care. Knee-deep in graduate school, I declined. Last thing I needed was *more* kooks and basketcases with access to a tip line.

I don't want to revisit that night. Sitting in my home office, I can't resist. I recall a quote from grad school and Oscar Wilde: "The only way to get rid of a temptation is to yield to it." I find most of Wilde's writing to be self-indulgent and sophomoric, but I never forgot that quote. So I yield to the temptation, give in, fire up another search engine, and read it all, from factual reportage to the madness of serial-killer cultists. I don't skimp or skim.

There is no reason for me to revisit these articles, the fantastical *or* the true—at some point I've perused them all. Nothing new is to be gained, the official version identical, speculated fates hinging on the whim of dead eyewitnesses, intrepid bloggers, and true-crime aficionados.

Theories change.

One part doesn't.

Because the central question remains: Where did Brooke go?

CHAPTER EIGHT

December 17, 1997, 8:22 a.m.
Twenty-Three Days Before the Disappearance

Brooke arrived for her morning shift at the Roseville Rest Home five minutes late, maybe seven, ten tops. Fifteen. It wasn't her fault. Traffic downtown was rerouted because of roadwork—although as far as Brooke could tell no one was doing much work, hardheaded men leaning on shovels, sitting on excavators, no one doing a goddamn thing except eating grinders and taking one big, long break. The roadways were a sloppy mess, cars at a crawl, red lights blinking everywhere, detours diverting drivers at a glacial pace.

As soon as Brooke stepped onto the ward, Michelle Penny, the home's supervisor, laid into her. Without the privacy of a closed door, Michelle admonished Brooke in front of everyone, deriding her for something that wasn't even her fault—why was it her problem the city was doing repairs during rush hour and the weather in New England sucked? Brooke couldn't defend herself, judged by onlookers. Didn't matter if most were heavily sedated and/or hard of hearing. It was humiliating. Brooke kept apologizing, hoping her boss would let it go.

Michelle wouldn't let it go, though. Hand on hip, toe tapping, finger waggling. Squawking haughty like a fat-assed, flightless bird. Michelle was what? Twenty-five, -six? A few years ago, they could've been in high school together, partying and having fun. Now, they were stuck playing grown-up in a rest home. The whole charade was ridiculous.

"This is the second time this month," Michelle repeated, belaboring the point, despite however many times Brooke acknowledged her mistake. "*Second*," Michelle added a third time.

"There was construction. It was a few minutes—"

"Try closer to twenty." Michelle pointed at the big round clock. "And it's *always* something with you, Brooke. *Always* an excuse."

"The road was closed—"

"Anticipate problems. Leave earlier."

Brooke nodded at the sage wisdom, promising, once more, it wouldn't happen again, anything to get this woman out of her face.

Eventually Michelle twattled off. How did women end up like that? Hair helmet and couch thighs, utterly joyless. Brooke knew Michelle's entire life revolved around this stupid job.

Brooke was straightening out her nurse's uniform, trying not to lose her shit, when Torie peeked her head out of the supply closest. Torie Dent was a couple years older than Brooke, a coworker and, at best, causal friend. They'd sometimes smoke and get high together in the parking lot after a shift. Torie was also the only person here under eighty for Brooke to talk to.

"Harsh," Torie said, waiting till Michelle disappeared around the corner.

In twenty years, Michelle Penny, with her pruned, scrunched-up bird face, would still be here. Brooke would rather be dead.

"She's such a bitch," Torie added, before tugging Brooke by the elbow, pulling them both into the supply closet. Locking the door, Torie revealed the wadded napkin, opening it to display six perfect white spheres.

Brooke's eyes grew wide.

"Mr. Peronace won't miss these," Torie said.

She wasn't wrong. Brooke was fond of Mr. Peronace, but the old man didn't have much time left. Besides, the Percocet were a snack compared to the morphine drip he had on tap.

Huddled around a disengaged mirror, Torie crushed the pills with a nine-volt battery, dusting them into a fine powder, using her finger to separate into several rows of fat lines. Torie took the liberty of going first, before passing the straw to Brooke.

Brooke snorted hard, a fast inhale hitting receptors in seconds, clearing up the fog if adding doubts to what she was doing with her life.

"What was that bullshit with Michelle about?" Torie asked.

"You said it. She's a bitch." Ten bucks an hour wasn't worth it.

"How are classes going?"

"Waste of time." Brooke hit another rail, tilting back her head, savoring the drip. No reason to tell Torie she'd quit Midfield State.

"Why are you taking them then?"

"Classes? I need to do something with my life?" Brooke said it like a question. Even she wasn't sure of the answer. For years, Brooke blamed her mom. Then Connie came back and died. Nothing got fixed. Worst of all? Brooke lost her convenient excuse. School, work, pills, powders. Stopgaps, band aids on broken legs. Brooke didn't have a good plan for the long haul. She needed to get out of Rocky Cove. A whole big world waited. A couple thousand bucks stashed in the bank wasn't going to cut it.

Torie snapped her fingers, calling Brooke's attention. "Good shit, eh?"

"I need money," Brooke said.

"Funny you should mention that..." Torie bent down for another snort.

Brooke laughed. "If you're asking to borrow some, sorry. I ain't got it. Life around the house is a mess. My father is barely able to keep up on the mortgage. My new baby brother Bobby is a serious drain."

"You hate him, don't you? Your brother Bobby."

"I don't know about 'hate.' But he's another mouth to feed. And he doesn't bring shit to the table." Brooke took the straw. "I want a place of my own."

"What about Mike?"

"What about him?"

Mike *did* work steady. Construction. Come a New England winter, a lot of workers were let go. Mike was entrenched enough that he'd avoided the axe. So far. Who knew how long that would last? He *was* generous—though less with money and more with drugs. But, like everything in this life, nothing is free. If Brooke wasn't taking Aaron up on his offers, no way she was making a deal with Mike.

"I'm not signing my life over to anyone." Brooke stood straight and leaned against the shelf, careful not to rattle metal and call attention to their hiding spot.

"He loves you?"

"Mike? He says he does. I don't care. Even if I *did* feel the same way—and I fucking don't—I don't want to be tied down to one guy. I still have things I want to do with my life."

"Like what?"

"Get out of this town for one."

"But you can't because of your dad? Bobby?"

"My father is always up my ass, but, no, I can't walk out on him. I lost my mom—he lost his wife. Plus, he's old and not well. Drinks like a fish, smokes like a chimney. He can't take care of himself." Brooke pointed through the door. "In a few years, he'll be stuck in this place. I don't give a shit about Bobby. Let social services take care of him. But my dad…" Brooke didn't want to talk about Paul. They had their issues, which had grown worse as Brooke got older. He was still her dad. Unlike Connie, he stuck around. That meant something to Brooke. "Someone is going to need to foot the bill."

"So it's just money," Torie said.

Brooke scoffed. "Just money?"

"What if I told you I have a way to make some? I don't mean chump change. I'm talking *real* money—money that'll set us both up."

Brooke rolled her eyes, overselling the skepticism. Get-rich-quick schemes didn't exist, at least none that weren't highly illegal. She also didn't walk out of the closet. There was one line left. Brooke held up the dollar-bill straw. Torie nodded to keep it.

Snorting it all, Brooke threw back her head, then wiggled her fingers, an invitation to share. *Let's hear your big plan. So I can say no and go back to killing time.*

Torie pointed at the residue on the tray. "Same way I got this."

"Stealing and selling drugs from dying, old people?"

"Most of them are end stage. This place isn't a rest home. It's a morgue."

"These meds are the only comfort they have. I need money, but I'm not robbing cancer patients. Jesus."

"You don't have to," Torie said. "But these people *are* going to die. And when they do, there's a lot of medication left behind—the good stuff. Dilaudid. Fentanyl. Pure, liquid."

"Yeah, meds that are recorded and kept track of. Logged and triple checked. They can't disappear and go unnoticed."

"Right. Except Billy Warren works here."

"Who's Billy Warren?"

"Night shift. Jack of all trades. Does most the cleaning. When someone doesn't wake up, Billy takes a break from unclogging toilets and mopping floors and is the one who moves the body and catalogues the medicine."

No surprise that Roseville would try and save a penny by having a janitor pull double duty.

"So?"

"So ... I've been sucking his dick for the past year and a half." Torie smiled wide, her attempt at sexy. Torie Dent wasn't the type of woman that drove men wild. She offered the one thing she had to sell. Everything is a negotiation. "And I've been getting ... perks."

"Percocet?"

"I meant perks. Benefits. But, yeah, those too." Torie leaned in to whisper, even though the girls were the only ones in the closet. "I have vials. Lots. I've stockpiled a stash. I'm thinking it's time to cash in."

Brooke wasn't stealing pain meds from sick people; however, if they were already dead... "Okay," she said. "What do you need me for?"

"You know those people, right?"

"Dealers? A few. None that would have that much cash."

"What about Mike? He parties hard. He must know major players. Ones that *would* be able to pay the big bucks." Torie licked a finger and ran it over the mirror, saliva sticking to every crumb, before rubbing them over her nasty, yellow teeth. "Swallow your pride or whatever you have to. This is our ticket out of here."

CHAPTER NINE

NOW

Lily is already seated when I arrive at the coffee shop, sipping an over-priced frothy concoction in an oversized mug. Hallowed Grounds, next door to campus, does tremendous business during the semester but remains empty during breaks. At this early hour, the inside is extra cold and sterile. The lights are low, all seats but one vacant.

Observations highlight a life of the mind. A coffee order doesn't tell one much. But there is a difference between a $1.90 house blend and a $6 double whipped soy cappuccino. Lily's attire, as well, doesn't betray a stray cat in search of free milk. Her healthy pallor and salon-styled hair paints the picture of a young woman who lives a comfortable life.

"Sorry for ordering first," she says, painted nails cradling mug.

"Not a problem." I unwrap the scarf strangling my neck, taking my time, deliberate. This stalling tactic allows the blood flow to return while I surveil. I'm searching for telltale signs of a liar. Eyes averted, skin peeled around cuticle, fidgeting, knee tapping—I see none of these things. Lily comes across like any of the students I teach at Uniondale, whose tuition is not cheap.

"Would you like something?" Lily makes to stand as I sit.

I motion for her to relax. "I'm fine for now."

Unable to request a driver's license, I'm forced to guess her age. *She's too young to be Brooke's daughter.* I want to put her at seventeen, maybe eighteen, making it impossible she is Brooke's child. At least not the one she was rumored to be carrying that fateful night. Then again, nineteen isn't out of the realm of possibility...

Lily and I navigate the uncomfortable. I smirk. She winces. Enshrined by the shoddy, amateurish artwork of undergrads—lopsided self-portraits with inconsistent light sources—I will not make this easy on her. Hands folded, eyes fixed, I wait. The onus of proof does not fall on me. I do not feel bad about this. For the twenty years Brooke has been gone, opportune strangers have contacted us. When my stepfather relocated to a full-care facility, these oddballs sought me out. Before Brooke went missing, I had no idea so many depraved, macabre factions existed, groups of warped and twisted individuals who band together, like role-playing geeks or fantasy football nerds, treating horrific crimes such as murder, kidnapping, and worse as sport, another hobby to pass the time, however gruesome. There are groups, shocking as it might sound, that regularly gather, tackling decades-old cold cases the police and FBI couldn't solve. On the few occasions I've been persuaded to meet any of these individuals face to face, I've only needed seconds in their company to recognize insanity. I do not feel this today. Instead of hope or closure, I experience the opposite reaction, angry that grifters have upped their game. Lily doesn't look the part. She is either a very good liar, or...

"This is weird," she says, making a face as if halting a giggle.

"I can appreciate that."

Lily bites her lip, and in the light of day, I'd be lying if I said I didn't catch shades of Brooke, a ghostly resemblance and reminder of our shared blood. What's left of it anyway.

Needing a distraction, I push myself up from the chair. "I think I will grab a coffee after all." And in case Lily is entertaining notions that I will accept her offer to pay, I hold up my hand to stay put.

Besides Lily and me, no other customers visit Hallowed Grounds. A hunched-over student worker stocks pastries. Seeing me, he stands up to take my order. Studying a handwritten, blackboard menu with limited options, I take longer than I need. My heart rate and pulse spike, body betraying mounting anxiety. On the outside, I hold steady, but inside I am spiraling.

I return with a coffee and the raisin scone I didn't want. Lily sits uneasy, apprehensive. I am still searching for clues, the body language that exposes a fraud. I detect nothing.

"You don't want to be here, do you?" Lily's words exude sympathy.

It's a bold strategy, this reversal to go on the offensive, and I respect her more for it. *Okay, Lily, let's show our cards...*

I nibble the extra-dry scone, smiling, in no hurry to swallow coffee to lose the lump in my throat.

"Brooke disappeared twenty years ago," I say. "Since then, several people have come forward making claims like you are." I hold up a hand. "No offense."

"No, it's okay. I get it."

"I'm reserving the right to be skeptical, is all. Brooke was—"

"Susan," she says, interrupting my clarification.

"Excuse me—"

"My mother's name. I didn't know her as 'Brooke Mulcahy.' I learned that at the end. The whole story ... about the disappearance." Lily pulls out her wallet and driver's license. According to it, she is nineteen, born roughly nine months after Brooke vanished. Perfect timing. The last name reads "Stillwater."

"Susan ... Stillwater?" I say. The name falls from my mouth like a stone. Plain, innocuous, ordinary. The opposite of "Brooke."

"I know this is weird..." The girl stops, tentative turning self-consciousness. "I don't even know what to call you."

"Robert is fine." Dr. Kirby is too formal. I am *not* granting this girl permission to call me "uncle."

"When Mom was end stage, she told me to get her laptop." Lily's eyes do not leave mine. I return her stare with equal intensity. "She pulled up the story on the web and explained everything—who she really was, why she had to leave. I don't think my mom wanted to die carrying that secret, y'know?" Lily turns toward the door. "Secrets can be a heavy burden."

The bell dings, followed by gust of icy air. A pair of co-eds enter. There is nothing interesting about either, but I arch my brow, studying both as if I know them. Lily watches me, while I watch the two order lattes to go.

"When I was home last semester—"

"Where's home?" I ask, happy to delay wherever this story is going.

"Bellemont. Small town outside Lake Champlain. During semester, I live on campus—"

"Where are you going to school?"

"Amherst," she says. "UMass. Creative writing."

Amherst is a top-ten program, and not easy to get into.

"I'm thinking of switching to something more practical," she adds, perhaps after seeing the face I make, which says that a creative writing degree is a waste of money.

"Such as?" I ask, sipping bland coffee that's gone tepid.

Lily seems taken aback by my interest in her scholastic career. She's not wrong. I don't care. I'm stalling, biding time, with no plan other than to prolong the inevitable. I sense she's holding back, waiting to spring an unscheduled witness, some shocking bit of evidence. I have no reason to believe this, just a gut feeling. One doesn't go through this much effort without proof to back up claims. A letter won't be enough.

"Poly sci? Philosophy?" she says. "I don't know. After Mom died, I took a semester off. I'm falling behind…" Lily pans out the window. "When I found your contact information… I wasn't going to bother you."

"This isn't a bother," I lie.

"After all this time, I wasn't sure … what the right thing to do was."

"It's a unique situation."

"I don't want anything from you," Lily says.

"I wasn't thinking that you did." My response is disingenuous, and we both know it.

"In the end," she says, "I figured you might have questions."

"A few."

"My mom was in an abusive relationship with this guy, Mike—"

"Yes. Mike Rakowski."

"Their relationship was fucked up." She catches herself. "Sorry. I meant—"

"I teach college. No need to curb your language. I hear 'fuck' sixty times a day—"

"Mike isn't my dad," she says. "If that's what you're thinking—"

"I'm not thinking anything—"

"My mom said she hadn't been with Mike … in that way … not for a long time." Lily's stare locks on me. "I don't know who my dad is."

"How do you feel about that?" I interject, borrowing a page from Dr. Amy's playbook. If years of therapy have taught me anything: people love to talk about themselves. Works wonders in therapy and sales.

Lily shrugs. "It is what it is." She takes another sip, blowing off questions of her parentage like the nonexistent steam on her cappuccino.

I'll admit it. She's got me hooked, curiosity piqued. I want to hear it all, the uncensored version. *Give it to me.* I want to know how my stepsister pulled it off. What happened that night? How did she escape in the snow and cold on foot, survive miles from civilization? How did Brooke—Susan—avoid detection all these years and stay disappeared so long. What was the reason she gave for never returning? *Let's see how well constructed this ruse is.*

Lily has her claws in, a look of satisfaction etched on those drawn red lips.

"What happened that night?" I prod.

"Mom had flunked out of college. Mike wasn't leaving her alone. She said…" Lily's eyes wane empathetic. "I don't want to make you feel bad, but she said you two weren't close, and that she fought with her father all the time. She used the car accident as an opportunity to walk away from it all, as a chance to start over."

"The police found her car. They canvassed the area. Brooke, your mom … Susan … was nowhere to be found."

"My mom said she got picked up."

"By whom?"

"Some old guy. Happened to be driving by at the right time. Asked if she needed a ride. He said he was on his way upstate. She asked to tag along."

What can I add to this? A simple solution to a complicated problem, nice and tidy. Might as well add a bow. The details have been well chosen. An "old" man, i.e., someone not acquainted with technology, unlikely to catch onto the impending internet explosion or read about a notorious missing person case; an old man who would likely be dead by now.

"Mom said the stars lined up that night." Lily beams, so proud of the foolproof details she's presented. "She'd been praying for a miracle.

She got one. Moved to a small community with a couple thousand residents. Cut and dyed her hair. Got a job—dental assistant. Good money for a college dropout. Easy to go unnoticed."

"And then what?"

"Then I was born." Lily brings the mug to her lips but doesn't drink right away. "You ought to know, your sister was a good mom."

We lock eyes and even though I can't see what's hidden behind the wide brim of the coffee mug, I know she is smiling.

If I had a hat, I might feel obliged to tip it.

With that, Lily sets down her mug, gathers her purse, and stands. "I should get back on the road. You have my number. Feel free to text or whatever. No pressure. It was nice meeting you." She slips her arm under the handbag strap. Coach, crossbody. I can't tell whether it's a knock off or the real thing.

"Almost forgot," Lily says, reaching inside. "I think she'd want you to have this."

The jewelry glistens in the overhead lights. My throat seizes up as Lily places the necklace in my open palm.

I stare down at the silver crucifix with Brooke's birthstone, and pray no one can hear my heart banging against its cage.

CHAPTER TEN

NOW

After Lily and I say our goodbyes, I go to the office. Pointless. Another wasted, unproductive day.

I've retreated to my car. The rain has gotten worse. It drapes in sheets. Even inside my luxury car with state-of-the-art heating, I can feel it, that cold rain. I cringe with each rolling, violent wave, recalling deluged days when my mother and I sought shelter from the storm.

Nothing rivals Diemen's winters. Like rapid-fire bullets. When surrounding areas are getting snow, sleet, and ice storms, the low-lying valley invites rain, which makes it worse—razor-sharp, subzero darts targeting exposed skin, piercing with deadly precision. Growing up, I survived all types of weather, the topography of New England and Upstate New York notorious for scalding summers and frigid winters. I hated rain most. I'd rather burn in the sun or freeze in the snow. Every time it rains, I feel like I'm drowning.

What will I tell Stephanie? I can't withhold information like this. My wife knows all about my conflicted relationship with my stepsister. At least the parts I've been able to articulate. I've tried to be forthright, honest, and truthful. How can I explain what Brooke was to me? I knew her as well as that girl seated next to me in the coffee shop this morning. Which is to say, not at all. I'd love to forget about that conversation. Secrets in a marriage are destructive.

I pull onto my street, a charming residential stretch peppered with ornate colonial-style homes. Nestled in the Hudson Valley, the square feet, sizable plot, and property value represent a long way from where I started.

It's almost five o'clock and, because it's winter, already dark, surrounding highlands slathered in deep purple as dark clouds descend to smother the valley. Peter does not have hockey practice today. Both my wife and son will be home.

As one starts dinner, the other finishes homework. Nightly routine. I debate whether to call Stephanie into another room. Do I tell her about Lily's visit now or wait till later? I see no reason to involve Peter yet.

When I open the front door and enter the foyer, Bridget, our yippy Yorkshire terrier, runs to me, barking and excited. I bend to rub him behind the ears, before he zips down the hall, through the kitchen, and to the glass porch door where he continues to bark. Bridget, despite his diminutive size, takes his guard dog job seriously, and there is no shortage of woodland creatures skittering in the shadows that demand his attention. I'm not sure why Peter wanted to call the dog, which is male, "Bridget." Stephanie speculated he had a crush on a girl with that name. The only Bridget I found in his yearbook did not seem the type you'd immortalize, and Peter doesn't seem to be noticing girls in that way yet. But we thought it important to give him agency.

I'm trying to maintain a smile for my family's sake. Stephanie sees the strain on my face before I get out a hello. Peter is already heading upstairs to finish his schoolwork. I make for the wine, pouring a healthy glassful, and take a seat at the kitchen table. My wife stops preparing tonight's meal, which is some new ethnic variation of chicken she's discovered—I detect hints of saffron and garam masala. She washes her hands to join me.

"What is it?" she asks.

I tell her about Lily, our coffee, and her claims.

"This girl stopped by yesterday? Why wouldn't you tell me?"

"Steph," I say, "we are going to be dealing with this for the rest of our lives. The story is everywhere online. There are entire organizations dedicated to solving what happened to her. Like book groups. But for serial killers and kidnappings. Kill clubs. These people are pathetic."

"What made you agree to talk to her then?"

"Curiosity? It's been so long since the last one." I swallow wine. "She knew things. Small details not online or in the papers. Her timeline after the crash ... where Brooke went, how she got there. Why no one was waiting at the accident site when police arrived."

"Do you believe this girl is your sister's daughter?"

"Stepsister."

"Half-sister."

"Same thing."

"That was twenty years ago. Did you ask to see ID?"

I throw up my hands. How can you ask for someone's driver's license under those circumstances? But yes. I saw her ID. "Her story made sense."

"Remember the last time? Twenty-fourteen, I think. That woman—what was her name? Toni? Tonya?"

"Something like that."

"The one who claimed she was Brooke's roommate? Said she and Brooke were best friends. What happened? We call the police, they go all the way up there, some rent-by-the-hour motel, and the woman is crazy."

"I know—"

"Notebooks scrawled with unsolved disappearances."

I sympathize. I don't understand it either, why some people are like this. I am being diplomatic, kind in my analysis. The truth is these people are depraved. It's cruel, how they reopen wounds, make you hurt, refusing to let you heal, twisting your insides for their warped entertainment. I don't voice any of this. I can't explain the whole story, not in a way that would make sense to my wife. I don't want to talk anymore. I rise to go to my office. I don't get two steps before she calls me back.

"How did you leave things?"

"I said it was nice meeting her."

Stephanie stands in the middle of the kitchen, hands wrapped in a dish towel. "I can't tell whether you believe her."

I hesitate. The truth is I don't know either.

"What was her name again? Lily?"

I nod.

"That doesn't sound like a name Brooke would pick. Not the way you describe her."

"According to Lily, she changed her name. New identity, small, nowhere town near Canada. Susan Stillwater. Dental assistant."

"And she passed away two years ago?"

I return to the kitchen to refill my pinot.

"Does it matter?" I say, adding more wine to an already full glass.

"This is still an open investigation. You have to call the police."

"Why? Like you said, last time we did, nothing came of it. What's changed? The girl—"

"Your niece."

"*Alleged* niece." I gasp, guilty of melodrama. I'm confused too. "She wanted to introduce herself. I didn't get the impression she's looking for a meal ticket or even to exchange holiday cards. She understands Brooke and I weren't close. Lily was passing through on her way to Amherst. Stopped to say hello, and now she's gone back to her regular life. Nineteen-year-old college students aren't interested in getting to know their long-lost uncle."

My wife is slow to agree. But she will. Stephanie doesn't want the headache any more than I do.

I come around to her side, kiss her cheek, and tell her I'm going upstairs to work before dinner. I almost make it to the vestibule before she calls me back yet again.

"That letter?" she says, referring to the missive from my dead stepsister.

"What about it?"

"That's the only proof she had?"

I shrug.

"It's been so long—are you sure that was even Brooke's handwriting?"

"Who knows?" I walk a few steps, knock on the wall, soft and reassuring, a call for luck. Never hurts. "Honestly, I think that is the last we'll hear from Lily Stillwater."

I round the corner, climbing up the stairs, patting the crucifix with Brooke's birthstone nestled snug in my pocket.

CHAPTER ELEVEN

December 23, 1997, 2:13 p.m.
Seventeen Days Before the Disappearance

"It doesn't work like that." Mike stewed in his tiny, filthy kitchen. Grease splattered and coffee stained, grout rife with grime.

"Yeah? Then how's it work?" Brooke leaned against the doorframe, adopting the casual body language of someone who didn't give a shit. With Mike, you couldn't let him know you *needed* him. On the drive over, Brooke kept reminding herself that sometimes you must make deals with the devil for the greater good.

Mike had the one-bedroom to himself, and the place smelled like him—a mixture of schwag beer, musk, and Fast Orange, the industrial-strength pumice hand cleaner he bought in bulk and kept stored in tubs under the sink. No matter how much he scrubbed, his hands never got clean. The apartment stank. Because Mike never did any dishes or laundry. Takeout containers and empty beer cans interspersed with soiled work clothes, pizza boxes with one slice of pepperoni left, weeks old. His big, untied boots, caked with sewage and sludge, sat in the middle of the hall, kicked off and tracking mud.

"For one?" Mike said. "You don't get to fuck half the guys in Rocky Cove and then come to me for fucking favors."

"It's not a fucking favor. It's a chance to make some fucking money. A business deal. We get it. You sell it. We split the profit three ways."

"I like three-ways." Mike smirked, oh-so-clever. He plucked his Marlboro Reds off the counter, swiping his long, greasy hair out of his face and lighting one on the gas stove. He tugged off his tee. He thought he was a real catch, Mike, with his muscles and clichéd spattering of tattoos. A heart. A cross. A naked sailor lady. And he *was* good-looking. Or good-looking enough for this town. Even after everything, Brooke couldn't hate him. Not totally. There had been a time she *did* care for him. In the beginning, Mike was different, funny and tough but tender too, and he … almost … got it. She used to love the way he'd look at her, the way he loved her, that all-consuming, I'll-die-without-you devotion. Back then, he wanted more and was willing to fight to get it.

The way he looked at her now was sad and pitiful. Like he still believed they'd be together. As if this were a phase Brooke would grow out of or he'd somehow turn into a better man. He couldn't see what everyone else did: Mike Rakowski was a loser, going nowhere. In ten years, he'd still be kicking around Eastern Massachusetts, digging ditches, drinking cheap beer, and getting plastered on the weekends. Brooke wanted more than big talk. Mike couldn't understand that. Mike couldn't understand a lot of things.

"Will Stimpy do it or not?" Brooke didn't know where Stimpy, Mike's drug dealer, got the nickname. Mike said it was from an old comic strip or some shit. Brooke had never spoken to Stimpy, only spying him from afar. He handled volume, though, she knew that. And the nickname sure fit. Short and squat with a lard mat of shellacked hair plastered to his skull, the guy didn't have many career options. It was either dealing dope or selling furniture at a discount outlet.

"I doubt it." Mike took a deep inhale, puffing smoke rings.

"Why's that?"

"Because he sells. He doesn't buy."

"Then how's he get the shit he sells—"

"And he doesn't know you."

"You know me."

"Do I?" Mike's face adopted a wounded expression. Coming from anyone else, the look might elicit sympathy. Coming from Mike, it made Brooke angry. He was manipulating her. Then to hammer the point home, he turned over his wrist, revealing the little moon, extending it forward, a sacred offering.

"Jesus, Mike." Brooke stuck her hands in her pocket, hiding the other half of the matching yellow tattoo. "We were barely seventeen."

"A whole three years ago."

"We were wasted."

"It was supposed to mean something."

To Mike, getting those matching tattoos etched deeper than a wedding vow. In sickness and in health. Till death do they part. Brooke would rather be dead.

Outside, buses chugged the line, horns bleating in between siren bursts. Fishmongers barked and street people screamed. Cops and rescue workers corralled the destitute, the criminal and wounded, as hard winter winds smacked the windowpane, glass caked and coated with film, obscuring how ugly it got out there. City life didn't seem so romantic anymore.

"What am I to you, Brooke? Friend? Ex? Fallback option? I sure as shit ain't a boyfriend."

Brooke darted past him and snagged the cigarettes off the stove. "You want to be my boyfriend again? That it?"

"I want to be something." Mike skulked around the dingy apartment, hot fluorescents from the bars and parlors hazing below, glowing pink, lime, and tangerine across cracked linoleum. Bugs skittered to escape the light. "Anything," he added, his voice cracking. He came nearer, head hung, meek and subservient. A big guy, he seemed so small.

In that moment, Brooke wanted to draw on better times. She tried to summon that first summer they got together. Connie had come back, Mike's dad was using him as a punching bag, and two troubled screwups found comfort in each other's arms. She smiled, remembering that cheesy Oasis song on the radio the first time they had sex in the backseat. Because at that age you really believe you will live forever and get everything you want.

She found Mike's hands, taking them in hers, running a forefinger across the rough calluses. Brooke affected a soft, vulnerable display, staring up at him with big, green doe eyes. She kicked off her shoes, letting him be taller. Because that's what he wanted, right? To be the man and have her barefoot in his kitchen. And if that's what it took, sure, she thought, why not? Best guesses and conversative estimates told Brooke they were sitting on *at least* fifteen grand worth of pharmaceuticals, maybe more. Her student ID at Midfield State's computer lab still worked. Researching narcotic wholesale wasn't easy. But rudimentary numbers were promising. Five grand each, free and clear. That had to be worth the bad taste this was going to leave in her mouth.

Brooke took his hand, guiding him to the bedroom. Looking into his eyes, she playfully pushed his shoulders until he fell back on the bed. She dropped to her knees and peeled off those dirty jeans. Brooke could be damned persuasive when she wanted to.

CHAPTER TWELVE

NOW

I'm woken in the middle of the night from a fevered dream, one of those tortured, tormented nightmares fueled by feelings of impending doom, but from which upon awaking you can't recall a single specific detail.

Bridget is barking. He's a sweet little guy, but there's not a sound or situation that doesn't cause him anxiety. I can empathize. Stephanie, as usual, is knocked out. Ambien and evening wine. Often Bridget sleeps in our bed. Something downstairs has caught his attention.

I steel my resolve for bare feet to touch cold wood. Bridget is relentless. I can hear him, running in circles on the kitchen floor. Heading toward the stairs, I pass Peter's room, my son fast asleep, and again I am gripped by the sensation I am losing my boy. I am a good father. I care about my son and his future, as any good father should. And yet when I try talking to him, I can't get out what I want to say. I want to tell him that I've been there and know how much it hurts. I want to promise him that it's going to get better.

Before I start downstairs, Bridget stops yipping at whatever furry critter has gotten too close to the patio door this time. I don't go back to bed, though. I sit on that top step and study the pictures running up and down the well. Most are of Stephanie's family, which is extensive. Her sister lives in Western Pennsylvania. They still manage to see one another several times a year. My wife is in regular contact with third cousins twice removed. I don't have *any* cousins. My mother and sister—half-sister—are dead. If my father is still alive, I wouldn't know it. I have Paul, who isn't related by blood or marriage, and with whom I never formed any meaningful relationship. There is one picture on the wall of my mother and me. An inconsequential photograph of an insignificant time that occupies no special place in my heart. I remove this picture from the wall and hold it in my hands. The photograph catches enough moonlight for me to rediscover my mother. I don't allow myself to think of her often.

For as hard as those early, tumultuous years were, I don't recall being unhappy. My real troubles began when we settled down, with Paul and Brooke. Until then, I had nothing to compare my life to; there was no contrast. Like being born blind. I thought everyone lived the way my mother and I did. Town to town, school to school, meal to meal. When I finally found stability, I didn't know how to assimilate. My mother, my only family to that point, was dying. I was used to fighting for food, scrounging for shelter, overcoming obstacles. To me, other kids were something in the way. I did my best to get along with others but when I couldn't convey what I wanted, I'd grow frustrated. Someone would say the wrong thing at the wrong time, make me feel stupid, and I'd flash.

I refocus on the picture, clutch it, study it, try and feel it. My mother and I are in a park. I don't recall who took the photograph. Since my mom is in it, it couldn't have been her. We weren't the type of family that could afford a fancy camera with a timer. I'm struck by how happy my mother looks. She is wearing a long green coat, the kind you find at Goodwill, on the rack so long they're practically giving it away. Her hair doesn't look like I remember. It's done up, as if she's gotten it styled professionally and wants to show it off. She has such a radiant smile. When I think back to my mom, I don't recall that. I remember sad, tired, scared, but never prideful. Plus, my mother didn't go to salons.

Maybe I'm reading too much into the moment, and it's simply a snapshot, a wrinkle in time. I put the picture back on the wall and start down the well, a predatory instinct to surveil the grounds and make sure all is okay.

When I hear Bridget's little feet pattering across the tile, I turn around, returning to my cold side of the bed.

The next morning, I awake, greeted by the delectable aroma of frying bacon. I think I must be mistaken—we seldom have bacon in the house, and I don't recall seeing any in the fridge. But sure enough, I round the corner, and there's my lovely wife, already dressed and made up, over the stove frying up a pan full of delicious, hot bacon. It's rare my wife rouses before me. Peter sits at the table, bleary eyed and drowsy. I check the clock on the microwave, surprised it's so late in the morning.

"Why aren't you ready for school?" I ask Peter.

My son tilts his head.

"It's Saturday," Stephanie says over her shoulder.

I have no reason to doubt her timeline but find myself adding days. The awards were Thursday night, so, yeah, that would be right. Days of the week make little difference to me. I spend them all the same, working. Which means after breakfast I'll be back in front of my computer. Then I think maybe today I won't work. Maybe today I will see if Stephanie and Peter want to do something. We can run errands as a family. Stock up at Sam's or Target. Perhaps catch a movie, have lunch in town.

I take a seat and Stephanie delivers my coffee along with the crisp strips of bacon.

"Well, this is a surprise," I say.

Her warm smile restores some of the faith I've lost overnight.

"I was thinking," I say. "We should go do something fun."

My wife raises her eyebrows. "Fun?" she replies, deadpan. "You don't do *fun*, Robert."

I force a laugh. "No, I'm serious. The three of us." I turn to Peter. "What do you say, champ?"

Peter looks confused. Maybe it's the "champ," a nickname I don't recall ever using.

"That *would* be nice," Stephanie says, kissing me on top of the head. "But I have plans today."

Bridget sits in the corner, strangely silent. He's not begging for food, which is a first. Hot sizzling pork should've sent him climbing walls. I want to ask Stephanie where she's going but the dog's stillness surprises, worries me. Waggling a bacon strip, I try to entice him over. Nothing.

I turn to my wife. "What's up with Bridget?"

"I don't think he's feeling well," she says, pointing toward the dog bed by the glass patio door. "Been curled up since I came down."

I catch Peter's eye. "Did you walk him this morning?"

Peter nods.

"I'm sure it's nothing," Stephanie says. "Probably something he ate."

"Peter, did Bridget get into anything on your walk? A trashcan? Garbage?"

My son shakes his head.

Stephanie composts the greasy paper towels, before setting the pot to soak, drying her hands. "I'll be back later."

"I didn't know you had plans," I say.

"Is that a problem?"

"No, of course not." I check with Peter, who scrolls through his phone. "Maybe Peter and I will do something."

My son does not look up from his screen.

Stephanie didn't want us buying Peter an iPhone. I argued prohibition never works, that temperance is key. I figured the longer we denied him what others in his class had, the more fixated he'd become, forbidden fruits tasting sweetest. Plus, I thought getting him a phone would help Peter be more social, make friends, start acting like a regular teenager. Instead, my purchase has created the opposite effect. The boy is forever in front of a screen. It's not healthy.

I hear my wife walk away, through the foyer, grabbing coat and keys. The door opens and shuts. At first my feelings are hurt she didn't want to spend the day with me. Then I acknowledge a last-minute idea sprung, my asking her to rearrange her schedule. I wouldn't appreciate that if she did it to me.

When I turn back to the table, I'm about to ask Peter what he'd like to do today. When my son was younger, he and I used to have these special "boy days." That's what we called them. Going to the movies, grabbing pizza and ice cream. He used to like that.

Before I can ask Peter if he wants me to check what films are playing, my son is already gone. I listen to him clod down the hall and up the stairs to his room. The door slams. Across the table, I see he's left his dirty plate.

I consider calling him back down to clean up his mess. Instead, I bring his dish to the sink, dropping it in the hot suds. I wet a sponge and sweep the crumbs from the table. The clock ticks. The appliances hum. A hard wind blows across the field.

I head upstairs to my office to work.

Midday, my hunger gets the best of me. I knock on Peter's door. No answer. I open it, in case he's wearing headphones, gaming, and can't hear me. He's not there. I come downstairs for lunch. Peter is nowhere to be found. After suggesting we do something, I didn't ask about his plans. I think of texting to check up, then tuck away the cell. I hope this means he's meeting up with friends and that they're doing something social and normal, and not holed up in a game shop.

Making a roast beef sandwich, I see Bridget still curled in the same spot I left him. He didn't move for the bacon. And now he's not excited about roast beef? Something *is* wrong.

I pick up the landline, which has emergency numbers scrawled on the cradle, and ring the vet. It's probably nothing, I tell myself, a stomach bug—I can't stand the thought of Bridget's being in pain. Yes, he's annoying with the perpetual yapping—I should be relishing the quiet—but I can't relax, too worried.

I tell the lady at the vet about Bridget's lack of appetite, careful to stress it's not an emergency—emergency visits cost more. She says to come right in.

I wrap the dog in a blanket and run to the car to avoid getting doused by the rains that have returned. By the time we enter the center of town, the rain has turned to snow, the pretty, fat-flaked kind that floats more than it falls. Like a lullaby. I don't get downtown often. There's not much to see. To get to the university, I generally catch the highway, bypassing all this. Ours is a pretty town, still clustered with mom-and-pop shops. We've avoided the fate that befalls bigger cities like Schenectady, Troy, and Albany, stamped with their Walmarts,

Home Depots, and Starbucks. Words like "idyllic" and "picturesque" get thrown about. Not every Northeastern town is an outtake from *The Saturday Evening Post*. That's what makes Diemen special. In a way, it is a time capsule. Of course, we have *a* Starbucks—we're not savages. Yet, we've managed to retain our humble origins and identity. This town is a village, a community.

Christmas lights still thread telephone poles, colorful ribbons on boutiques and cafés. A giant wreath circles the big round clock at the bank. A sense of holiday cheer lingers, carrying with it expectation that maybe this year will be better than the last.

The lady at the veterinarian clinic takes my information. A moment later, the vet comes out. I don't know this man—Stephanie brings Bridget for his check-ups. Maybe because of this, this lack of familiarity, the vet—who introduces himself as Ken—does not come across as genial or warm. He's curt, brusque. I imagine Stephanie coming in, with her natural beauty and brighter personality, and getting a different reception.

I follow as Ken takes Bridget to the back room. Repositioning his stethoscope to listen to the dog's heart and lungs, the vet asks the standard questions. Has he been eating okay? *No, that's why we're here.* Sleeping okay? *How would I know? I sleep too.* Did he have any reactions to the latest round of inoculations? I answer to the best of my ability. Working from campus, I don't spend as much time with the dog as Stephanie does, and I am not familiar with the frequency of immunization shots. I don't know why Ken is asking me this. He's the vet. He should have all this information in his chart.

When the vet opens Bridget's mouth, the dog whimpers. He tries again and the dog shudders, cowers. Ken pulls back, a perplexed look overtaking his face. I've never heard Bridget cry like this before. It's a soft, thin, weak wail. The dog's mouth is wide open. Given Bridget's pained expression, I expect a bark or howl to emanate; instead, all that comes forth is a dry, dusty wheeze. Like a raspy cough.

The vet stares at me. His eyes convey a mix of concern, fear, and contempt. "Did someone hurt this dog?"

"Excuse me?" I say, feeling defensive, though I'm not sure why.

Ken keeps scratching behind Bridget's ears. The dog does not seem soothed. I can see the vet is trying to word something delicate, and I can't, for the life of me, understand what that might be. Bridget is not old—five years—and fear of disease, such as cancer, has been ruled out by his question whether someone hurt the dog.

"I understand this breed is vocal," the vet says as if empathizing with me.

"Yes," I agree, "Yorkshire Terriers can be yappy." I wish he'd get to whatever point he is trying to make.

Ken the vet doesn't say anything. We stand like that, eyeing one another with uncertainty.

"What's wrong with Bridget?" I ask.

Ken keeps staring at me like I'm a monster who keeps his dog outside in the winter. Which, of course, is not true. Bridget has his own bed indoors, is allowed to sleep with us, and he eats better than most humans.

"His vocal cords are seared," the vet says.

"What do you mean, 'seared'?"

"Burned." Ken can't hide his disgust—for *me*. I'm trying to wrap my head around how Bridget seared his vocal cords. I voice the one thought floating around my brain—Bridget must've found a piece of sizzling hot bacon that somehow fried itself out of the pan.

"Bridget will eat *anything*," I say, going for lighthearted. "Even hot oil—"

"No," the vet says. "Nothing he ate. Someone burned this dog."

"I don't understand—"

"You see it more in the South," Ken says, cutting me off, scratching his chin and trying to come to terms with an atrocity. "I mean, you hear stories of..." The vet gathers himself. "Mr. Kirby, someone scalded this dog's vocal cords. On purpose."

"What—how...?"

He shakes his head. "Heat up something metal. Coat hanger would be my best guess. Force the dog's mouth open, shove the hot tip down his throat, burn off the vocal cords."

"Why—why on Earth would anyone do something like that?"

This is the first time Dr. Ken has an answer ready. The way he shares it, like it's the most obvious answer in the world, makes me feel like a moron.

"To stop him from barking."

CHAPTER THIRTEEN

December 25, 1997, 11:43 a.m.
Fifteen Days Before the Disappearance

After Connie left, Brooke and her dad didn't make a big deal out of holidays. The one exception: that first Christmas Connie was back. That had been a nice Christmas, with a real ham, salty and juicy, and actual green things like vegetables and a salad. That year they had presents too, lots of them. Thoughtful ones, wrapped pretty, and stacked under a fat blue spruce tree. On Christmas morning, they'd all gathered in their pajamas, eating cinnamon buns and drinking hot cocoa, coffee without splashes of alcohol, the household full of joy, mirth, and good tidings. While Christmas carols played on the stereo, Brooke and her family, old and new, tore open emerald and gold wrappers beneath twinkling multi-colored lights. They already knew Connie had cancer, even if her mom downplayed how serious it was, how metastasized the tumors had grown, how soon she'd be gone.

That Christmas, Brooke's mom had bought her a necklace, a crucifix with her amethyst birthstone. It was beautiful. Brooke didn't know how her mother got the style just right—white gold not yellow, which Brooke hated because it looked so tacky. Mother and daughter never talked about accessories or fashion, and Brooke wasn't the type to wear much jewelry. She loved that necklace, vowing to never take it off.

That Christmas felt like a lifetime ago.

This Christmas was the fourth since Connie died. A pallor of gloom hung over the home. Brooke hadn't had time to clean, the place cluttered with Bobby's dirty plates, junk food wrappers, and soda cans. Random, rank socks littered the living room.

Brooke had dug out the old plastic tree, the one they used while Connie was missing, from under the stairs, setting it in the corner, leaning against the wall because she couldn't find the stand. No one bothered to decorate it. Brooke felt compelled to put a *few* boxes underneath, so it didn't look so bare and pathetic. In the morning, the makeshift family—Brooke, Paul, and Bobby—exchanged gifts. No one made cinnamon buns. No one played Christmas carols. Paul's coffee came with a heavy pour of whiskey.

No one knew what to get Bobby. He wasn't into sports, didn't have a fashion style. Most of the time he played video games on a portable handheld device. Brooke didn't know how any of that stuff worked. The boy *did* read books, weird science fiction and fantasy ones. Brooke didn't recognize the titles, except the one about that hobbit. Brooke told her dad she'd buy Bobby a wizard book, even though at fourteen, she wondered if Bobby was too old for that stuff.

That was how the day started. Paul, bleary eyed from booze— Brooke was surprised he'd gotten out of bed—three sad sack strangers stationed around a pipe cleaner tree. The only reason Brooke was doing any of this was for Bobby. Every kid deserves a Christmas. Seeing him sitting there, cross-legged on the floor in his goofy plus-sized pajamas, staring into space, Brooke rummaged for kindness—he'd lost his mom too.

"Merry Christmas, fecto," she said, mussing his hair, handing him his present.

"Thanks," he said, tearing off the paper, before adding, "I already read this one."

It got worse from there.

Since Mike had agreed to set up the drug sale with Stimpy, Brooke couldn't avoid inviting him over. She'd been hoping he'd decline, say he had something better to do. Of course, he didn't. Mike relished having Brooke all to himself. Which was what he wanted. Her, to be his and his alone. Soon, Paul would head off to the bar, Bobby would hide in his room, and she'd be stuck with him.

When Mike arrived, he was already drunk. Normally a six-pack kind of guy, he walked in reeking of the harder stuff, cheap scotch and well bourbon. He confessed coming from an all-nighter with his construction buddies, which had turned into a morning crawl, last call to opening bell. His red-rimmed eyes said the bender had been fueled by a healthy helping of blow.

The first thing Mike did when he walked through the door with the frozen chicken thighs—meat Brooke asked him to grab for Christmas dinner—was mash his face against hers, right in front of Paul and Bobby, who stopped playing his handheld video game to gawk. In their living room foyer, Mike mauled her, one hand clutching uncooked poultry, the other groping and trying to feel her up. Possession. An animal marking its territory. Brooke tried to wriggle free. Paul didn't like Mike but steered clear of Brooke's love life. Times like this, she wished he'd interfere. Paul grumbled about needing air and headed out back for a smoke. By the time Brooke pried Mike off, he was laughing and hooting, the forced exuberance of a drunk. Bobby remained on the floor, chubby tummy poking out between the holes in his pajama top. Mike flopped the dethawed chicken on the counter. Gobs of viscous meat stewed in warm, pink poultry blood.

"When did you pick these up?" Brooke asked.

"Last night."

"You've been carrying them around, bar to bar, with no refrigeration?"

Mike shrugged, unwrapping his winter layers, and plopping in the big chair in the living room, cracking a beer, kicking out his big, booted feet caked with mud. Not willing to risk salmonella, Brooke dropped the chicken in the trash bin and opened the drawer that housed the takeout menus.

From the kitchen, Brooke listened as Mike went after Bobby. The cruelty wasn't as obvious to Paul. Or maybe he didn't care. He'd granted a final wish to a dying woman he loved.

Take care of my son, please.

Of course. Paul would promise Connie anything. In her dad's mind, "taking care of" meant food, clothing, shelter, and medical insurance. And he provided those things. But Paul wasn't a hands-on parent—he hadn't been with Brooke either. Paul might've turned out better if his heart hadn't been broken. Or maybe her dad wasn't the nurturing type. Brooke was stronger and could weather neglect better than Bobby, who clearly needed guidance.

Brooke tried picking up the parental mantle. She was the one who made sure Bobby had his forms signed for school, who made sure he had presents to open, birthday cake candles to blow out. Despite her issues with Connie, Brooke took her mother's dying wish to heart.

"Hey, numbnuts," Mike said. And after a few seconds, when Bobby didn't reply: "I'm talking to you, dillweed. What you doin' with that thing?" That "thing" being the video game their mom bought Bobby her last Christmas, stretching dollars she didn't have as far as they would go.

"Leave him alone, Mike." From the kitchen, Brooke sifted menus, trying to decide between pizza and Chinese.

"You ain't playing with friends," Mike said. "Do you *have* friends?"

Water burbled in old copper pipes.

"You don't got no girlfriend." The sound of snapping fingers, then louder: "Hey, fuckball. I'm talking to you." A beer breaking free from plastic rings. Another tab cracked. "You a homo?"

Brooke slammed down the menus. "I mean it, Mike! Leave him alone."

"You like to suck dick? That it?"

Brooke waited for Bobby to stand up for himself and show Mike he wouldn't be pushed around—which was essential when dealing with a bully like Mike, who would push until he couldn't push anymore. But Bobby didn't do a damn thing. Maybe he *was* gay. Brooke didn't know, didn't care. Then Paul shouted from the back porch, his face pressed to the cold glass. Brooke couldn't hear him, making for the back door.

"Chinese!" Paul shouted through the window.

Brooke had turned around, ready to choose from an assortment of fried dumplings, egg rolls, hot and sour soup, boneless spareribs, Kung Po chicken, maybe some of those green onion pancakes too, when she heard the commotion in the living room, as if someone had jumped up and kicked the coffee table, jostling remote controls, magazines, and empty glasses.

"I take it out, you suck it?"

A second later came the strike and sound of a video game sent careening across the room, smashing against the wall, shattering into hundreds of tiny pieces.

Brooke ran into the living room. Bobby was crying. Mike zipped up his fly, laughing.

"What the fuck is your problem?" she said.

Mike waved her off, staggering from his spot, weaving past, making for the back porch to join Paul for a smoke.

Brooke stood at the edge of the room, searching for how to console Bobby, who remained sitting Indian style on the floor, sobbing, sniffing back excess mucous that ran from his nose into his mouth. The whole scene made her sick.

"You can't let people push you around, fecto."

Bobby didn't glance up, didn't break from his crying. What was she supposed to do? Hug him? Let him cry? Tell him it would get better? Before she could do anything, Bobby pushed himself up from the floor and ran to his room.

Brooke went back to the kitchen to order the food.

The kid was too soft for this world. Sooner or later, it would eat him alive.

CHAPTER FOURTEEN

NOW

Sitting in my car on Main Street, I find Diemen doesn't look so pretty anymore. What kind of monster hurts a dog? I once read an interview with Stephen King where he talks about having a villain injure a dog—I can't recall the name of the book. King did it to illustrate how evil the man was. I remember thinking at the time it was funny. Not the subject matter, which is horrific. But because in that interview, King said he got more angry letters about that one scene than any of his other books. I was struck by that. The man writes about killer clowns eating children, satanic orgies, serial killers, and a vast assortment of other ghastly beasts—yet to demonstrate the worst of the worst, the most unfathomable of evils, he had to harm a dog.

Pulling in the driveway, I see Stephanie's car and am wondering how I tell her about this. Coming on the heels of Lily's visit, I'm questioning whether I have to tell her. I'm not contemplating dishonesty for the sake of personal gain; I don't want to scare her. Bridget doesn't go off leash—he's a runner—which means someone has been *in* our house. We lock our doors at night. Usually, sometimes, once in a while? But not last night apparently because someone walked right in. That was the sound that woke me up. I'd sat on the stairs, doing nothing, while someone mutilated our dog.

I enter a dark house and find my wife, sitting alone at the kitchen table with a mostly empty bottle of white wine. With the lights off, evening gloam casts her in a deathly pall.

She doesn't ask where I've been or why I'm cradling Bridget like a baby. I place down the dog, more tender than usual, and he scuttles off to the corner to hide in his bed. I wish I could do the same. The sun has set, scarring the winter sky rusted violet.

Stephanie stares at me. I see the pain in her eyes.

"Peter." It's the first thing out of my mouth. I say it without thinking. Something bad has happened to my boy, my deepest fear.

"Peter's fine," my wife says. "He's at Carol's house."

Carol is a friend of my wife, and an odd place for our teenage son to visit. Even when we used to need a sitter, Carol isn't the type of person who watches your son. There's nothing wrong with her. She's terrific for girls' nights out, even if she's a little wild for her age. She's far from a derelict or alcoholic—we don't have those sorts in Diemen—she owns, doesn't rent, has a good-paying job, eschews chain restaurants. She's just not a "kid" person.

I'm trying to wrap my brain around what's happening in my kitchen. Of course, you can't articulate such a sensation in the moment; you need reflection. Real time does not afford that. This is happening as I think it. In the moment, all you can do is process what you see, which leaves you lagging, playing catch-up because the next moment has already arrived, stamping its newfound implication, which is yet to be reconciled. I experience conflicting stimuli, trying to sort what belongs, casting aside what doesn't, compartmentalizing this recent intel into an updated worldview. Standing in my kitchen, remodeled at no small cost, staring at all the cold granite, marble, and gleaming metal, I can't create a new picture or, more importantly, see where I will fit in it.

"Robert," she says, and I can hear it in my wife's voice. That one simple word, my name—it sucks the air from the room. The shift, the change in tone—even with the heat blasted toasty, there is a drop in temperature. We can feel these things, intrinsically know when our world is about to be turned on its ear. "Sit down. Please. We need to talk."

Never in the history of conversation have the words "we need to talk" been followed by anything good.

I turn back to the counter, pulling down a glass. "This sounds like a wine-first conversation," I joke. Joking comes easy. It's a defense mechanism. It gives one time to protect those parts that can still feel, still hurt, still bleed. "Can I get you a glass?" I add, ignoring the bottle or half-empty glass in front of her. I reach for the cabinet that houses stemware, self-preservation telling me to stall as long as possible. Whatever is about to happen is not anything I want to hear.

"No. Please. Robert. Sit."

I stop searching for glasses. I will not be pouring any wine.

Taking my seat, I can't help but feel I've entered a negotiation.

"Go ahead," I say, as if my permission is required for Stephanie to speak.

"This isn't working, Robert."

Like an idiot, I struggle to grasp what "this" is. In eight seconds, I will hate myself twice as much because, right now, my eyes fix on the iPhone that has come up in her hand, brain wiring doing its best to spare me humiliation by offering solution via simple appliance repair. Her phone is broken.

Something is broken all right. It isn't her phone.

"I've been feeling so alone for so long," she says. "You come and go, hiding in your office. You don't talk to me. You never want to spend time with me or our son—"

"What are you talking about? This morning I asked if you wanted to spend the day together."

"I already had plans."

I throw up my hands, dropping my jaw with exaggeration and forcing a laugh. Even now, I play the clown. Go for the cheap laugh, and let's move past this.

"First time you've asked in ages," she says. "I assumed you'd be working like you do every weekend."

"Forget this morning. Water under the bridge." I thumb into the dark, evoking brightness and optimism. "Let's do something now. We'll go into town. Grab dinner, a movie? We can pick up Peter first—"

"It's too late for that."

I look at the clock, pretending she means the time of day.

Stephanie doesn't dignify my charade.

I reach for her hand. "What do you want?"

She pulls it away. "A husband. This feels like we're roommates."

"Roommates?"

"You never touch me."

"I touch you," I say flummoxed, treating the statement as preposterous, while also trying to recall the last time we really had sex, made love instead of a quickie to service basic human needs. I can't think right now. Married couples often go spells without sex. It's not ideal. Life gets in the way. We both have lives. Hers is more social. I'm a professor and an author. This isn't grounds for separation.

"I think we need time," she says.

"Time? To do what?"

"To reevaluate." She turns away, staring across our little valley into the black country night, toward the tiny white lights dotting the hillside.

I trace her gaze. I want to know what she's looking at, what's out there, what else has caught her attention. Or maybe I don't want to know.

When I was younger, between semesters at college, I worked for a local contractor in the summer, painting houses. Lousy pay but I liked being outdoors and left alone. There was one day where I was up higher than I should have been, given the weight I was carrying and my unfortunate lack of coordination. There was a small section I'd missed, and it was driving me nuts. I've long suspected I have a touch of OCD. I extended too far and lost my footing and could feel myself falling back, and in that split-second I processed several thoughts at once, but the two most important were: one, if I fell from that height, I'd break my neck. And two: I didn't have time to be "thinking" about anything. Dropping bucket and brush, I leapt for the ladder, a lemur to a tree. The bucket fell thirty feet to the grass and sidewalk, paint splashing, rolling a wave of red that could've been my blood, as I managed to grasp a single rung and hang on.

That is how I feel now. I am falling backwards. I don't have time to think. I need to jump and find something to hold onto and not let go or I will die.

"I know I've been distracted," I say, trying to locate the precise facial expression that conveys pain, confusion, and regret. I need to adopt it, project it, own it. But emotions that complex are not always easy to identify or implement. Pursed lips, furrowed brow, and sad eyes won't remedy this. *We need more.* Anxiety and nerves kick in. "Th-the NEH grant t-took up a l-l-lot of time," I stammer, like I often do when I get overwhelmed. I hate when I stutter. I feel like that fat, cross-eyed little boy again.

"This isn't about the grant," she says. "It's been going on for a while."

I try and think of those words. A while. I don't recall "a while." Until eight minutes ago, I'd have gone on record, hand on Bible, that Stephanie and I had a great marriage. There are fights. Every couple fights. Rough patches come with the journey. But I experienced no disconnect between us. Stephanie is my best friend. All this time, I thought I was doing a good job, which of course is relative, subjective, and objective depending on point of view. Right now, that assessment is not shared by the only person whose opinion matters.

The doorbell rings. Who rings a bell this time of night? It's pitch black out. No one's called to announce their arrival. The last thing I need is an interruption. I don't have time to waste. I must find my rung and hold on.

I don't move. Neither does my wife. The bell rings again, followed by a loud, urgent knock.

"Are you expecting anyone?" I ask.

Stephanie shakes her head.

I fumble for reassuring words, a means to delay the inevitable, but I can't get anything out. Not wanting to risk stuttering again, I rise from my chair, walk down the vestibule to tell this kid or whoever is out there to take whatever they are selling and get lost.

Through the big bay windows, I see the blue and red lights swirl, painting white walls patriotic, and I accept my night is about to get a lot worse.

CHAPTER FIFTEEN

December 28, 1997, 10:07 p.m.
Twelve Days Before the Disappearance

"You ain't fucking coming inside," Mike said from the backseat of
Torie's battered and rusted beater, alternating his glare between Brooke
and Torie up front, resentful of being stuck in the back yet relishing his
being needed so much.

They were at an impasse, an old-fashioned Texas standoff or however that saying went. Mike said he worked alone. Okay, cowboy. Torie
didn't trust Mike and wouldn't let the drugs out of her sight, which was
why she insisted on driving. Brooke didn't trust Mike either. He was
going to skim off the top—that was the price of doing business. What
worried Brooke most was Mike was a fuckup. And he found new ways
to fuck up all the time. Even when the route to the hoop was straight
and unguarded, he managed to miss the shot. Brooke also knew this
was out of their hands. That's why Torie came to her in the first place.
Mike knew Stimpy, and Stimpy wasn't letting them inside—drug
dealers are apprehensive about meeting strangers, and for good reason. Brooke had watched enough Discovery Channel reenactments
to know odds don't always favor the dealer. Wires, stings, informants,
operations, raids, busts. No one's doing felonies for free. If it was up to

Brooke, they would've given Mike the drugs and waited for him at her house. The risk you take. "No fucking way," Torie had said. Now they were stuck here, in this neighborhood, at this time of night, which was the last place Brooke wanted to be.

Behind the abandoned mills and closed-down factories, slow creeks trickled like a chunky, meaty gravy, feeding toxic pools that sludged beneath industrial slate skies. Feral cats hissed as they prowled for fish heads, and the unwanted warmed fragile bones over oil barrel fires. River Gate was already the skids, and this neighborhood, dubbed Crooked Row, made the rest of town look glamorous by comparison. On their way here, they'd driven through downtown, a collection of bars that never closed interspersed between dollar stores and rent-by-the-hour motels. Everyone on the street had the same look in their eyes, hatred for just being born. That was city center, with at least a few 7-Elevens and liquor stores, markets with actual food, which lent a resemblance to society. Where they were now, the outer rim of River Gate, people stopped going through the motions. Hooded figures lurked in the shadows, shifting wads from jacket pockets to stuff more cash. Runners pedaled and darted beneath stoops and gutters, passing packets to palsied palms in the weak light of the moon.

Brooke wasn't expecting the Four Seasons in Back Bay. Still, she was surprised by the squalid conditions of Crooked Row. Once a viable waterfront haven and key cog along Southern New England's wheel of commerce, River Gate never recovered from the recession of '61. In the decades that followed, lax laws and legal loopholes regarding the disposal of hazardous waste muddied clear channels, and the once-vital seaport turned into little more than a beachfront dump. In the '90s, the EPA stepped in to combat the damage, sealing off the waterway River Gate had been named after, closing bay and harbor access to avoid further pollution. By then it was too late.

Brooke had learned a lot about regional history during her two and a half semesters at Midfield State.

"Hey," Mike said, catching Brooke's reflection in the mirror. "You're the ones who wanted to come along."

"I'm not handing this over," Torie said, holding up the paper bag full of narcotics so everyone could see. "How do I know you'll come back?"

"Shut the fuck up," Mike said. "I'm her best friend."

Best friend? Brooke felt sorry for Mike. After they made this sale—twenty-five thousand dollars wasn't out of the realm of possibility—Brooke planned to take her cut and never see the asshole again.

"Torie," Brooke said, gesturing over the headrest. "Look around. These aren't apartments you just walk into. How does Stimpy know we're not cops?"

"Do I look like a cop?"

"No. But that doesn't mean you weren't popped and are wearing a wire."

"A ... wire?" Torie tightened the tee shirt over her tits.

"That's how guys like Stimpy think." Brooke touched her arm to show they were on the same team. "I know it. You know it." She pointed out the window. "The people in that house don't." Then peering back at Mike: "How long will this take?"

"A fucklot shorter if she shuts the fuck up and lets me go inside." Mike pulled his Zippo and lit a cigarette.

"Don't smoke in my car."

He slapped his Zippo head shut and blew out a lungful, because Mike Rakowski was the kind of guy who carried a Zippo, and nobody told him what to do. "Stimpy already knows I'm coming and what I'm bringing. If you'll let me be on my way..."

"Fine," Torie said. "But if you're not back in fifteen minutes, I'm walking up and ringing the bell. Or knocking. Or screaming your name from the street."

"Yeah," Mike said, snaring the paper bag, kicking open the door and flicking his butt into the swirling, frigid winds. "You do that."

"Get fucked, Mike."

He tucked the scrunched-up bag inside his coat, blew a kiss, and disappeared into the night.

"Your boyfriend is a real asshole," Torie said.

"He's not my boyfriend."

"Then what is he?"

Brooke had been trying to answer that question since she'd first met Mike Rakowski. Eyes adjusting to the darkness, she watched him enter the duplex. Like the rest of the squat, ugly structures, it was square, brown, and made of hard material, brick, concrete, scar tissue. The reminder that children lived here, evidenced by the rusted bicycles and deflated sports balls, gutted. Tomorrow, Brooke would forget she was ever here. These kids should be so lucky.

Tall fronds rustled along the water's edge. Unmown grasses and untended weeds scraped against the hull of the car with each icy gust.

Ten minutes turned to twenty, twenty to thirty, Torie's anxiety getting worse by the second, panic she insisted on voicing.

"No one's even in there," Torie said.

"Someone is in there."

"The lights are all off."

"They're probably in the back or basement."

"Mike probably took off," Torie said. "I'm going inside."

Brooke stared at her, wordless. They both recognized the empty threat. Torie could say it all she wanted. She wasn't getting out of this car. Torie fell back into the ruptured seat, fiberglass tufts poking out. "How long are we gonna sit here?"

"However long it takes."

"This is bullshit!"

By now the streets had settled, sordid activity dried up, the scene dead. No one tossed tiny balloons from second-story windows. No hoodrats huddled on stoops; no bicycles or runners spirited into the distance with a week's pay.

The cold, black night felt too quiet.

Brooke sensed the encroaching doom before she heard the sirens or saw the lights, a split-second intuition. Fight-or-flight adrenaline kicked in, screaming for her to get out of there.

And then there they were, four squad cars, screeching brakes in front of the duplex, slamming doors followed by bullhorn demands.

The women ducked, Brooke's eyes fixed on the ignition, gesturing for Torie to turn the key, step on the gas, go! Why had they parked so close to a drug den? Why had they come at all?

Torie froze, paralyzed by fear. Brooke prayed the police wouldn't notice their car.

First the flashlight shone through the window. Then the cop rapped on the glass.

Brooke caught the glint of gunmetal as she slowly brought her hands into view.

CHAPTER SIXTEEN

NOW

"Mr. Kirby?" the officer inquires. Beyond his shoulder, a younger man stands, his thumbs looped in his belt, guarding the bottom of the stairs. One hand reaches over and brushes the grip of his gun, readying the draw should the fugitive make a run for it.

"Yes, I'm Dr. Kirby." Normally, I don't correct with "doctor." Yes, I have the degree. I don't save lives or replace hearts. Right now, I'll take the deference. I can feel Stephanie's looming behind me.

"Mind if we talk inside?"

"What is this about?"

"We received a call from Pets and Pals Veterinary Clinic." The officer gazes past me to make eye contact with my wife, as though trying to elicit communication via secret signal, blink twice if your husband is a monster. "About your dog..." He peers down at his notepad. "Bridget."

This, of course, catches Stephanie's attention. She rushes forward, squeezing under my arm, out in front. "Bridget's inside," she says, turning back to stare at me and join the police in their prolonged accusations.

"The vet at the clinic called about possible ... animal abuse."

Stephanie's eyes, which were already leery of me, grow more disenchanted.

"Robert," she says, formally addressing me by name as if we haven't been married over a decade. "What is he talking about?"

"Someone ... burned Bridget's throat. Deliberately. To stop him from barking."

"And you didn't think to tell me?"

"Gee," I say, slathering words with sarcasm, "I guess I had something else on my mind."

"Who would do such a thing?" Stephanie pivots up the steps, hurrying down the hall to the dog. I'm left with the cops. I understand they have a job to do but their timing couldn't be worse.

"Is this necessary?" I ask. Unable to add the truth, that my marriage is crumbling as we speak. They can't know that. I come across like an insensitive jerk, my impetuous tone implying they've interrupted a luxurious champagne bubble bath. This section of Diemen carries that reputation. Which isn't fair. It's a well-off part of town, in a better-off part of the state, but trouble finds everyone.

"We treat allegations of animal abuse seriously, sir."

Rolling my eyes, I further cement views that I'm a self-centered ass. I want to catch who did this—of course I do—there's also such a thing as priorities.

Now we are in the kitchen. Stephanie cradles Bridget, who, given the situation, looks appropriately skittish. He tries to bark, like any time he encounters strangers, but all that comes out is a dry, dusty cough. I make to scratch him behind the ears, show them that Bridget is not scared of me, but when I come closer, Stephanie, my wife, who up until a half hour ago was an ally, snatches back the dog. To the police, I'm sure it looks like both are terrified of me.

This is Diemen, though. I'm a well-respected professor, the recent recipient of a prestigious National Endowment for the Humanities grant, and, goddamn it, they have to show me some respect.

"Can you tell us what happened, Dr. Kirby?"

"If I knew," I say, "don't you think I'd have told the vet?"

I must project that I don't care what the police think—I didn't do this—there is no reason to act guilty when I'm innocent.

They wait for more.

I groan and recap waking to Bridget's barking, how I, i.e., not my wife, disrupted my slumber in the middle of the night to investigate. When Bridget stopped barking, I'd assumed it was a deer or raccoon that had him riled up. I add how I—again not my wife—took the day off of work, dropping everything to bring the dog to the vet. I say this with the rightful indignation of the good guy.

"Dr. Ketchum said—"

"Who's Dr. Ketchum?" I ask.

"Bridget's vet," Stephanie replies, coolly, and I'm aghast she has the nerve to act self-righteous.

"Ken Ketchum?" I repeat, turning to the cops. "Sounds like he could be one of you boys. Ken—Catch 'em!" It's a stupid joke, but I'm trying to cut the mounting tension.

"There's nothing funny about animal abuse, sir."

I want to say, "Lighten up, Francis," alluding to a line from an old movie, but I don't, fearing I'll look extra prissy. I try to think how a normal person would act in such a moment. *Offended. Yes, that is the play. How dare they come in* my *home and imply I would harm a sweet little dog like Bridget.*

"Why would I think there is anything funny about someone harming my dog?" I stand as upright and stiff-shouldered as I can.

"Perhaps," I add, "instead of interrogating *me*, you should be out catching who did this." I know I am parroting lines from cop shows like *Law & Order*. I'm not steady on my feet and can feel myself wobbling. I'm getting riled, finding it harder to breathe. Or maybe it's because I've locked my knees to stand taller, which runs the risk of passing out. I pull out a stool at the counter, plunking myself with determined grief. I can't lose my composure, completing the portrait of a hair-triggered, temperamental psycho. "Sorry," I say. "As you can imagine, this is quite upsetting."

No one replies. I can feel their eyes on me. I am aware my blood pressure is spiking, a return to the old days when I'd get overwhelmed and lash out. I struggle to keep "Bobby" where I buried him, deep in the recesses of my past.

"Have you had any recent altercations?" the cop asks. "Run-ins with unhappy neighbors? Perhaps someone angry the dog barks so much? Relieves himself on their lawn?"

The nearest house couldn't hear Bridget if he was ten feet tall. Which I make sure the police know. Besides rejecting the premise of his question, I reiterate the neighborhood we live in.

"How about disgruntled students?" the cop continues, fishing. "Coworkers?"

"Ortho Warsh," I blurt.

"Robert!"

Like Ortho Warsh is this paragon of virtue and not a flaming asshole. I want to say, *Well,* somebody *came onto my property, enticed my dog close enough to maim him.* I can't find the bravado needed to fuel such a bold stance, so I remain silent.

"Who is Ortho Warsh?"

"He's a colleague of Robert's," Stephanie interjects, saving me from further embarrassment. "But he didn't do this."

I know Ortho didn't do this. I took the question at face value. They asked if I'd had "any recent altercations" with "coworkers"? All I did was respond with the truth.

"Ma'am," the cop says, "we're trying to see if anyone harbors ill will toward you or your husband." He points past Stephanie's shoulder at the glass patio door. "Is that usually locked?"

"Yes," I say.

The cop walks over and slides open the unlocked patio door.

"This is a very safe neighborhood," I say.

"There was a girl," Stephanie says.

I know this must be addressed. Lily. Constant variables, newly introduced integer. I can't articulate, my soft brain tongue tied, stress tripping up inductive and deductive reasoning skills. Still, I don't want to talk about Lily. Because then I'll have to talk about Brooke. And everything will change.

"Lily Stillwater," I say. "She came by my office at Uniondale. Claiming to be my niece." I pause. One, two, three. "My missing stepsister Brooke's daughter."

Right as rain, at the mention of Brooke's name, I sense the collective mood in the room soften. The sympathy card, which I hate playing. Doesn't matter if I'm a state over and twenty years removed; everyone knows the story. Suspicion turns to pity. I'd rather they think I'm an animal abuser.

The police wait for me to say more, watching, as does Stephanie, engrossed by tales of my tragic history, which I am again exploiting, whoring out my traumatic past. I also have no choice.

Talking about Brooke's daughter means talking about the night of the disappearance, dredging it all back up, the loss, the scars that can't heal because the wound refuses to close up and scab over. I talk. They listen. I keep it as brief as possible. I don't care about Lily—I don't have reason to believe or doubt her, and I am not protecting her. I also can't believe that a nineteen-year-old co-ed is slinking onto my property, breaking and entering, prying open a dog's mouth, and inserting a piece of metal hot enough to cauterize internal organs. Then again, I can't imagine *anyone* doing that. Of course, hearing about the timing of my meeting with Lily sparks the cops' imagination. I am not at odds with their agenda. Foremost on my mind, however, is my floundering marriage. I feel like a guy standing on a station platform in the rain with a comical look on his face because his insides have been kicked out, and, yes, I did just watch *Casablanca* on Turner Classics, but I can't bring up any of this, these tangential thoughts, regardless of cohesion, because they'd translate as elusive or disjointed to the outsider who isn't privy to points of origin. And goddamn I can't articulate that right now.

When I'm done recapping my infamous history, the first cop, the older one with the buzzcut who has done most of the talking, and whose name badge I might be able to read were I so inclined, asks if I have a phone number for Lily.

I toss back my head. Yes, I do. I don't see the point in calling. Even if she *did* do something so heinous, what do they expect? Her to confess?

I pass along the number and try to look pleasant as I do so. If she didn't do it, I can't imagine what the poor girl will think. And if she *did*, I'm not sure I want to hear it. What if she *is* related to me?

By supplying what I know—the college she'll be attending, the hometown she claims to be from—I try to assure myself I'm glad this is out of my hands.

But I can't lie to myself anymore.

I know we are just getting started.

CHAPTER SEVENTEEN

NOW

After the police leave, my wife and I stand in the kitchen, at opposite ends. I thought Stephanie was my best friend, a person I knew as well as I did myself. Now she is just another mystery I am unable to solve.

"What now?" I ask.

"I'm going to go stay with my sister."

"In Pittsburgh? So that's it. You're moving out, twelve years of marriage done? That's great, Steph."

"I'm not moving out," she says. "I need time. I think you do too."

For as angry as I am with her, I must admit, on some level, I know she is right. If Stephanie were to stay, I would exact my revenge, passive aggressively, piece by piece, until she was hurting like I am hurting. It's a petty trait, and one that I am not proud of. I am vindictive. If I have to pick sides in the Bible, I favor leaving the world blind. Of course, I know the Bible is fiction, and not even good fiction, but my mother, God rest her soul, was a true believer. I don't care how many years pass, when you grow up indoctrinated into the faith, skins do not shed so easily.

"What about Peter?" I say. "School?"

"He can miss a little time. I'll call his teachers."

"Hockey?"

"He hates hockey."

No. I shake my head. "You think you're taking *my* son?" This is a hill I can die on, the loyal, proud father, position beyond reproach.

"I'm not 'taking' your son. I think he's better off with me. For the time being."

"And why's that?" I say, walking into her trap. "Because you love him more? Are the better parent? More responsible? Better person? What?"

"No," she says, lucid and calm. "Because some lunatic is lurking around our house? Breaking in? Hurting our dog?"

"No one is 'lurking.'" My words lack conviction.

"Then who injured Bridget?"

"We don't know if *anyone* did. Who is that vet, Ken?" I'd never met him before today. I'm sure he's qualified. Doesn't mean he's infallible. I don't see how what he's suggesting is even possible. The precision and expertise, the medical training one would need—

"I was already planning on taking a break," Stephanie says with an exhausted sigh. "This doesn't change anything."

I close my eyes, let my thoughts settle. I *do* need time. I can't repair the damage done. Not like this, not when my emotions best my intellect. I'll make the situation worse. I don't fight her. "Fine," I say, dismissing my wife and family with a flick of the wrist. Take my son. Take my dog. Go. I'm a goddamn country song.

My wife starts to walk away. She doesn't get three feet before I call her back.

"Do you still love me?" It sounds so pathetic, the way those words fall from my mouth. I am opening myself up to devastation—you never ask a question like that, not when you are this vulnerable.

Thankfully, Stephanie says, "Yes, Robert. I still love you."

Watching her pick up Bridget and walk out, I don't ask any more questions, choosing faith over truth.

When she is gone, the big house feels cold, empty; I am alone. Surrounded by luxury, I find no comfort—the Varianne curved sofa and Cavallo recliner, the Jasmine fossilized clam coffee table might as well be cardboard boxes and grad-school Furio. I am not piling on misery or woe to milk self-pity; I am not trying to make myself feel worse. This observation lands a long way from delusional. I *am* alone, the house *is* empty, and without anyone else here to keep me company it is too goddamn big. These … things … that are supposed to represent success or status symbols mean nothing; they are vapid, soulless, overpriced objects. I do not turn on the lights, allowing darkness to descend, sweep in over the woods and envelop me. I sit in a chair at the kitchen table and stare out the big glass patio door, into the dense forest that juts against our property, the impenetrable trees that create a wall behind which anyone can be hiding. This is not the first time I've been left alone—Stephanie and Peter have taken vacations without me while I've stayed behind to work—but this sensation I experience now is gutting. I feel their extraction, my wife and child, the hurt, addition of pain by subtraction of love. Because Stephanie and Peter define me, occupy every inch, and their removal leaves a gaping hole in my chest where a heart should be.

Tonight, I can't bring myself to sleep in our bed, opting for the couch, which is where I often end up sleeping most nights anyway. I tend to work late into the night, and when I go to lie down, I often find Bridget hogging my side of the bed. He's a small dog, but he sprawls, covering more space than one would think possible. I could move him.

Sometimes I do. More often than not, however, I leave them both in peace, heading to the couch so as not to disturb anyone. This is where I sleep now.

When morning breaks, there's that split-second where I am oblivious, *tabula rasa*, a blank slate. Nothing has changed. Schrödinger's sad sack. My family is both in the other room and they are not. Each is possible but neither outcome carries consequence. Then it all comes rushing back, striking me like a nail pounded into my forehead, splitting bone.

Stumbling into the kitchen, emotionally hungover, I power on the espresso machine. Rain pelts the patio and sliding glass door, waves of water whipping with the wind. I look over the muddy fields of slop and sludge, toward the treeline. I open the glass door, step onto the patio, searching for a set of footprints. Pointless. Any possible prints have long been washed away. The time to do that was last night, before the storm, but the police were too busy grilling me, my wife too consumed with executing her plan of escape, which had to be months, maybe years in the making. As I went about my business with a goofy grin on my stupid face, believing all the lies I've told myself. I feel like a chump. That was one of my stepfather Paul's favorite words. Get pushed around at school, beat up by another boy, rejected by a girl. "Don't be such a chump, Bobby."

It's raining harder now. I am getting drenched, soaked by a bargain baptism. Then, beyond the fringes of my property, as I trace the wood line to the nearest street, I see the car. It is red, or maybe that's rust. Through the pissing rain, it's too far to make out much. No make or model. It sits there, idling, in the distance. A regular old car. I know it is not from Diemen. This car isn't one of ours. There's no law against a driver, of whatever means, pulling over, perhaps to take a phone call or check an address. I pull my glasses from my pocket, strap them on, fogged up and wet. I still can't see, the car swallowed in the heavy fog and mist that accompanies winter rains in the lowlands. Maybe it's a boyfriend killing time, a girl waiting on a friend, an out-of-towner, confused. It doesn't have to mean anything. The way the car is parked, though… Leaves me uneasy.

I step into my rubber boots and slide open the door. I don't grab a winter coat because that is in the mudroom, by the foyer, and I am too invested now to turn back. I am in my tee shirt, pajama pants, and galoshes. The rain soaks me to the bone. I walk across the platform, descend the stairs, into the squall, moving toward the old red car. I don't get ten feet before the driver, whoever it is, spins off, rushing down the road.

My landline rings on the wall next to the patio door.

I see "Diemen PD" on the caller ID, answering it while still half outside.

"Dr. Kirby," a gruff voice announces, while I stand at the edge of a monsoon like a fool. "This is Officer Cook." And when I don't respond, he adds, "From last night?"

The man on the phone does not sound like the cop from last night.

"Wanted to let you know, we phoned the number you gave us for Lily Stillwater. Are you sure you wrote it down right?"

I become aware how drenched I'm getting, or it finally starts to bother me. I duck back inside, leaking pools of cold rainwater to the floor. Staring down at the mess, I feel like I am melting.

"Dr. Kirby?"

"I'm here. I didn't write down the number. She wrote it down for me."

"The number you gave us is for a nursing home. Nothing in Bellemont. We also called Amherst. There is no record of a Lily Stillwater enrolled there. Not this semester. Or last."

I try to think what this might mean. The early hour and lack of caffeine doesn't help formulate thoughts.

"Can you think of anything else she told you? Anything that might be of use to us?"

Like what?

"Well," Officer Cook says when I don't answer, "if you do think of anything else, please give us a call—"

"Wait," I say. A thought tickles the back of my brain.

"Yes?"

"You said that number was for a nursing home?"

"Correct."

"What was the name?"

I hear papers rustling on the other end. "Roseville Rest Home." He waits. "Does that name mean anything to you?"

"No," I say, thanking him for the call and hanging up.

I grab my wallet, keys, and cell, and make for the front door.

The pitter patter of the rain off the car roof is maddening. I fire up the engine and crank the radio to try and drown out thoughts. A talking head chirps about seasonal cinnamon recipes, promising to return with more baking tips after this fundraising break. I pull up an app and type in "Roseville Rest Home." GPS says it's a two-hour drive.

I tell myself this will be good. It's been a while since I visited my stepfather.

CHAPTER EIGHTEEN

December 29, 1997, 5:44 a.m.
Eleven Days Before the Disappearance

Before her father picked her up at the River Gate precinct and bailed her out of that dank, rancid jail, Brooke had a lot of time to think. Which wasn't easy to do given the foul stench and limited space to hide from it. The stainless-steel toilet overflowed with browned, soggy papers and God-knew-what else. No one bothered to clean up the other side of the holding cell, where a homeless woman had puked. Poor thing lay face up, inches from beefy pink vomit, remnants dribbling down her chin. Brooke should've at least rolled her over so she didn't choke. Brooke had her own problems to worry about.

What a clusterfuck. The cops had found Mike inside Stimpy's, smoking and playing video games with a couple hoodrats, neither of whom were Stimpy. The vials, pills, and assorted meds sat in the sack next to Mike. They were easy to trace back to Roseville Rest Home, since no one had bothered to scrape off names or labels.

Paul and Brooke fought the entire way home, hurling insults, pointing out all the ways each had let the other down. Even as she defended herself—highlighting hardships like her dead mother—Brooke recognized how bratty she was being. More than most, Brooke knew that life wasn't fair; that the world owes you nothing and it gives you even less. This insight didn't ease the pain. To survive this life means to play the cards you're dealt. Brooke hadn't been dealt the worst hand. But the cards she held landed a long way from a winner.

Slamming the truck door with a parting "fuck you," Brooke stalked up the steps, as Paul peeled out in reverse, speeding down the street to finish getting drunk somewhere else.

In these moments, when Brooke was raging, she needed to be alone. So she could calm down and not kill somebody. She would've had that space. Except now goddamn Bobby was living here. Soon as she walked through the door, there he was, staring up through thick glasses, goofy look plastered on his stupid face, big book sitting open in his lap. It was six in the morning. What fourteen-year-old boy wakes up at six in the morning? To read a book? Not playing video games. Not jacking it to the JCPenney lingerie catalogue. Regular teenage shit. No, a book. He was such a dweeb. He kept staring at her without meeting her eyes. Brooke had grown certain her brother had mental problems. She knew Connie drank and partied before finding Jesus. Next time she was on a computer, she'd check the effects of alcohol on fetuses, look it up online. Would make an interesting topic for an abnormal psych paper when she got her ass back in gear and returned to school.

Brooke threw her bag on the table, knocking over the bowl with the extra keys and random junk, bills she'd have to open later and pay, because if she waited for her father to take charge, the power company would leave them all in the dark.

Bobby blinked, staring silent.

"What are you looking at, fecto?"

On one hand, Brooke understood her disdain for her new brother wasn't rational—she had taken psychology courses after all. He was a symbol, her disgust a projection. Bobby represented the reason her mother abandoned them. What did they call that? Transference? That wasn't Bobby's fault. He was a kid, the by-product of a million-to-one shot of some squirming tadpole latching onto one unlucky egg. Right place, wrong time. Or the other way around. Who gives a fuck?

Bobby didn't answer. Just sat there in his oversized pajama pants and stretched-out tee shirt, stained with an assortment of foodstuffs. A fat, helpless lump. The kid tried to hide his weight by wearing bigger clothes, which only made him look fatter.

Brooke couldn't help herself.

"Fucking retard!"

She stomped up the stairs to her room, slamming the door, throwing herself on the bed.

College dropout, aimless, drifting, about to lose her job as soon as the police talked to the nursing home about the stolen drugs—and they would—how could they forget to scrape off the labels? Now she was facing criminal charges and possible prison time? Best-scenario was probation, but that shit still went on her permanent record. She'd have to include it on every job application till the end of time. *Fuck. Me.*

Grabbing her Discman, Brook snapped on the headphones, cranking the volume, hoping Screeching Weasel would drown out the noise in her head.

Outside garbage trucks lumbered along her street, big green monstrosities rumbling over ice, snow, and crusted mud in the early dawn, hungry bellies grumbling to be fed. A fast, funny thought flashed in her head. It could all be over, like that. She could throw herself away with the rest of the trash. Curl up in a ball and go to sleep in a can, let robotic arms toss her into the hopper, wait for the packer to crush her skull before they peeled away her remains. Cart off what was left of Brooke Mulcahy to some landfill where she could rot in peace, let circling seagulls pluck out her eyes and feast on soft tissue. Then again, there had to be easier ways to turn out the light—which was how she thought about it, not as death or something as desperate as suicide— this wasn't a "cry for help." Just turn out the light and go to sleep and not have to wake up and deal with this bullshit anymore, because she was sick and tired of living the same day again and again. You spend all your time doing shit you don't want to do to get to the one thing you almost enjoy, which is over before it starts. Every day Brooke watched people who seemed delighted to be alive. Whether it was throwing a ball in a park or playing fetch with a dog or catching snowflakes on their tongue, flinging a frisbee, doing jumping jacks, whatever these normals did to pass the time, they appeared tickled just to be here. She saw a bumper sticker last week: *Every day is a gift. That's why it's called "the present."* Made her want to puke. Brooke wasn't like that. Not even close. Every day was a burden. And the weird part? This morning, she wasn't even *that* depressed. Yeah, the holding cell sucked, and its stink stuck to her. What she was feeling now was general unsatisfaction, run-of-the-mill, ordinary "what's the point?" She objected to evolution's basic design. Even when everything was going her way, which wasn't often, life was, at its best, only … okay.

Now this headache. She'd have to get a lawyer. Brooke couldn't afford a lawyer. Not a good one anyway. The court would provide a public defender, some deadbeat who'd urge her to plead out. What could they prove? She'd been sitting in a car. Mike was the one who got caught, in the house. Yes, the discarded medications read "Roseville," but anyone could've dug them out of the trash bins. Right now, all they had on her was being in the wrong neighborhood at a suspicious hour.

Unless Mike turned on her.

In the end, that's who it all came down to: Mike. Brooke wasn't worried about Torie, whose fortune was tied to hers. The police would try and use Mike's arrest to catch bigger fish, other dealers, spin the catch up the line. Was Mike willing to rat out Stimpy or would he keep his mouth shut? Everyone knows: you don't talk to the police. If Mike didn't want to cut a deal, the cops would come down harder on him, and that's what Brooke feared. Ratting out a pusher gets you shot. Saying who you got the drugs from in the first place? Might not be as sweet a deal, but it was a helluva lot safer bet. Let her and Torie take the fall to save his skin. Mike wouldn't do that to her. Would he?

Brooke couldn't think. She needed a shower to wash away the stench of that grimy cell, the puke and the shit.

Grabbing underwear from the drawer, she exited her room, entering the small bathroom across the hall. She turned the knob as hot as it would go, letting the water steam. Brooke had begun to get undressed when a noise in the hallway made her stop.

The bathroom door, which she'd shut, was ajar. The old door had a hook-latch lock, which, if pushed, left a crack to spy through...

She heard the heavy footsteps plodding down the stairs and a door slam below her feet.

Bobby.

Pulling her jeans back on, Brooke hopped into both legs, stumbling into a run, racing downstairs.

Shaking the handle to his room, she found the door locked. "You little pervert," she screamed, banging with the flat of her palm. "Open up!"

Bobby said nothing.

"Fucking little shit!"

Brooke kicked the base of the door, anger boiling over. It was more than being spied on by a pervy little brother, more than the invasion of privacy. It was the encroachment on her life, this unwanted intruder in her home, her space, *her* world. She wanted her old life back, the one that was the normal amount of fucked up where she could ignore her drunk father and the stupid, needy boys; where she could get a moment's peace to rest or party or shower without having to worry if the door was all the way closed.

It wasn't until she heard the wood splintering that Brooke realized the full force of her fury.

From inside the room, Bobby finally made a sound—a high-pitched squeal, a little girl eeking at the sight of a spider.

"I'm … so-s-sorry," he cried. "I had t-t-to use the b-bathroom."

Backing away from the cracked door, Brooke could still hear the sobbing, the chest-heaving snot bubbles in between the stuttering. And she hated him all the more for it.

"Stop crying!"

Bobby cried harder, which made Brooke hate him more.

Squealing truck tires skidded into the driveway.

Brooke's day was about to get a whole lot worse.

CHAPTER NINETEEN

NOW

Time manipulates perspective. The more of it that passes, the less we have left to fill. Which is both good and bad. When you don't know better, you can still be wowed by wonder. Like when you're a kid, how the summer seems to last forever. This transcends ignorance is bliss. You're clueless in the grand scheme, an insignificant dot on this spinning big blue orb, whose nuances and intricacies are lost on you. You can't miss what you never had. Conversely, the older you get, the more freedom and independence you gain, the more you comprehend and the smarter you grow. Part of that, however, is accepting how much there is *to* know and how little of it you grasp and never will. With time and space, this infinite pool of knowledge expands at a rate exponentially faster than you can learn, meaning you literally grow dumber by the day, hour, minute, second.

The drive to the Roseville Rest Home takes longer than the two hours GPS allots, traffic on the Mass Pike heavier than usual due to the wet wintery mix. Tractor-trailers, side by side, clog the pipeline, mud flaps caked with silver naked ladies and hard brown ice. No one is happy about it. It's all blaring horns and flashing lights, screams trapped behind the glass, angry people stuck between places they don't want to be.

I fan through satellite radio, scanning the frequency, from alternative to comedy to sports to news to pop. Nothing soothes. A cornerstone—my rock-solid marriage—has been removed. I feel like Yeats' second coming prophesy. I've lost track how many times I read that poem in college. I'm not a fan of the genre but that piece always moved me. Things have fallen apart. Without my wife and child, my center cannot hold.

The Roseville Rest Home crests a knoll, encased by evergreens, tips frosted with snow. From afar, the scene looks pretty. Like so much of this life, however, it is an illusion. Get closer and you see Roseville for what it really is: a place where the old and useless go to die. The exterior is faded, cracked, colors drab, browns and oranges, hints of puke green that thread the ugliest gradations in between. The nursing home resembles an old Howard Johnson's restaurant, with its speared church temple and severe pumpkin roof. Cheap, demoralizing. I try to remember when Howard Johnson's stopped being a restaurant—I am pretty sure they've gone out of business altogether. I recall eating there with my mother. Or am I inventing a memory, subverting, conflating, creating an alternate reality from something that never was?

Stepping inside the old nursing home, I am hit by the awful smell, an olfactory nightmare of discounted foods purchased in bulk, the kind that comes in five-gallon buckets—low-sodium soups, rehydrated vegetables, potted proteins to be heated in microwaves and slipped in shallow bowls, delivered on cafeteria trays, left for the infirmed to lap with all the dignity of a dog.

The first room is the common area. Dated. But not too bad. Teal and brown, burnt umber and goldenrod, worn, frayed rugs, lamps that don't turn on. Goodwill on a better day. Paisley print couches and thrift store seats go unoccupied. Old, withered people slump in wheelchairs.

Curved spines, worn vertebrae, and decades of bad posture twist and contort fragile frames, arthritic necks no longer capable of supporting a fully developed human skull. Weak blue light from an antiquated television projects onto cheap wood paneling. The ceiling dips extra low.

"Can I help you?" The woman before me plasters a well-intentioned smile but can't hide the exhaustion of what must be a soul-sucking job, to be surrounded by so much decay and death.

I explain who I am and what I've come for. She tells me to wait here. Old people glance in my general direction but never quite make eye contact, as if squinting through the evening gloam to make out a street name or identify a species of bird.

A moment later, another woman rounds the corner. Pear-shaped with a stiff hairdo, she beckons me into the hall, where I expect her to lead me to Paul's room. Instead, we remain rooted in the corridor, whose aesthetic development halted deep in the last century. I know Roseville isn't five-star accommodation, but I don't recall its being so low-rent either.

"Mr. Kirby," the woman says, tone so grim and resigned I am certain Paul has passed. "It's been a while."

I don't recognize this woman. I have never met or conversed with her. Social graces dictate I must offer perfunctory excuses. I've been busy. I've been working. I have a family. None of this is a lie, even if they skirt the real reason why I don't visit often.

"It's been three years," she says.

It has not been that long. Perhaps a year. Two at most. No way three years have passed since I last saw my stepfather.

"You haven't returned our calls."

It's true that I've received a few calls from the nursing home. None of the messages conveyed urgency.

"Your father—"

"Stepfather," I correct. "And not even that." I will not explain our convoluted history.

"He doesn't have much time left. He is lonely. He has no one."

"I'm sorry," I say, interrupting. "Have you not been receiving payment? On time and in full?"

"There is no issue with the money, sir. I would simply urge you to visit him more often. It's imperative for a resident's emotional well—"

Enough with the guilt trip. I tell her I live a state over, with responsibilities of my own. I am well aware Paul is an old man with no family. I pay the man's bills, his entire stay here on *my* dime. I've done my part.

Instead of apologizing, she says, "I knew your sister." Which catches me off guard.

"Excuse me?"

"She worked here. Your sister. Brooke. Did you know that?"

I shrug. Sure. Maybe. Why not? Brooke worked a few jobs, one of them, yes, at a hospice or whatever, something else in eldercare.

"Michelle?" the woman says. "Michelle Penny." She waits for me to acknowledge this revelation.

I'm not sure the response she's expecting. I don't recall Brooke's mentioning someone with that name—I barely remember my stepsister working here in the first place. Why this supercilious lady is telling me any of this, or why I'm supposed to care, perplexes. It's another baffling exchange added to a recent spate of them.

Like she's won an argument, Michelle pivots and wattles down the hall. Reluctantly, I follow, silently irate over having been admonished by this stranger for not having done more on top of the too much I already do.

We pass tall, thin machines with monitors, twisty tubes, and screens, casting elongated shadows, crooked fingers beckoning this way come. The glum well is choked with the stench of the dying. There's no other way to describe it. The human body, like all living things, is not designed to last. It breaks down, erodes. Dust to dust. Just a matter of time before these impermanent shells give out for good. Life itself is a contradiction. We are born into this world dying. Living healthy is just the slowest way to kill yourself. Tonight. Tomorrow. Next week, month—maybe the patients get another year—but no one is walking out of here.

I'm not fooling myself. I know what I did. I could've taken in Paul, but I was under no obligation to do *anything*. When I left grad school and married Stephanie, I went above and beyond. Learning he was behind on his mortgage, I offered to take it over for him, paying his bills, repaying his debt, getting him above water. I bailed him out, saving his home before the bank could swoop in and give him nothing. Instead of letting him freeze and starve, I've kept him fed with a roof over his head. Sounds like a good trade to me.

When Michelle delivers me to Paul's room, she stops in the doorway, blocking entrance.

"We have implemented comfort measures," she says. "Do you know what that means?"

Yeah. I get it. Paul is not long for this world.

Michelle smirks as though I've been taught a lesson. The only "lesson" I've learned is how vital my involvement has been in keeping this fragile, fading, old dying drunk alive as long as I have. Paul Mulcahy was not a nice man. I'll always appreciate the help he lent, providing shelter and insurance, which the state also affords. The man was an asshole. He may not have beat Brooke or me, but violence was always on the table. Paul was an emotionally abusive alcoholic, with a hair-trigger temper, who never once made me feel wanted or loved. I was a burden to him.

Michelle moves aside. I step into the room. Paul looks half of what he was, and he wasn't much to begin with. He sloops crooked in his bed. I dip my eyes to meet his vacant gaze, wave a hand. Hello? Anyone home?

It takes a moment for Paul's eyes to focus, before they go wide. "Bobby!"

No one calls me that anymore. I hate the name, which paints the picture of a fat guy who still lives at home with his mother and eats too much pasta. I raise no objections, however, permitting the nostalgia. I can't get inside his head. I don't know what he recalls from our brief time together, if he's skewed history and fabricated the sketch of a loving relationship. If so, good for him. Let him hold those memories dear.

From the corner of my eye, I'm surprised to catch Michelle Penny, still standing at the edge of the frame, arms akimbo. I turn to the nice lady director, tell her, in no uncertain terms, she can go. Thanks, that will be all, please leave, direct deposit on schedule. Then I close the door so I can get a minute alone with the worst years of my life.

Staring at the old man's wizened, slacken skin, I don't hazard to guess his age. I honestly can't remember. Seventy-five, eighty? Older? His person betrays a hard-lived life. I wasn't the guy's biggest fan. Still, I don't like to see any living creature suffer. By the way his upper and lower jaw conjoin and collapse, as if one half is swallowing the other, I can see he's lost all his teeth. His lips flap when he speaks and his chin tremors when he doesn't. His eyes retain enough of a spark that I see he's still in there somewhere, if compromised and diminished. I only need a few answers and am hoping he's cognizant enough to give them to me.

"Hello, Paul. It's nice to see you."

"Bobby!" he says.

Sliding over a chair, I force a smile, doing my best not to retch at the smell, which is, to put it mildly, putrid. Someone needs to give the man a sponge bath. The yellow taint to his flesh is indicative of long-term alcohol abuse and irreversible liver damage. Old, dead skin flakes in fat swaths, like when you chip slivers off the wall to match color at the paint store.

"How have you been?" It's a stupid question—the man wears an adult diaper—but I maintain my smile.

"Bobby," he repeats. This time the name is sadder, almost slurred. I can't tell if this is because of the missing teeth or the copious amount of opiates surely pumped into his veins.

Beyond his shoulder, a framed photograph sits on the medicine cart that doubles as a bedside table. I stand and reach beyond him to retrieve it. The photo shows Brooke, Paul, and my mother. They are waterside, by a river or a lake. Summertime. Brooke is maybe five, so it's before I came into the picture, pun intended. I show it to him, which is unnecessary since he sleeps with it beside his bed.

He nods, grins, but says nothing.

I study the composition. Other than my not having been born yet, I can't deduce many particulars, like where this photograph was taken. I think of asking him to recall details but know it's pointless. I do know one thing: this picture was not here when I brought him in.

I return the photo to where I found it.

"Bobby," he says.

"How are they treating you?"

He attempts a smile.

"That's good," I say, hoping to elicit another word out of his mouth beside my loathsome childhood name. "Got everything you need?"

"Bobby," he says.

"Yeah, you said that, Paul." I reach out and take his frail hand, careful not to squeeze too hard. In his prime, Paul was not a big man, but he was tough, wiry and wily, a scraper. I still remember the time he and Mike Rakowski got into it. I don't know what provoked him, but Mike *was* a big guy, and stronger. Mean too. Paul went after him like a jailhouse rat, snapping, slashing, gashing, trying to gouge eyes out, until I broke it up. Now he's wasted away, withered, like a wilted, neglected house plant. I won't be able to stand this place much longer, with its foul smells and maudlin ambiance. I need to ask what I need to know and get out of here.

"Paul—" I start to say.

"Bobby."

"Yes. It's me. Real good to see you too. Does the name 'Lily' mean anything to you?"

"Bobby?"

"Lily," I repeat slower.

"Bobby?"

"Lily Stillwater. Sound familiar? Ring a bell? Evoke … anything?"

Paul takes a moment to think. He's thinking hard; I can see he wants to make me proud with the right answer.

"Bobby?"

"No, Paul. This would be a … younger girl. Nineteen?"

He shakes his head. I contemplate how much weight to assign his answer. His speech is impaired, communicative abilities all but gone. Is he able to comprehend the question at least? If I were to hand him a pad of paper and pencil, could he write a response? Judging by his blank expression and atrophied limbs, I conclude the answer is a hardy "no."

I say I have to get going and turn to leave. This will be the last time I see Paul Mulcahy alive, if that's what you'd consider his current state. I won't see him for the funeral either. There won't be one. Paul has no family, no friends. Why pretend otherwise? Several thousand dollars for a hole in the ground and a modest headstone no one will visit?

On the dresser by the door, several greeting cards stand propped up. Perhaps one is from Lily? Even a generic one without an address. At this point, I'd welcome any clue to help me gather information and track her down.

Although the penmanship appears to be feminine, upon closer inspection, I now see all the cards are from Aaron Reardon, Brooke's former preppy best friend. I never had issues with Aaron, who was such a good guy, how could I? Everyone liked Aaron. Except Mike Rakowski. I am not surprised Aaron would take the time to send holiday, birthday, and "thinking of you" cards to a dying man. It kind of pisses me off, though, which is immature. The gesture is sweet. Aaron loved Brooke, and this is a nice way to honor her memory. It's also overkill in its consideration. I start to count the cards but stop after ten. I read a few. The messages, simple well-wishes, imply a deeper connection, as if the mutual loss of Brooke forever tethers the two together. Aaron is no more blood to Paul than I am.

I glance back at Paul, who grins. I consider asking him about Aaron, if he visits or if they talk, but there is only so much one can infer from a response of "Bobby!"

These cards shouldn't be a surprise. I remember once overhearing Brooke talking on the phone, explaining why Aaron was the one guy she *wouldn't* sleep with.

"He *is* sweet," Brooke said. "He's really caring and a good friend." Then she paused. "But he's also, kinda, y'know, boring."

A nice, sweet, caring, boring guy who would make time to send periodic, thoughtful greeting cards to an inconsequential dying drunk like Paul Mulcahy.

I realize Paul has been talking to me this entire time. I think I catch actual words. When I turn to give him my full attention, however, he's staring out the window at a crow perched on a street sign.

I don't bother with a second goodbye. Walking out, I snatch a greeting card with a phone number in case Paul "needs to talk." How sweet. As if Paul Mulcahy could pick up a telephone and carry on a conversation.

CHAPTER TWENTY

December 29, 1997, 6:35 a.m.
Eleven Days Before the Disappearance

Brooke left Bobby whimpering in his room to go deal with Mike. She knew she'd have to sooner than later, but this was sooner than she'd expected. Or was ready for. She'd been out on bail a couple hours and would've liked time to rest, think, decide how she was going to handle this shitshow. As much as she hated Mike right now—and in this moment, the fire was all consuming—she had to play nice. Brooke had yet to meet with a lawyer, but if Mike told the police where he'd gotten the stolen medications, she was screwed.

At the porch steps, Brooke found Mike leaning against his truck, door open, engine running, smoking and stewing. Dawn was breaking, reds and purples layered thick like European oils from the art class Brooke had taken at Midfield State. A fire sky.

Brooke stopped on the porch, lording over him. She folded her arms and tried to look tough.

"What the fuck were you two doing out there?" Mike slammed his truck door. "I told you not to come."

"Why the fuck were you taking so long! You left us out there on the side of the road for two goddamn hours."

"It wasn't two hours."

"It was two hours."

Mike blew past her, up the stairs. She didn't budge. He didn't flick his cigarette into the snow, even though he knew Paul didn't want anyone smoking in the house; even though he knew Brooke would be the one who got blamed. Mike Rakowski didn't care about anyone or anything but himself.

"It's not my fault Stimpy's house got raided," Brooke said, shutting the front door.

"Um, yeah, it is. Cops drive by, see two white girls sitting in a car on the side of the fucking road after midnight. What the fuck you think they're going to do? They know Stimpy's house. It's called probable cause."

"Sitting in a car isn't probable cause."

"It's whatever the cops want to call it." Without asking, Mike went to fix himself coffee. "You couldn't keep your head down?"

He flung open the cupboard, cluttered with foods that would never expire or get eaten, canned fish, evaporated milk, biscuit mix, stacked haphazardly with no rhyme or reason, the pantry stash of roommates with nothing in common.

"Why did you and what's her name have to come in the first place?"

"Because Torie doesn't trust you?"

"I give a shit." Mike slammed down the coffee tin, rifling shelves, casting aside boxes and loafs of bread. "I should've told her to fuck off." He turned to Brooke. "Where're the filters? How do you find anything in here?"

Brooke pointed at another cupboard. "Like you should talk. I've been in your apartment."

"Right. I forgot. You're so fancy! You own. Or, should I say, Paul owns."

"It's my house as much as it is his."

Mike plucked a filter, dropped it in, and grabbed the coffee tin. Ripping off the lid, he dumped what seemed like a half pound of coffee, black grounds spilling everywhere, before punching the machine to brew.

"Can you try and not make such a mess? Who do you think cleans up?" Brooke threw back her head. "How did you even get out?"

"Like you give a shit." Mike sucked on his cigarette. "I didn't have Daddy's help, that's for sure."

"If you're gonna smoke, can you at least crack the window or open a door?" Brooke dropped into a seat at the kitchen table, shaking her head, disgusted, though at what in particular, she couldn't be sure. Mike? The situation? The cluttered house? The inclement weather gathering off the sea? It was all the same, one big, sloppy mess. All she knew for sure: she'd get stuck dealing with it.

Mike dropped his butt in the sink and turned on the water, washing away the evidence.

"What happens now?" she said.

"Prison?" He laughed.

Brooke didn't.

"I don't know," Mike said, cracking the window above the sink, waving to disperse lingering smoke. "Court date is January twenty." He sneered at Brooke. "Daddy's not getting me get a lawyer. Gonna have a goddamn PD."

"My father isn't rich."

Mike gestured around the kitchen, pointing up at the ceiling and the extra space of a middle-class existence. "You got this house. Which is more than me. I don't got collateral. You're gonna get a real lawyer. Me? Whatever dropout public defender dillweed they assign. That was a lot of dope they seized. It's all labeled with Roseville Rest Home." He caught her eye. "*I* don't work at Roseville."

"Are you threatening me?"

"I'm not going to prison for this shit. I already have a record."

"Drunk and disorderly, Mike. A couple nights in a holding cell. You're hardly a seasoned ex-con."

"Judge don't care. Record's a record. You're lily white." Mike dropped his hands and his entire expression softened, hostility giving way to imploring.

"You want me to admit the drugs were mine?"

"You'll get a lighter sentence than me. Probably community service and probation."

"Probably." She laughed. "No way, Mike."

"Keep out of trouble for a couple years and it goes away."

Around the corner, a door opened and slammed, followed by the sound of feet pattering across the floor, pounding up the stairs, before another door opened and shut as fast.

Mike pointed at the ceiling. "The fuck?"

"Bobby," Brooke said. "Caught the little shit trying to watch me shower."

Mike laughed. "Maybe he ain't a fag after all."

"No, just a pervert."

Mike pushed himself off the counter, reaching out to touch her hair. Brooke recoiled.

"How long we known each other?"

"Too long," she said.

"We're still friends, right?"

She didn't answer. She wanted to. She wanted to say, "Friends? Are you out of your fucking mind? Fuck no, we're not friends. We're not *anything*." Anytime Mike touched her, Brooke felt squeamish. It had been almost six months since Brooke let him fuck her. He'd push, she'd fight him off, get him to settle for handjobs, or blowjobs if she needed something bad enough. Why should she have to do anything for Mike Rakowski? Why did she always seem to need him? She hated him. She wished he were dead. Or at least gone. But prison? Brooke didn't want Mike sent to prison. Because they *did* have history. A long, shared, mutually troubled one. There was a time when she had no one but Mike. Before, during, after Connie. The depression, the anger, the hopelessness. The worst of the drugs. The heartache, the pain, the desperation. What she'd gone through, they'd gone through together, Mike's home life as rotten, as broken. Those nights she wouldn't come home, sleeping beneath the train tracks or out by the quarry, Mike was the one who held her tight, who listened to her cry and kept her warm. Friends like Aaron could never understand that. What Mike and Brooke endured was a war. It wasn't the same as men and women who fought and died, like in Iraq or whatever. But the experience for them, the damage it inflicted, was as real.

Thinking all these things, Brooke felt Mike burrowing into her neck, hands reaching under her shirt. She pushed his hand away. He kept pawing. She felt his hot breath on her skin.

How do you cut a bond you no longer want when roots burrow that deep?

Brooke stared over his shoulder, eyeing the steak knives.

CHAPTER TWENTY-ONE

NOW

Back at my house in Diemen, I call Stephanie, who doesn't pick up. I leave a message to tell my son I love him. I ramble more than I should, talking about this recent uneventful day, trying to infuse my speech with confidence and constancy. Life will continue. It's hard to project these qualities and ideals with patience and poise in a fifty-seven-second message. When I blather about the weather, I worry I'll stutter, and end the call, feigning another important one coming in. After I hang up, I realize that strategy was horrible. For years, my wife has derided me for putting work ahead of our marriage. And I just told her I can't talk. Because of work. I'd kick myself harder except for the stuttering. It's a defect I've worked hard to overcome. When it returns, as it will during times of stress, I'm reminded of the life I fought so hard to leave behind.

I fall into a seat at the kitchen table. Another gray day casts its pall. Why did Lily leave a contact number for Paul's nursing home? I can't shake the question. In the beginning, Paul and I were in frequent contact with authorities. We kept one another abreast of developments, however feeble, despite the miles between us. Years have passed since then. If there were updates, police would let me know. And Paul? He's gone. The man I saw today, for all intents and purposes, is already dead.

Digging through an upstairs office drawer, I find the contact number for Ed Zambrano, a Rocky Cove detective. When did we last speak? Four, five years ago? I don't know if the guy is still a detective or if the case is even active.

When I call Zambrano, he informs me he's no longer in charge.

"Jurisdiction is tricky," Zambrano says, explaining the nuances of investigating a missing person case. "If the crime takes place across state lines—Brooke's car was found in Vermont—state troopers get involved."

He drones on about procedure, which I am less interested in, and I recall this particular trait of Zambrano: he is a talker, although he seldom says anything useful, another reason I stopped shopping for updates.

"It's more complicated," he continues. "Because of the potential abduction angle, the Feds might want a say, too."

"But there haven't been any new developments?" I never believed rumors Brooke was picked up by an opportunistic sociopath.

"Not that I know of," he says.

I'm pretty sure I hear him eating on the other end. Something leafy, crunchy. A salad with apple, walnuts, a pear. It's a three-minute phone call. How hungry can a person be?

"Anyway," Zambrano says. "We don't have the manpower down here. When they pulled me off the case eight years ago—"

"That long?" I could've sworn we'd spoken more recently than that. I haven't talked to any other detective.

"Maybe longer?"

"We spoke five years ago," I say, with confidence. "When that crazy lady claiming to be Brooke's roommate contacted us."

"No," Zambrano says, chewing. "That wasn't me."

"I passed along her contact information."

"Like I said, Mr. Kirby, that wasn't me." He chomps another bite. "I remember you."

I suppose I should be impressed he remembers me after all this time. To tell the truth, I don't care. If he can't help me, he's wasting my time.

I hear him put down his lunch, rattling a drawer on the other end. "You're gonna want to call Vermont. You got a pen?"

I tell him to go ahead.

"Vern Tuepker. Last I knew he was running the show up there."

Last he knew?

I phone the Vermont State Troopers, which proves less efficient. The maddening process leaves me on hold several times with multiple transfers, serenaded by synthesizer saxophones and tinny keyboard beats. It's like a time machine. More than the muzak, I have been transported back to another world, this vanishing. My mind races, turns on itself, and I find myself growing angrier. Each time someone picks up and tells me to "please hold," I want to reach out through the receiver and strangle them.

After almost ten minutes, I am finally connected to Tuepker's voicemail, where I leave as succinct and detailed a message as I can, suppressing my disgust at the unprofessionalism of what is supposed to be law enforcement. I end the call, uncertain I've conveyed the correct information, my temper flaring. I can't remember if I even left my number, I'm so worked up and pissed off over the ten-minute game of phone tag.

Lightning crashes. Thunder booms. Rain pelts the glass. I am not surprised by lightning in the winter. Though often associated with summer, lightning is more common during the cold months.

Something to do with warming trends over the Atlantic. Why my brain retains such useless information, I do not know. I sit at the kitchen table, eyes drawn to the refrigerator and all the happy magnet moments plastered on the door, which reminds me how alone I am now. The rain smacking glass is the saddest sound I've ever heard. The wind picks up, slapping buckets. It's violent, unnerving. Like a reckoning.

Why would Lily leave the number for the Roseville Rest Home? The thought loops. Combined with the lightning, thunder, and rain, relentless as a dental drill in my skull, I fear I'll go mad.

My work as a civil engineer concerns patterns, grids, logic and cohesion. Order. This is chaotic. That woman director, Michelle, saying Brooke used to work for her makes me remember the stolen medications, adding another wrinkle that I am unsure how to incorporate. Now other parts return—how angry Paul was after that arrest, how much worse Mike got with prison hanging over their heads—and at the same time the specifics are hazy, like retelling a story or joke you heard secondhand, rendering you unable to remember why you found it so poignant or hysterical in the first place. I recollect details of the arrest, which took place a few weeks before Brooke disappeared. Paul had to put up the house to keep her out of jail. When I bought the house from Paul, I had to pay off that debt. This is fact. The rest lies beyond the peripheral, beyond the scope of what I can see.

I need help. Reaching out to Mike Rakowski isn't an option. Even if I knew how to get in touch, I wouldn't. Instead, I retrieve the greeting card from the nursing home, and ring up Aaron Reardon.

"Bobby Kirby!" Aaron's unabashed enthusiasm rivals a drunk girl hearing "Brown Eyed Girl" for the thousandth time on a college bar jukebox.

"How are you, Aaron?"

"Terrific. Just terrific." He laughs, a high-pitched, giddy squeal. So much joy. "Wow. It has been a long time, eh?"

"Too long," I say. It hasn't been too long. If I didn't see his name and number at the rest home—and if I didn't need some assistance now— we aren't having this conversation. Everything about Aaron screams high school pep squad demanding more school spirit.

I don't want to play catch up or hear about what the guy has been doing for the past twenty years. No doubt he's done well. Aaron was student council president, debate, chess, and scholastic team champion, a winner. Manners, however, dictate otherwise.

As expected, Aaron is thriving. He has his own business. He explains what it is, something to do with rehabilitation and helping people get back on their feet after hard times. There's a charity compo- nent. No surprise. Aaron Reardon was always trying to make the world a better place. He jabbers. I half listen, tuned out, staring through streaked glass at the churning sky unleashing holy hell. I'm thinking of Stephanie and Peter, how I'm going to reinvent myself this time. He yammers about giving back to the community, his wife and three wonderful kids, whose names I don't catch. I think it's two girls and one boy, or the other way around. I interject a few "greats" and "wonderfuls," to confirm I'm paying attention.

"Aaron," I say, cutting him off, "I don't mean to reopen old wounds—"

"What's on your mind, Bobby?"

"I go by Robert now."

"Sorry. Robert."

"It's about ... Brooke."

"Brooke." His voice takes on somber reverence, infused with melan- choly, fondness, and sense of loss. The ratio of ingredients is spot-on, a master class in grief. "I think of your sister often."

"Stepsister. Yeah, it still hurts." That isn't lip service, and I'm not commiserating because I need something. The more time passes, the more I can't pretend Brooke's brief stop in my life didn't leave a deep, lasting impression. She is the ghost I can't escape.

Maybe it's because I know Aaron really did love Brooke that I open up. Or maybe the honesty that pours forth owes to a breach in the dam, unrelenting pressure compromising structural integrity, cracking walls, which leaves me gushing more intimacy than I am used to because I need to share it with someone, and Aaron seems willing to listen. I tell him about seeing Paul, about my wife, child. I leave out the dog. Aaron is a sensitive guy. I don't want to alarm him.

I gaze over the backyard, through the pounding rains, trying to shake off ridiculous notions there is a femme fatal out there, a nine-teen-year-old psychopath with a coat hanger and blowtorch. I switch the call to speaker, even though I won't be able to hear as well, and walk to the patio door, double checking to make sure it is locked.

"That's so great you visit Paul. I know he wasn't always the warmest father figure."

"All in the past. Listen, Aaron, the real reason I'm calling is I got a visit from—I don't know how to say this without its sounding sensational. Over the years, people have come forward claiming to know what happened to Brooke..."

"What is it?" Aaron's wishful thinking hangs in the air.

"A young woman stopped by my office claiming to be Brooke's daughter."

"What—when? I mean, who—what?"

I search for signs of movement in the forest as I give a rundown, a brief recap of Lily's visit: the alias Brooke lived under; their adopted hometown of Bellemont, Vermont; the supposed college, which turned out to be a lie; the phone number leading to Paul.

"Jesus," Aaron says, which might be the closest I've heard the guy come to swearing. "Plus, all that's going on with your wife and child? Dear God, I am so sorry. How can I help?" At this point the earnestness is so palpable it feels like a third person has entered the conversation.

The storm continues to assault the black forest, swaying treetops and limbs, whipping twigs into a swirl. If my tiny dog was still here, I'd be worried about a tornado whisking us off to Kansas.

"I don't know if the girl was telling the truth," I say, turning from the patio. "Like I said, I've gotten many strange calls over the years. Something seemed different about this one. You were Brooke's best friend, right?"

"I like to believe so."

"The rumor. She was pregnant. Do you think it could've been true?"

"Your sister confided in me about *everything*." He chuckles. "One of the perks of being stuck in the friend zone." He stops chuckling. "She never told me she was pregnant. But..."

"What?"

"I know it's not fashionable these days, and don't get me wrong—I support a woman's right to choose—but I don't believe in abortion. Personally. For me. I've always felt that way. If Brooke *was* pregnant and having doubts about whether she wanted to keep the baby, I'm not sure she'd come to me. With everything else in her life, it might've been too much."

He's talking about more than the stolen medication and arrest.

"By 'everything else,' you mean Mike. Yes, he was an asshole."

"He was worse than that. Mike Rakowski was abusive, emotionally *and* physically."

"You're not the first person to point that out. No one understood why she dated him."

"That's the thing. They *weren't* dating. Brooke had broken up with Mike. But he wouldn't take no for an answer. He forced his way into her life, made himself indispensable."

"Indispensable?"

"They moved in the same ... world, let's say that. You know your sister partied, right? Mike was the hook-up for pills and pot, other drugs. She was dependent on him. Whose idea do you think it was to steal pain medications from the hospital? Who set up the sale? Heck, I wouldn't be surprised if Mike tipped off the cops himself."

"Didn't he get arrested too?"

"Mike was always getting arrested. He knew how to play the game. Brooke gets charged? Now she needs him. Needs him to take the rap. Which he'd be happy to exchange. For a price."

"You're telling me he'd ... force ... Brooke to be his girlfriend? Have sex with him?"

"Mike wouldn't need permission for that."

"What are you trying to say?"

"Rape." Aaron chokes on the word. "What kind of a monster forcefully imposes..."

"You think Mike—"

"I don't know. We're talking, right? Speculating. I *do* know, for a fact, that your sister wasn't *with* any other guys. Not like that. She'd been having, let's call it 'a crisis of faith'—she was trying to change her ways. I don't want to talk bad about her..."

"Just say it."

"Your sister slept around. I can't say she was 'celibate' toward the end—she was messing around with plenty of guys—but she'd drawn the line at sleeping with them."

"And you believed her?"

"Why wouldn't I? Brooke *never* lied to me. She'd withhold information, not wanting to hurt my feelings." He chuckles again. The rollicking
joviality tap dances on my last nerve. "You know I had a crush on your
sister, right?"

"Wow. Really?" *Only the worst kept secret in town.*

"Big time. She didn't think of me that way. My point: she could
confide in me if she was abstaining from sex. Now you say a girl—nineteen would be about right—comes to you, claiming to be your niece—"

"*If* Lily is telling the truth. She lied about college, and she gave me
the wrong phone number."

"A wrong number. That led to her grandfather."

Winds continue to whip, a whirl of sights and sounds, memories
and conjuncture. It's too much. I fear a blood vessel in my brain will
burst and I'll succumb to an aneurism. I start seeing double and am
having a difficult time breathing.

"Are you okay, Robert?"

"Overwhelmed, is all," I say, feeling drawn to the front door. I can
sense someone out there.

"Let me help," he says. "I have accesses through my work—rehabilitation is tied into the state system, boring stuff you don't need to worry
about. I can get addresses, social security numbers. Susan Stillwater,
right?"

At the front door, I check to make sure it is locked. Deadbolted
too. Then I see it. Out the window, a car. Red, rusted. It faces my way,
engine running, billow of smoke adding to gloomy fog and further
obscuring. It stares at my house, high beams fixed on me.

CHAPTER TWENTY-TWO

NOW

"You should call the cops," Aaron says when I tell him about the car watching me.

"I don't want to involve the police."

"Robert, if someone is threatening you—"

"I might be mistaken. Overreacting. It could be a neighbor's car. Or a friend of theirs." I peek back out the window. I know what I've told Aaron is a lie. This isn't a neighbor's car. *They've come for us.*

"You need to call the authorities," he says.

I watch the dark road. Rain races through headlights, streaks of white tearing through black. The downpour splatters furious, smacking off everything—roof, doors, windows.

"Want me to call them?"

"No," I say, "it's fine." As I say this, the car backs up, makes a U-turn, drives off, brake lights a blur, forget reading a license plate. I *feel* like it's the car I saw earlier, the red and rusted one across the field. With the storm, I can't be sure of a color or condition of an exterior. *We're making things up.* "It's gone."

"Good," he says. "You relax. I'm going to make some calls."

I have no idea what Aaron can or can't do. My nerves rattled, I'm anxious to end the conversation. He tells me to sit tight, take it easy, and above all to "be kind" to myself.

After I hang up, I check all the doors and windows, scanning up and down the street like a wingnut recluse paranoid about 5G and chemtrails. All the while, I'm thinking about Aaron's decree. *Be kind to myself.*

Being kind to myself has never been easy. Beating myself up comes more naturally. We reformed Catholics carry our sins—forgiveness has never been part of my skillset. Especially when it comes to forgiving *myself.* With Stephanie and my son gone, I internalize how much of this is my fault. This guilt stems from my mother, the catechism of self-flagellation. I've tried to reconcile that early, intense religious experience with the man I've become, softening the harder edges of zealotry. I want to incorporate what I've learned from this life of the mind, while not eschewing faith altogether. Though I celebrate science and the quantifiable, I also find solace believing there is a God, a speculative answer to an unknown element. I want to believe that we are more than human skin housing suffering—we have a higher purpose, a reason for being here, a soul. It's hubris to believe we have it all figured out. Kindness? I am not blameless. I *have* prioritized the wrong things, neglecting my wife and child. I've had great excuses—wanting to succeed to provide for my family; to lead by example and be a better role model for my son; to give them the most comfortable life possible. The best schools for Peter. Luxury for Stephanie. But how much of that is true? We already have money. One can always use more, of course. I also know the thrill I receive from outside validation. I bask in praise and adoration. I live to be celebrated. It is the fuel I run on. Why do the opinions of strangers mean more to me than the respect of my own family? Am I being too hard on myself? Do I deserve kindness? Forgiveness? When you're raised to believe God is always watching, you don't get to choose selective moments when He looks away.

Despite Aaron's parting wish to be kind to myself, I am not up to the challenge. In fact, it only makes me yearn to hurt more.

When I wake, the storm continues to rage and a hard rain falls, echoing throughout these empty halls.

My cell rings. Stephanie.

"Sorry," she says, without remorse. "I didn't get your message last night."

I want to ask why not? Did she not have her cell with her? She always has her phone with her. Who doesn't have their cell phone with them? *She saw our name on the caller ID and chose not to answer it.* I clamp my teeth and grit my jaw to hold my tongue.

"That's okay," I say. "I was just checking in." Rising, I pluck my sweatshirt from the chair. The house is freezing, and here I stand, too despondent to reach for the Nest and warm my aching bones. "How's Pittsburgh? Your sister?" I wait. "How is Peter?"

"Peter's fine." She pauses. "He has his own cell phone."

I know that, I want to say. I'm the one who advocated for him to get it. She was against it. I fought for him. Does she remember that? Does he? *He's taken her side.* I voice none of this. Instead, I ask, "What did you tell him? About us?"

"Nothing. He thinks we're visiting his aunt."

I want to press. Peter is not an idiot. He knows we wouldn't take him out of school during the semester. He knows I would not let him skip out on his obligations or hockey. I want to ask what *she* thinks, to demand how much longer she's going to carry on with this bullshit. My instincts, so often wrong in these circumstances, cannot be trusted. I maintain decorum and thank her for returning my call. *Keep it cordial, polite, sane.* I say to tell my son that I love him, and that I'm here when she's ready to talk.

That's it. Stephanie gives me nothing else, and the call ends. I reflect on the foreign, cold conversation. I stare at the cell's screen, looking at how short the call was. Less than a minute. I converse with telemarketers longer than that. When Stephanie and I first began dating, we could speak for hours, about everything and nothing at all.

My cell immediately rings back, and like that all is right with the world. Stephanie has come to her senses. She's going to tell me how much she loves me, misses me, that we are still a family and she's coming home with my son.

When I slide on the phone, I catch "Vermont State Troopers" across the screen.

"Vern Tuepker," a man's deep voice announces. "What can I do for you?" Vern Tuepker does not sound like a man who wants to do anything for anyone.

I remind myself I am allowed to inquire about a case involving a biological relative, twenty years later or not.

Though I shouldn't have to, I reiterate who I am and why I am calling.

"Yes, Mr. Kirby," Tuepker responds with an aggravated groan, as though I am holding up this morning's bowel movement. "I am familiar with your sister's disappearance."

I do not correct him that Brooke was my half-sister, stepsister, skipping ahead to the reason I called.

Tuepker launches into a perfunctory recap of events, rehashing details I already know. This is done as part of department protocol, a checklist to avoid accusations of wrongdoing or—heaven forbid—cause for a grievance filed. Unlike Ed Zambrano, however, I don't feel comfortable cutting

Tuepker short. He's authoritative, commanding, intimidating. I have to listen as he repeats persons of interest, which includes Brooke's former lovers, such as Mike Rakowski and her ex-basketball coach Rod Collins, both of whom I know about, both of whom have been cleared. I do learn a few new particulars, like how Collins' wife divorced the Division II coach prior to his fatal heart attack that ended his 2015 season.

"That's it?" I ask when he's done. "No other leads?"

"It's a cold case, Mr. Kirby. Unless someone comes forward with new information, I'm afraid we are at a standstill." He pauses. "Do *you* know anything new?"

"I do not," I tell him. "But as you can imagine, it's hard to let go." Even after two decades. I start talking about my position with the university, my recent award and grant. I am not sure why I feel the need to impress this man. Except to convey I am above reproach and not someone easily dismissed.

"Yes, Uniondale," Tuepker says, yawning. "Good school."

I wonder how a Vermont cop knows about a small, private, exclusive Upstate New York university. *They've been keeping tabs on us.* Of course they have. I'd been living with Brooke when she went missing. Despite my young age at the time, I wonder if they suspect me, before shaking off the ludicrous notion.

"When cases drag on this long, Mr. Kirby, it is doubtful we will ever find out what happened to the victim."

Victim.

That's it. Dead end.

Then he says, without provocation, "You want to look at the evidence?" This surprises me. "Maybe a fresh set of eyes catches something new."

I'm stumbling over words, unable to ask what I want, the way I want to ask it, strategies, like where do I start?

"Tell you what, Mr. Kirby," Tuepker says. "The evidence is too much to photocopy and ship. Why don't we grab lunch?"

"I'm in New York—"

"University is still on holiday break, no? I'm only an hour or so away. How's this afternoon?"

The drive from Diemen to Briarboro, the small town just over the border from Massachusetts into Vermont where Brooke disappeared one fateful, snowy January night in 1998, isn't far—it's under two hours, even with slogged-down winter traffic. I'm not passing up the opportunity, even if I'm not sure *what* that opportunity is. Tuepker, who wasn't receptive initially, offers to meet for lunch, volunteers to share evidence? *What's the catch?* Then I realize there is no "catch." This costs him nothing. It's a quick-fix checkmark to prove he's still doing his job. In the end, he gets a tax write-off for a free meal.

For my part, I am happy to leave behind the gusty rain of the valley, trading it for the soft snowfall east.

The tavern Tuepker suggests is called the Brown Bear, a log cabin replica off the interstate designed to hook tourists with its manufactured motif. Good ol' throwback folksy America, where everyone wears overalls, says "y'all," and they have maple syrup on tap. Sure enough, the inside captures every rustic, postcard stereotype, a Cracker Barrel for folks who want a shot of hard liquor with their burger and beer. From the rocking chair out front to the whimsical signage, the Brown Bear is designed to recall an era that, in all likelihood, never existed.

Waiting for me on tavern's porch, Vern Tuepker doesn't match his deep, burly voice. Expecting a giant, I am instead greeted by someone closer to William H. Macy, diminutive, withered, with a weathered, scruffy face, emphasized by languid eyes and the puffy bags beneath them. In his arm, he cradles a box, roughly the size of a shoebox, which I assume is the evidence. He holds it close to his chest, unwilling to let go.

We sit at the bar. Tuepker takes off his wide-brimmed brown hat, smoothing the few straggling hairs that remain. Patrons wave and smile, which tells me this is a regular stop for the trooper.

"Surprised to hear from you." He signals for a beer. "Family members tend to be more, let's say, persistent."

I reiterate the party line, how I didn't know Brooke that well, how we didn't have the same last name. When people question my relationship with Brooke, that answer usually suffices. With Tuepker, it does not.

The bartender brings his beer, and asks if I want one, too. I have no intention of drinking—I'm driving. I ask for a coffee, which I am told isn't made and that I'll have to wait.

"Did you know I was there that night?" Tuepker says. "The night your sister cracked up her car."

I shake my head. I'm not sure why this revelation surprises me. He is a Vermont State Trooper, a veteran of the force.

"I would've liked to speak with you sooner," he says.

"You could've called." I resent the implication, as if I've been hiding or withholding information.

"You were just a kid, weren't you?" The way Tuepker says this unnerves me. It does not exonerate but rather implicates. He is stating fact, but it feels salacious. I want this evidence he's offered and then to get away from this man. He is not an ally.

I glance around at the customers, realizing I was wrong about the Brown Bear being a tourist trap. It's a local spot. Everyone in here looks the same. They all have that same crooked expression you find in these tiny country towns, eyes too close, features pinched, either from alcoholism or inbreeding.

"Yep," Tuepker continues, picking up a conversation he's been having with himself. "I was there that night. Terrible. Car all crumpled, front end smashed to shit. Ever see the pictures?"

I shake my head no.

Tuepker reaches into the shoebox-sized case, retrieving a single glossy photo, which he slaps on the bar. It shows Brooke's old car, pointing in the wrong direction, nose driven into an embankment. It does not look like an accident one walks away from.

"Skidded off the ice." He points at the picture, its fields of white, surrounding mountains, and trees of evergreen. "We searched for days. Experts think she hit her head, wandered off in the storm. Except the witnesses—"

"Hope Washington and Nathaniel Jones."

"Correct," he says, sounding impressed. "So, you *did* follow up?"

I want to ask how he thinks I'd forget an event that has defined my entire existence. His attitude comes across as combative. I convince myself this is projection, that the perceived aggression is imagined; the state trooper has a naturally sour disposition. When Tuepker stares with blatant disdain, I tell myself he has one of those faces, what the kids call "resting bitch face." I've watched him interact with locals, exchange pleasantries. People seem to like him, and he them. He does not, however, like me.

The bartender sets down the black coffee. "No milk or sugar. Sorry." He walks away. I don't drink my coffee black, but I am not raising objections. I've seen this movie before, this town where they don't take kindly to strangers.

"Used to get calls," Tuepker says, side-eyed. "Not so much anymore. People with theories. Telling us their deep, dark secrets." Now he glowers at me, unbreaking.

"So those files?" I say, speeding along the process.

"Why do you want to look at them?" he asks.

Why? *For one, you offered?* I stammer another answer, one more neutral and unobjectionable, repeating I would like closure. His expression says I am lying. *He's privy to secret information.* Lily? Our dog Bridget? My current estrangement from my wife and child? I do not know. This is twenty years. I am meeting with a man I've never met, who says he was there that night. No matter how nice I play or what reassurances I give, he holds me in contempt.

"No tracks," he says, picking up the photo, which he stashes in the box, before closing the lid.

This man is not sharing evidence. He is not giving me a damn thing. He wanted to meet me, face to face, in person. *He wanted to look us in the eyes and see for himself.*

I pretend to glance at the time and say I need to get going.

"Funny thing is ... Bobby ... there was a man," he points out the window, in the general direction of the Green Mountains, "living in those hills. And would you believe it? After your sister goes missing, they found two bodies buried under his floorboards. And get this ... *Bobby* ... this man was, in fact, in the area that night. A psycho killer. Talk about bad timing. How you like that?"

I hate that name. Bobby. I am not correcting him. He's baiting me, a drunk man picking a fight. I, too, have heard this "serial killer" theory, which always struck me as preposterous, too convenient, too ... contrived, is the word I'm looking for.

"You probably want to know his name, eh? You suddenly interested in what happened to your sister and all."

I open my mouth, unsure how to respond. I came here hoping for answers about Brooke's possibly being pregnant. I have no interest getting drawn into a game of cat-and-mouse.

"That's the Feds," he says, brushing me off, polishing his beer, and waving for another. "Once serial killers and kidnapping are in play, that's their ballgame."

I wince a smile, chuckle, which is part swallow and half snort, my heart in my throat.

Tuepker whips out a piece of paper. He's already taken the liberty of writing down a name and number, information he could've given me over the phone.

I glance at the contact info. Paraskevi Pallotta, FBI, Boston.

"Call her," he says.

Tucking away the paper, I snatch my coat, pull a five for the coffee, and mutter goodbye. Tuepker never reacts, doesn't say a word.

Sitting in my car in the parking lot, I stare back at the bar, shaking. I'm enraged, beside myself, although I can't articulate why. *He wasted my time.* Vern Tuepker didn't accuse me of anything. *He lied about sharing evidence.* The conversation carried an implied, subversive threat. I can't pinpoint what that threat was. I fire up the engine and punch it in drive, getting on the road as fast as I can, while reminding myself to stay under the speed limit and not violate any traffic laws. I keep watching the rearview for trooper lights. They never appear.

With each mile behind me, I exhale relief. I look at the paper Tuepker gave me, the number for Paraskevi Pallotta, FBI investigator out of Boston. I don't know how much stock to put into what Tuepker told me—kidnapping and serial killing always seemed so far-fetched. I decide to call anyway, surprised to not only reach a live person but Pallotta herself.

She sounds friendly. Especially compared to Tuepker. Pallotta suggests meeting. Tomorrow, coffee, Boston.

I am already headed east on the highway, like I knew this would happen.

Before I hang up, she says, in a casual aside, "It'll be nice to talk to you in person. As far as I'm concerned, we solved this case ages ago."

CHAPTER TWENTY-THREE

December 31, 1997, 7:01 a.m.
Nine Days Before the Disappearance

"You're just like her!" The factory gray of Paul's grease-stained one-piece uniform draped off his wiry frame, a comical sight, David Byrne's oversized suit.

Never a big man, her dad had been losing weight. She could hear him vomiting in the bathroom most mornings. It was hard to watch, his decline. Maybe they should talk about his drinking? Then this morning he'd barged through the door, amped up, hurling coats and kicking chairs, rousing her out of bed. Now they were in the kitchen having another knockout, drag-down fight.

"You have no fuckin' common sense!"

Forget trying to help her father—Brooke was pissed for having been woken up for this bullshit. Admonishment for how she lived her life? From Paul, a mess of a man on his best days? Hilarious. Never mind killing himself with hard liquor and stomach ulcers, her dad never recovered from Connie. He'd loved her mother so unconditionally, he'd been a punching bag for the woman when she was alive, and now that she was dead, Connie's stranglehold had only grown tighter. Paul was collapsing under the weight of added responsibility. He couldn't take care of his *own* kid, let alone Connie's bastard addition.

Just like her? What a joke! She was *nothing* like her mother. What did Paul know about her life anyway? Their shared loss could've brought them closer, forged a bond; Paul couldn't see it, though, so gutted by *his* sorrow and *his* pain; he was unable to recognize his own flesh and blood was hurting too.

"I give up," Paul said. "You don't fuckin' listen to a thing I say anyway." Her father ripped off a coverall button and popped open a beer. "You know I had to leverage the house, right? The only thing I own. Get you out of jail."

"What do you want me to say?"

Paul spun around, stabbing at her with the cigarette and lighter he held. "Nothin'! There is nothin' you can say. You keep fuckin' up, there won't be no one left to let down. 'Cause no one will believe in you anymore. Words are empty. You have to *do* it."

"Because you're *such* a man of action." Brooke's stare narrowed. "All you do is sit around, getting pissed, pining for Mom. She's dead! And she only came back to die because she needed someone to watch after Bobby!" Brooke didn't care if her weirdo half-brother was listening. She was sick of him using up the hot water and eating all their peanut butter. "She never gave a shit about us!"

Her father had a hair-trigger when it came to Connie, her mother a topic off-limits. Brooke braced for one of Paul's violent outbursts. He'd been teetering on edge. When he got pushed over that line, he couldn't control himself. To his credit, Paul never hit Brooke, not even a swat on the butt when she was a toddler. Abuse comes in all forms. When triggered, Paul would unleash a string of profanity, voice adopting a terrifying timbre. He'd start knocking over chairs, throwing shit—mugs, bowls, glassware—chucking anything he could get his hands on— dishes, cups, dinner plates. They'd smash against the wall, landing close enough to make it clear if his aim wasn't a little off...

Brooke grew up scared of her father. Brooke wasn't scared anymore, and it had been a long time since he could make her cry.

Bring your worst, Dad.

This time, however, Paul didn't pick up any place-setting. He dropped his hands, like a resigned gunslinger in some old western knowing he no longer had the drop. In that moment, her father never looked older. He seemed to age ten years in ten seconds.

Paul turned to the east, where the big window framed the clouds smothering the low winter sun. It was heartbreaking to witness, light fading, darkness invading. When he'd told her that "no one will believe in you anymore," he hadn't been talking about Brooke. It had been a rare moment of self-introspection for her dad.

"I'll fix this," she said. The arrest was her mess.

Her dad didn't respond, studying that dim, distant dot in the sky as if it housed ancient wisdom. The pained expression on his face conveyed he wanted to say something. One last nugget of advice to pass on before he retired to pasture. Her dad had never been great expressing himself. Paul Mulcahy was a man born of a different era, part of a generation that landed jobs straight out of high school, grinding away in the factory at night, returning home each morning, a little more dead inside. Soon, he'd wilt, perish, dust to dust. This conversation was more than Brooke could hope for.

"I'm sorry," she said.

"All I wanted was a better life for you."

Regulating emotions didn't come easy for her dad. They'd been in the kitchen for the past half hour, hurling insults and pointing fingers, Paul on the precipice of losing his shit. Now he'd gone the other direction, one-eighty, turning that anger inward. Brooke knew she inherited the mental problems and depression from her father as much as she did her mom.

Paul stepped to the table, pensive, tired. "Mike is bad news." He dropped in a seat, bouncing the cigarette butt off a dirty plate.

"I know." Brooke joined her father at the kitchen table.

When Mike was over, Paul wasn't mean or rude to him. In fact, it was often the opposite. The two would share beers and smoke on the back porch, a boys' club. They'd talk about the Patriots or Red Sox, make racist or sexist jokes. To the casual observer, the two men seemed to get on fine. But when Mike was gone, Paul didn't hide his disdain. Then again, anyone around Mike for more than two minutes could see the guy was trouble. Take away his good looks, he didn't have much going for him. And he wasn't *that* good-looking. In quieter, more reflective moments, Brooke wondered if she kept Mike around as punishment, because a deep, dark part of herself wanted to suffer, didn't believe she deserved better. Brooke couldn't articulate the intricate psychology behind such self-destructive behavior. At Midfield State, she'd studied the fringes of self-hatred, -loathing, and -compassion. But she'd dropped out before these terms became part of her vocabulary.

"All a parent wants," Paul said, "is a better life for his kid."

Breaking his own rule, Paul lit a Winston at the table. He didn't bother to open the back door or crack a window, blue smoke swirling above his head.

Paul tried to smile. "I was watchin' a movie when I got off work the other mornin'. Couldn't sleep. Can't remember the name of it. This old father was talkin' to his son about the day he was born and what a magical moment it was. I can't remember where I was when you were born. I wasn't at the hospital. And not because I was at the bar or workin' or anything like that. It was different in those days. We checked your mom in. Couple days later, I came back to pick you both up. First time I saw you, you were already days old. I think about that a lot."

Brooke didn't know how to respond. So she didn't say anything.

Paul, never one to open up, was talking, and she didn't want to startle or shock him back into silence. Who knew when—if—there'd be another chance?

"Best thing I ever did with my life," Paul said, eyes dewy, "was havin' you. I know I fucked up a lot of shit. I felt sorry for myself. I wanted her back. Seein' you reminded me she was gone, and I wasn't the best father I could be, and…"

Brooke knew he was trying to make a point, and she could guess what that point was, but waiting for him to reach it was awful. She leaned over and grabbed his hand. "You were fine," she lied.

"No, I wasn't." Paul dragged on his smoke, sipped his beer, craven face turned toward where the sun used to be. "This isn't a pity party, and I'm not tellin' you this so you'll forgive me. I'm tellin' you this so you don't make the same mistake. I don't want you to wake up at fifty and see you've pissed away your life."

Paul dropped his lit cigarette in his half-full beer, rising from his seat. Fifty wasn't *that* old, but they'd been a hard fifty. What the factory and alcohol hadn't destroyed, the broken heart took care of.

Grabbing his big black coat off the back of the chair, he stopped at his daughter's side. "You get one life, kid. Don't give it away."

After her father walked out the door, Brooke remained at the table. The house was quiet. If Bobby was home, he must be asleep. Then she heard the clodding feet scrambling up the well. He had been eavesdropping on their entire conversation. Little shit.

Her father was right. It was time for a clean break, rip off the band-aid, jump in the cold water, whatever analogy Brooke needed to take out the trash and be rid of Mike Rakowski for good.

With the court case looming, Mike would milk it. Didn't make any difference how mean or nice she was to him, if she gave him the occasional handjob or let him grind up against her. Mike wanted Brooke, to be with her, near her, to make her his and his alone. Possession. Mike was going to hold this arrest over her head until he got what he wanted, which was *her* under *his* thumb, fat in a kitchen with a crying baby at her feet, out of options, dependent on him. In the end, Mike might not throw her under the bus. In the end, Mike might do the right thing and find a way to keep Brooke out of it. But she'd pay, one way or the other.

Brooke wasn't going to wait to find out. Like her old basketball coach Rod used to say before she ruined it by fucking him: sometimes the best defense is a good offense.

She didn't know what happened inside Stimpy's that night, all her information coming via Mike. Her lawyer would urge her to settle and make it as painless as possible.

The cops wanted to scare her.

Lawyers wanted a quick payday.

Mike wanted her held hostage.

Each of these options took the control out of her hands.

It was time to seize that control back.

CHAPTER TWENTY-FOUR

NOW

I book a room at a Holiday Inn off the Mass Pike. Hotel rooms come with tiny refrigerators to make it feel more like home. In the morning, I skip the complimentary continental breakfast, opting for a nearby Starbucks, before hitting the Mass Pike for my meeting with FBI Agent Paraskevi Pallotta.

Northeastern scenery whips by; fields of amber grain glisten in the cold, new day sun, slim stalks poking out beneath the thin blanket of overnight snowfall. I am thankful to be in a moving car. To most, seeing rest stops and roadsides doesn't inspire fondness. For me, they evoke security. Even though my childhood with Connie was anything but stable, I never feared being abandoned. She kept me close, like a mama bear and her cub.

I dial in satellite radio, searching for old-school, road-trip music, a classic from Cat Stevens or Steely Dan, the music my mother used to groove to. Before I can settle on anything, a call bleats over the Porsche's sound system. Aaron Reardon.

"Hey, Bobby! Excuse me, I mean, Robert!"

Aaron's perky enthusiasm hasn't changed in twenty years. Every salutation brims with unbridled optimism.

"Are you driving?" he asks.

"I am," I say, drawing out words because I don't want Aaron to ask where I'm going. I am one stop from our hometown, and though I have time to kill, I'd prefer not to kill it over coffee with Aaron Reardon. Of course, that's exactly what he asks.

"Boston?" he says. "Will you be passing Rocky Cove? Got time for a quick bite? I can sneak out for an early lunch. Be great to catch up, talk in person—"

"I'd love to, Aaron. I've already passed the exit. Plus, I'm meeting someone."

"Oh."

"No, it's good," I assure him with specifics to get his mind off hurt feelings. "An FBI agent working Brooke's case. She says she has important information."

"That *is* good. Next time!"

I wait for him to talk—there's a reason he called. I watch the Rocky Cove exit buzz past, feeling better when the lie becomes true. "Was there something you wanted?"

"Right! I *did* call you! I was going to tell you that I have a friend who works at Amherst. She's going to verify if this Lily is a student."

"Don't bother. Police already checked. She's not enrolled, this semester or last."

"Let me give it a shot."

"Have at it," I say, not adding it's a waste of time. Let Aaron feel like he's helping.

He chatters away, until I tell him I need to focus on the road and hang up. The long stretch offers little to look at, but it beats small talk with Aaron Reardon.

As I approach Boston, traffic grinds. By the time I reach

downtown, I'm reminded why I hate big cities. Chaos. Disorder. Towns, even smaller ones like Rocky Cove, display cohesion, shopping centers and supermarkets that resemble actual grocery stores and aren't crammed into a brownstone, sandwiched between double-decker apartments and nail salons. And Boston is the worst.

City planners appear to have been drunk when laying out city grids. A civil engineer, I take personal offense. In Boston, there are no "blocks," where four rights can correct a wrong turn. Nothing is straight. It's all circuitous, former horse-and-buggy paths paved into the hillside. Driving around Chelsea, I can't get my bearings, which fills me with a sense of dread, as if something wicked this way comes. In New England, the ghosts of the innocent burned at the stake never feel far away.

I find the Dunkin' Donuts, which is wedged between a hip and trendy yoga studio and an overpriced juice shop. A gaggle of young, impossibly in-shape women in tight-fitting pants pose with remarkable posture, toting rolled-up mats and looking extra excited to stretch their chakras.

I open the door. The bell dings. "Dr. Kirby?"

If I didn't know better, I would've pegged Agent Pallotta as one of the yoga juicers. She's not as young as the girls next door but still younger than I'd expect an FBI agent to look.

I tell Agent Pallotta to call me Robert. She says first names are great. I try to say hers and mangle it. She says "Vivi" is fine. And here we are already making friends.

"Hope you don't mind Dunkin' Donuts?" she says.

"I'm from Massachusetts. If I didn't like Dunkin' Donuts, they'd revoke my citizenship." It's a stupid joke but one called for in these situations. Truth is, I hate Dunkin' Donuts. The coffee is horrible, and after your teens, no one can eat a donut. If it wasn't such a regional staple, Dunkin' Donuts would've been put out of business ages ago.

We take our hot bean water to one of the few tables, which seats us by the window and the ponytail congregation out front. The glass barrier can't protect us from the bursts of sporadic laughter and grating enthusiasm.

"I'm glad you called," Vivi says. "I've wanted to reach out to the family for a while."

"If you wanted to reach out," I say parroting, "I'm not hard to find."

"That's not what I mean." Vivi hefts a folder from her bag, drops it on the table, and holds up a hand. "Let me start over. Officially, we don't know what happened to Brooke. That's the agency's position. I, however, believe otherwise." She waits. "I still have supervisors and protocol to follow—"

"I understand," I assure her. "If I were a reporter, this would be off the record." Like when a friend says they can't share a secret, but if you can *guess...*

"Yes. Not because what I'm about to tell you isn't true. I wouldn't share it if I wasn't one hundred percent certain. This information hasn't been made available to the public. It's unprovable now, after so many years—"

I intertwine two fingers. "Scout's honor."

"You were in the Boy Scouts? So was my brother—"

"No. I lied. I couldn't think of any other way to reassure you."

Vivi laughs. It's a terrific laugh, her entire person in on the joke. You can tell a lot about someone by the way they laugh. How uptight they are. How compassionate they might be. People say eyes are the window to the soul. I disagree. Eyes can do anything you want them to. Lie, deceive, manipulate, patronize. But a laugh? A real honest-to-God laugh? Where you leave yourself exposed and vulnerable? There's no greater height to fall from.

Vivi waves her hand in front of my face to redirect my attention.

"You still in there? Your eyes went glassy and far away."

I assure her I'm fine. *Then again, if Vivi has extensive files on our case, she knows all about us*—how they sent me away, how doctors patched up my broken brain. *We are better now.*

"Are you familiar with the various theories?" Vivi says, picking up our conversation. "About what happened to your sister?"

"Stepsister. Half-sister. Same mom. And yes. There's been no shortage. I had to stop paying attention." I begin to recap some of the crazier conjecture when she interrupts me.

"Do you enjoy teaching at Uniondale?"

"I—yes?" I pull away, quizzical. "Sorry. Not sure what my job at the university—"

"Nothing," Vivi says. "Trying not to overwhelm you." She laughs. "One of the reasons they stick me in archives—I don't have the greatest people skills. I tend to blurt."

"Are you always this ... forthright?"

"You mean am I always not full of shit?"

Her laugh kills me, like a knife to the gut, so genuine. I wonder if I've ever experienced such unfettered joy in my life. How can a federal agent, who must see the worst mankind has to offer, be so carefree?

Vivi plays with her hair, starting to tie it back in a ponytail, before stopping. A yoga girl prances outside the window and grins, as if witnessing the awkward splendor that is a first date.

I can see why yoga girl would make that mistake. That smile, that laugh, and now I'm uncomfortable. I'm a happily married man.

Except I'm not, at least not the "happily" part. *You shouldn't be thinking what you're thinking, Bobby. Those are bad thoughts...*

Then Vivi returns to business, mood vacillating so fast I'm left speculating. We *were* flirting, right? How attune am I? How much am I projecting?

"I'm sorry to say," the agent continues, "Brooke is unlikely ever to be found."

That sobers me up. "That's a pretty definitive statement."

"Does the name Samuel Erskine mean anything to you?"

I shake my head.

"Definitions of 'spree' and 'serial' killers muddy the waters."

"Serial killer?"

"I'm sorry." Vivi winces. "Did I mention my people skills aren't so great?"

I swear I catch her blushing, which makes this one of the stranger exchanges I've had. Here we are tossing out witty one-liners over casual, nonverbal cues—I'm certain we shared a moment—in between talk of mass murder and horrendous fates.

"It's okay," I say. "I didn't know Brooke well. She was a stranger. I am familiar with the rogue serial killer theory. I've always thought it fringe, radical." I wait. "Out there."

Vivi pulls a pair of eyeglasses from her bag. With them on she resembles a more grown-up Zooey Deschanel. Then again, most attractive women with dark hair, glasses, and bangs look like Zooey Deschanel.

"Samuel Erskine is a man we've long suspected of being involved in the disappearance of two women. Not suspected. Known. Definitely." She makes sure she has my undivided attention. "And likely a third."

Vivi doesn't need to add who that third woman might be.

"Your sister's roommate said—"

"Brooke didn't have a roommate. She lived at home. With Paul and me."

Vivi appears confused, before perusing official documents. "Torie Dent?"

I shrug, neither in the affirmative nor negative.

"Your stepfather said—"

"Paul is not my stepfather. He and my mother were married. Then they weren't. I came along after they weren't. And Paul isn't saying *anything* these days. Unless you count repeating the same nonsensical phrase over and over."

"You *are* captious," Vivi says.

I can't help but smile. "Captious" is one of my all-time favorite words.

Vivi dives back into the paperwork. "According to Ms. Dent's testimony, Brooke was in an abusive relationship—"

"Mike Rakowski. He was an asshole. Everyone who met the guy will tell you that. If I never speak to the sonofabitch again, it'll be too soon. But Brooke didn't have a roommate. She lived at home."

"Anyway," Vivi says, agreeing to disagree, "it appears your sister was planning to start a new life. Those plans were interrupted. Permanently. Sam Erskine moved throughout the Northeast. He came from money. He may've killed others out of state, perhaps farther south. Unknown. Mom was a doctor, dad a lawyer. Had a younger brother named Troy, who was also an attorney." I'm having a hard time following Vivi's logic, which zips and jolts all over the place. "You remember the Unabomber?"

"Who doesn't remember the Unabomber?"

"To give context," she says. "Like Ted Kaczynski, Sam Erskine was another nihilist who willfully cut himself off from civilization. Money not being an issue, he had plenty of places to stay throughout New England. Family properties. Cabins, hunting huts. He was quiet, unobtrusive, kept a low profile. Neighbors said … wait for it …" Vivi points a finger at the page. "Neighbors describe Erskine as 'polite and well-mannered' and were 'shocked to learn he was a killer.'" Vivi shakes her head. "No one ever suspects the good-looking, middle-class white guy."

Vivi's exotic features shine. Paraskevi Pallotta. Greek? Italian? Last name sounds Italian. Stephanie and I have visited Italy a couple times, most recently when Peter was seven. I pledge to see Venice again before it crumbles into the sea.

Vivi motions to hold on, shifting papers. "From January seventh to February fourth, Erskine was staying at a cabin outside Briarboro, Vermont, the little town where your sister—half-sister—had her accident. In the mountains. That one month—not even a whole month. Three weeks and change. The property was one of many that belonged to the family. We believe that is where he brought the girls."

"Girls?"

Vivi watches out the window as the yoga gaggle returns indoors for the next class. "Erskine transported the corpses. From … elsewhere. We found remains of two women within vicinity of the property." She stops, hand up. "Not Brooke. The other women we know he killed. After Samuel Erskine killed himself—" Vivi mimes a two-finger blast under her chin "—his brother Troy came forward. He'd been cleaning out the cabin, found his brother's old writings, which paint the picture of a disturbed young man. I can't tell you when or where Sam Erskine killed the other two women." She lowers her head and glances around. "But he killed those two women."

Her frequent starting, stopping, pausing, and redirecting would normally irritate me—I loathe scatterbrains. Something about this woman, despite the horrific subject matter, is intoxicating. It's driving me nuts trying to put a finger on what is so bewitching about her. She's quirky. I am not a fan of quirky.

"We found blood. In the cabin. Not belonging to the two women. Troy didn't come forward until it was too late. Erskine was always disappearing, threatening to stay gone. No one checked the cabin, which was more of a hunting blind. Do you know what that is?"

"A small hut for hunters to hide and shoot things."

"I'm trying to explain how a sibling could be missing so long and no one cares."

For a second, I think she means Brooke, me. *That makes you a bad brother, Bobby.* Vivi must see this.

"I'm talking about Troy Erskine. *His* story. What I think?" She leans in with a sultry whisper. "Parents died, left him the money, didn't want to deal with his crazy brother. Blood was too contaminated to get a useable sample."

"Blood? From the two women?"

"Brooke's."

"Wait. You just said you can't prove Brooke was there."

"We can't."

"Then how can you be so certain it's Brooke's blood."

Vivi returns a peculiar look, as if just now remembering a vital detail she's forgotten.

"Because after the crash," she says, "we know Samuel Erskine picked up your sister."

CHAPTER TWENTY-FIVE

December 3I, I997, 5:I3 p.m.
Nine Days Before the Disappearance

Stimpy's place didn't look any better in the light. Not that there was
much of it left with winter hijacking the sun so early these days. Since
last time Brooke was here, most residents' feeble stabs at festive had
been cleared away and boxed up for next year. A few oversized colored
blubs hung from sporadic gutters. A couple mangy wreaths dotted
the occasional door. One deflated Santa. Set against the squalor of
Crooked Row, these paltry efforts rendered the neighborhood more
wretched.

Brooke started partying in junior high, her drug use at its worst in
high school, peaking senior year. Pot and pills, mostly. She'd done the
harder stuff, too, when opportunity arose. Outside of coke, opportunity
didn't arise much. In her graduating class, Brooke was known as the
wild girl, a reputation graded on a curve. Rocky Cove was a suburban
town where "wild" meant getting drunk in the seventh grade or snorting white lines, ninety percent of which was baby powder. It's easy to be
a one-eyed queen in the land of the blind. There was always a broker,
a middleman, a go-between. Brooke never had to deal with men like
Stimpy.

As she'd explained to Torie, Stimpy's was not a regular residence. You couldn't go up and knock on the door or ring a bell. She was breaking an unspoken rule by heading into the duplex without an invitation. Brooke anticipated reluctance, resistance, problems. But Brooke was a pretty girl, and pretty girls could talk their way into—and out of— many things.

Now she sat on a ratty couch, being told to relax, which was impossible to do. Forget the booming bass shaking walls. It wasn't that the people, whose complexions didn't resemble Brooke's, spoke languages Brooke did not understand. There was no one specific issue; rather, it was the entire presentation, the way these men and girls carried themselves, everything about them cold and hopeless and hard.

No one spoke to her. Men who resembled wet rats with tattooed teardrops stood in the shadows, smoking chemicals that stank of bleach and toilet cleaners. They wore skull caps, hoodies hiding wife beaters. No one looked at her. No one ignored her either. She could feel their passing glances, verifying she hadn't moved. Where could she go? Her path to any door was blocked. She was in it now.

With nothing to do but wait, Brooke replayed ten minutes earlier. Standing on that cold porch with its dim yellow bulb encasing a million dead, dry bugs, back when she still had a chance to turn around, go home, and not make this mistake. She'd felt the stern tug of common sense, endured its insistence to change course. She'd heard the voices, the music, smelled that smell classic rock radio had been warning her about since she was a kid. Brooke's body tingled, down to a cellular level, screaming at her this was a horrible idea. She hadn't listened.

That was the worst part, knowing how preventable this was, that she'd willingly turned a blind eye. She'd rung that bell of her own accord and when the door opened and the man asked, "The fuck you want?" Brooke still had the chance to run—no one was going to chase after her, they'd close the door, mutter, "Crazy bitch," allowing another strung-out junkie to scurry away, unharmed. Who cares what they thought?

Instead, Brooke stood her ground, acting tougher than she was. She said she wanted to see Stimpy and wasn't leaving until she did. That decision wasn't tough—it was stupid.

She'd gotten what she wanted.

Careful what you wish for...

Brooke watched shadows creep and dance up the walls, loud cars with spent mufflers cruising the block, coughing exhaust, shotgun blasts that made her flinch. Brooke wasn't some ingénue, a phrase she'd picked up in the one Shakespeare class she'd taken—she loved the lilt of that word, its soft, rolling sounds, so elegant. She could never use it around her friends. If she were hanging out with them, she'd say this wasn't her first rodeo or find another dumbed-down cliché. She liked "ingénue" better because the word wasn't meant for her. It reminded her the future was unwritten and she could reinvent herself any day.

First, she had to get out of this mess.

Brooke tried to convince herself she was overreacting. She wasn't some sheltered suburbanite who thought every dark-skinned kid ran with a gang. These men—boys—came from a harder side of life, sure. Their worldview had been shaped by a different set of circumstances. That didn't make them criminals. Maybe they stole, did illegal drugs... Okay, that would make them criminals. Then again, so was Brooke. She was here because she'd been arrested. An accessory charged in commission of a crime. Which sounded less menacing, the more she thought about it. Never mind the arrest, she'd done the same drugs as these guys. Don't be a hypocrite, she told herself. Don't be a baby. Sitting on that ratty couch, none of this internal pep talk moved the needle.

Brooke was in trouble. She knew it. And she couldn't fix it. This was when it hit her: she wasn't walking out of here unscathed.

"You."

He didn't look any different than the other druggies in this place—hard, lean, mean, sagging baggy jeans, resigned to a life he had no possibility of escaping.

The man jerked his head. "Let's go."

He kicked a door open wide with his bright white, unlaced sneakers. A set of stairs led to a dim basement, where voices whispered in hushed tones.

"What you waitin' for?" he said, nudging her forward.

Brooke took a tentative step, feeling the man loom behind her. She'd hit the point of no return. Her only choice: to venture further into the unknown and find what waited on the other side.

When the door closed, the music muffled, and the muttering stopped.

Then she heard the lock tumble, sealing her in darkness.

CHAPTER TWENTY-SIX

NOW

Vivi and I order more bad coffee I don't want while she shares the devastating details I both long to learn and wish to forget.

The FBI has evidence. Irrefutable, ironclad. Toll road footage of Samuel Erskine's van, license plate numbers, gas station stills from the night in question. And sitting up front in these photographs, besides Erskine and in plain view shotgun, a black-haired passenger. I don't need a computer to tell me who that woman is. State-of-the-art facial recognition technology does anyway, confirming with ninety-nine percent certainty.

Brooke.

Vivi takes her time showing me these photos, answering my questions, chief among them why this information wasn't made public. The FBI agent out of Boston explains the peculiarities of due process. Innocence and guilt have rules to play by. There is a greater picture at stake, ongoing cases where victims might still be alive. Deals to be made, trades bartered, criminal lowlifes who will rat on one another to shave a month off a sentence. This is the bureaucracy of prosecution and incarceration, the way this information is gathered and released; how department officials determine whether they want to run with information based on the likelihood of charges, indictments, and the percentage rates of convictions. In the end, Agent Pallotta says it all comes down to answering one simple question: does paying back Paul justify the cost of nailing Peter to the wall?

"Unfortunately," Vivi says, "Erskine will never be charged in your sister's case, and that means the file will never officially be closed. It now belongs to a giant section devoted to limbo. We know who it did, but with no body recovered, no DNA admissible, there's no way we could prove it from a legal standpoint." Vivi stops to point again at the photograph of Brooke in the front seat of a serial killer's van. "Doesn't mean he's not guilty."

I stare and try to convince myself it *could* be another woman who looks remarkably like Brooke, same height, hair, and bone structure in the front seat; I know that's a lie. As sure as I'm still living and breathing, it's her.

"I hope this brings you some peace," Vivi says.

I remain silent, reflecting, searching out holes to poke, entertaining possibilities something is missing. I fixate on specifics and details of the conversation. If I am to shut this door, I must do it for good.

"What about the witnesses that night?" I ask. "The ones who saw Brooke's car. Hope Washington, and what's the other one's name? I'm drawing a blank. The drunk guy coming from his second-shift job?"

"Nathaniel Jones."

"Are they alive?"

Vivi peruses files, thumbing pages. "Hope Washington passed away in twenty-twelve. Complications from diabetes."

Then she surprises me.

"According to what I have here, Nat Jones is still with us. He's an old man. Not sure how much use he'd be. We are going on twenty years."

"And he was inebriated."

Vivi nods, stops, watching me stare at the photograph of my dead stepsister. "What are you hoping to find, Robert?"

"After Nat Jones left—how long until she was picked up?"

"There was about a ten-minute window before police arrived."

"Erskine was, what, stalking her?"

"We don't think so. Happened to be passing by."

"That's one hell of a coincidence," I say.

Vivi's face exudes compassion. "I know this is hard to hear."

It's not that, I want to tell her. I can't explain why I'm so disquieted. She wouldn't understand. *Couldn't* understand. Despite this new ironclad evidence, which I can see with my own two eyes, it doesn't feel right. A random serial killer? *It's too tidy.* An unsatisfying conclusion. *Why look for more trouble?* Because I want—I *need* this to be over.

"Do you have the contact information?" I ask.

"For whom?"

"Nat Jones."

Vivi reopens the folder but doesn't read.

"I'd like to talk to him."

"You just acknowledged he was impaired—which the police already—"

"I'd still like to talk to him."

"Nathaniel Jones is eighty-one years old." Vivi flips through pages. "I don't even see a phone number, let alone email."

"Mailing address?"

"Are you planning on writing him a letter?"

"He was the last person to talk to my sister. Maybe he can remember something she said, something that would let me…"

I leave it there, let the sentence trail off and allow Vivi to finish the thought, fill in her own blanks. Because I know whatever she chooses to insert in its place will be better than anything I can come up with. I have no doubt, Vivi, who seems like a decent, honest person, will settle on a decent, honest answer.

The Haystack Mountains clip Briarboro proper, which brings heavier snow. The higher up I go, the worse it gets. The address I have for Nat Jones is far up in the clouds, a nowhere street buried among a no-man's land. Each turn delivers me deeper into darkness, farther from civilization, no lampposts or guardrails, barely enough room for one car to hug narrow lanes and squeeze beneath rocky overhangs.

It's daytime. I should be able to see. The mountain range obscures whatever weak light is not swallowed by cloud. Wrapped in thick, impenetrable fog, I find myself navigating half blind in driving, drifting gusts.

I keep assuring myself this isn't a waste of time, that Vivi's files are up to date and Nat Jones isn't dead. I overlook red flags, like the man not having a telephone or email. I eschew these facts out of necessity. I need this recluse, geriatric wino who stumbled upon a car accident more than twenty years ago to clear me of wrongdoing. *This is the last man to talk to her. At least the last one we can talk to.* Right now, I need Nat Jones more than he can possibly know.

Traversing the remote cliffside, I invent a ramshackle shed perched on a parapet, a shoddily constructed homestead warmed by a puffing tin stove, sleepy hound dog curled at the foot of an old man gnawing corncob as he languidly rocks on the porch despite subzero temperatures, savoring spiked sweet tea. Like so much of my life, it is a fantasy.

Instead, I find considerable acreage and mature landscaping. A paved driveway delivers me to a modern-looking house with tall glass walls. Even the truck I park alongside appears to be a newer model Dodge.

When Nathaniel Jones opens the door, he squints, understand-ably confused. I don't imagine many unannounced visitors come this way. Then again, without a cell or email, there is no way *to* announce. I explain who I am, what I'd like to talk about, why I'm standing on this stranger's front steps in a blustery storm.

After I finish, I anticipate befuddled silence. I'm asking Nat Jones to recall fleeting minutes from nearly a quarter century. Why should this old man remember a damn thing about that night just because its specter haunts my dreams?

To my surprise, he says, "I'll never forget that night. That poor girl..." He clears a path, welcoming me.

I enter a comfortable home with contemporary décor, which again refutes my prejudice of a mountain man who hunts his own moose meat and ladles moonshine from a pail.

He asks if I'd like something to drink. I say whatever is fine. I wait for variations of rotgut and whiskey. Instead, the old man puts on water to boil, before he sifts through boxes of herbal tea in a cupboard, reading the names of myriad blends I couldn't care less about. I finally convince him to pick. I should be more appreciative. The delay offers opportunity to prepare my interview. Because that's what this is. An interrogation. Perhaps all Brooke's secrets didn't die with her...

Waiting for water to boil, I feel my mind turn on me as it begins constructing outrageous scenarios where Nat Jones knew Samuel Erskine, his brother Troy too. *They were all in on it.* I don't have a cause-and-effect chain for these far-fetched theories. Just an old man living in a house that's too nice for a retired factory worker. Or maybe Nat Jones is a relic from a forgotten era of American history when a man didn't need fancy degrees or a well-off spouse to retire comfortably.

After Nat returns with hot tea on a plate and finishes listing all the possibilities to spruce up my chamomile—honey, sugar, milk, cardamom—when I finally have his undivided attention—I can ask what I've come here for.

"I was returning home from work," the old man says, without hesitation. He points at the big glass wall with his sugar spoon. "It was a lot like today. Only nighttime. Snow really coming down. Colder. Icier. Never had much streetlight up here." He flicks his spoon at fields of impenetrable white. "Your sister slipped off the road."

I glance out the window, marveled by how silent and secluded everything is.

"It's nice having privacy—closest house is half mile through those woods. It's also scary not knowing much about your neighbors."

"Are you talking about Sam Erskine?"

Nat blows on his tea, takes a sip. The mug reads, "World's Best Grandpa." I don't see pictures of any children in frames. Not on tables, not hung from walls. The old man takes his time, rubbing the white scruff on his chin, before joining my gaze out the window.

"Mr. Jones?"

"It was big news up here," he says not looking at me. "A killer. Living in those woods. Like something out of a horror picture."

"Did you see Erskine that night? His van? It was white, no windows. Must've stood out."

"Nope. Like I told the police. I never met Erskine. If I glimpsed him at the market or post office, I wouldn't have known it. I read about what he'd done in the papers. Awful. Monster."

"You think Sam Erskine took her?"

"Not for me to say." Nat Jones shrugs. "Dates match. Math adds up. They never found your sister's body, right?"

"I met with an FBI agent earlier today. She had proof Erskine picked up Brooke. There's footage from cameras, tolls. My stepsister was definitely in his van."

He shrugs again, as if to say, *Well, there you go.*

"How was she when you stopped?"

I'm interested in observations, behaviors, impressions. *Did Brooke say anything pertinent?*

"Shook up," he says. "Car bashed in. Lucky she was on two feet. It was close to zero. I tried to get her to come back here with me and wait for the cops. I told her she'd get frostbite out there. She said she'd already called for help and they'd be there any minute. Which wasn't true. She couldn't have. Not as many cell phones back then—"

"Brooke didn't have a cell—"

"Even if she did," he continues, ignoring my input, "no service up here."

"How long did you talk to her?"

"Five, six minutes."

Decades and age erode memory, but Nat Jones seems to recall the event as clearly as last week, all the odder because of implications he'd been drunk at the time, an important detail I don't feel comfortable addressing. Thankfully, he doesn't make me.

"I'd just come from Tommy's Place," he says. "This little roadside bar I often stopped by after work." He retrieves a shiny coin from his pocket, holding it up for me to see. "Ain't had a drink in thirty-eight years. I just liked the people, y'know?"

I nod like I understand. Though I don't. Why would an alcoholic tempt himself like that? Of course I don't know if Nat Jones is lying. The police believed he was drunk, which was why they dismissed his testimony.

"When I got there, your sister was standing outside in a blizzard, hugging herself, shivering. Broke my heart to leave her like that. Like I say, I couldn't get her to come back with me. Can't say I blame her. Stranger, side of the road, late at night... I should've waited with her.

I could see I was making her nervous though, me sticking around the way I was."

"Did … she say anything else?"

"Such as?"

Was she pregnant? Did she hint at sexual assault? Instead, I ask about Mike Rakowski. "Did she talk about the crazy ex-boyfriend she was running from? How about where she planned to go?"

Nat Jones shakes his head no. "Car was so cracked up, she wasn't going nowhere. She'd tipped over into a culvert. Car kinda tilted on its side. Driver's door too kinked to open. She'd had to kick through the windshield to crawl out. Cars back then wasn't like they is now, glass that rain like diamonds. Glass all broken in jagged shards. Your sister was lucky to be wearing a thick winter coat. I could see the padding shredded. Before I left I asked if I could help retrieve her possessions inside the car. She said no. Said she had everything she needed."

"What did she have with her?"

"Nothin,'" Jones says. "Not a damn thing."

CHAPTER TWENTY-SEVEN

December 3I, I997, 5:53 p.m.
Nine Days Before the Disappearance

The first thing Brooke noticed when she saw Stimpy's face was the nose. Or lack thereof. It was impossible to miss. Mike had told her that Stimpy was named after a cartoon character. The name made little sense to Brooke; She never read the comic strip or saw the show. Who cares about a name? You think Mike would've mentioned the nose? In the middle of Stimpy's head where a regular nose should be, his face sported a disfigured bulb, the pulp of which had been suctioned back into his skull, creating a series of concave bowls, like an inverted Russian doll. His nostrils, two red slits, angry and infected, looked painful to the touch, and a dark golden crust burbled around their outer edges. Brooke had enough nursing training to recognize the signs of cocaine nose, which is what happens when the acidity of coke erodes the septum and foundation of the proboscis, and cartilage breaks down. Brooke tried to redirect her gaze elsewhere. *Don't stare, don't stare, don't stare…*

"What you want?" Stimpy asked, his voice a high-pitched, nasally whistle.

Brooke strove to remain nonplussed. Like the distorted sound and collapsed thing in the middle his head were totally normal.

"You fuckin' deaf or sumthin'?"

"Sorry," Brooke said, even if she wasn't sure what she was apologizing for. "I'm Mike Rakowski's..." She caught herself.

"His what?"

"Girlfriend," Brooke said, opting for the easiest explanation.

"Mike Rakowski?"

"Yeah."

"He's a piece of shit."

As wide as he was tall, Stimpy reclined in a plush chair, fitted in a terrycloth jumpsuit, flanked on each side by a pair of skinny men with black hoods. Stimpy tugged the terrycloth around his crotch. Brooke didn't want to speculate what was going on underneath.

Light from the streets above struggled to penetrate the narrow basement windows, thick blankets tacked over thin slots. Behind Brooke, in a dark corner, two girls sat on the floor, infatuated by bright, shiny objects. Brooke hadn't gotten a good look when she walked in—these weren't children; they weren't women either— more like light, wispy fairies. Brooke tried to ignore them. Every few seconds the clanking clink of metal on metal dinned, followed by stifled giggles.

"Take off your shirt," Stimpy told Brooke, who choked back a laugh, like it was a joke.

No one else was laughing.

Brooke shook her head slow, still unsure if he was being serious.

"How I know you ain't got no wire?" Stimpy said. "Take. It. Off."

Brooke stalled, stammered.

Stimpy opened his tracksuit jacket, displaying the handle of a gun tucked snug against his fat stomach. "Bitch, I ain't askin' again." He pulled the gun, arm extended, hand cocked sideways like a Spike Lee flick. "Take off your fuckin' shirt!"

Slowly, Brooke undid her top, peeling it from her shoulders. She didn't get far before Stimpy told her to stop. This wasn't about seeing if she had a wire. He wanted her to know he had all the power. She was in his world now, and he could make her do anything he wanted.

"Sit," Stimpy said.

Other than a small couch off to the side, piled high with electronics, wires and cords intertwined, writhing like serpents, there was nowhere *to* sit.

Stimpy, seeing her confusion, slapped his thigh. The flesh beneath his tight tracksuit jiggled like Jell-O. He squealed with joy.

Brooke didn't move.

"I'm fuckin' with you." Stimpy pushed himself to his feet. He called one of his boys, whispering in his ear. Then Stimpy juked his head, beckoning Brooke to follow to the near wall where a refrigerator, one of the few furnishings in the basement, hummed too loudly. Stimpy kicked the base of the door and the buzzing quieted. "Fuckin' piece of shit," he muttered.

There was a stark contrast between what Brooke had seen upstairs and this basement. Neither was glamorous. But upstairs was a party, people getting drunk and high. There'd been a big television and video game console, lamps and tables. There was music and dancing and kissing. Upstairs was a good time. She'd been uneasy, surrounded by smoke and thumping bass, the uncertainty of her alien status, but it was better than this isolated basement with its cold, sodden smells. Mold trapped in the plaster feasting on the lack of oxygen and dearth of light, sounds trapped in space, eerily muffled. It struck Brooke as strange, the sad exiled king alone in this dingy cellar.

At the fridge, Stimpy opened the door, retrieving a jumbo Ziploc baggie stuffed with white powder. "Wanna get fucked up?"

Behind her, the basement door slammed. When Brooke turned, no one else remained.

Stimpy dragged a small folding card table out of the shadows. Unsealing the fat Ziploc, he toppled a mound of white powder. Pulling a credit card from his pocket, he separated the pile into thick lines, and then jammed a rolled-up dollar bill inside his angry, red nostrils. Bending, and with great effort, he inhaled extra hard. It sounded like a congested pig over a trough in a rainstorm, all wet smacking. Futile. When Stimpy lifted his head, the line of drugs remained unchanged, barely a dent. Disappointment colored his face. What little powder he had managed to levitate temporarily flurried back out his nose, snow-flakes drifting.

"Sonofabitch!" Stimpy's eyes narrowed and pinched tight, which accentuated the knotted deformity in the middle of his face. Brooke tried to pretend she didn't see the damp, bloody straw he held out for her to take. She felt her pockets, thanking God for the crumpled five-dollar bill. Brooke flashed her best pretty girl smile, rolling the five into a straw and leaning over before he could be offended. A quick sniff and she tasted the antiseptic drip of Novocain, followed by the numbness only good cocaine delivered, drugs that hadn't been stepped on a dozen times. The ringing in her ears was instantaneous. It grew more intense until Brooke started to get dizzy. She reached out to steady herself on the refrigerator.

"Shit no joke," Stimpy said, proud of his product.

The rush was the kind she used to pay extra for. Now she prayed for it to stop. Stimpy had lost interest, head back inside the fridge, big backside poking out, a bear with its snout stuck in the honeypot.

"Sorry 'bout before," he said, pulling out. "Can't be too careful. Cops be sendin' pretty girls strapped all the time."

Stimpy smiled, his concaved nose puckering deeper. As unpleasant as his face was to look at, Brooke preferred that to his grating voice, which mimicked a deaf person trying to speak. Brooke felt bad for drawing that comparison.

Brooke doubted the cops were setting up elaborate stings—Stimpy wasn't big enough to warrant that kind of attention. Then again, what did Brooke know about this world? It was one she skirted the edges of, visited occasionally; she didn't live here.

Stimpy opened the top to the freezer, retrieving a bottle of Jägermeister. The sight alone made Brooke want to retch. The first time she'd gotten drunk, out-of-her-skull, puking-all-night hammered was from Jäger bombs. Who drinks that shit after high school?

He didn't bother with glasses, tipping back the bottle, funneling the licorice-infused, medicinal liquor down his open gullet. The gurgling sound in his throat, amplified by his nasal disfigurement, hit her gag reflex, and then she couldn't stop thinking about the rest of the carnage lurking inside cranial walls, the erosion, lesions, the open sores and discharge. By the time he passed the bottle, Brooke couldn't put the brakes on her imagination. Vivid pictures of contamination filled her mind, squirming bacteria and worms crawling around his mouth, the process sped up like science class films illustrating the life and death of a plant or mouse, remains decaying in the dust, absorbed by the earth to feed other slimy things that slithered on their bellies. Brooke couldn't put her mouth the same place Stimpy's had been. Polite refusal wasn't an option. She accepted the bottle and pretended to take a swallow. Brooke did her best not to breathe, not to smell or taste whatever Stimpy had left on the rim. An impossible task. Whether she really inhaled the rot was irrelevant; she believed she had, feeling Stimpy's sick all over her skin, parasitic hooks digging, which caused Brooke to dry heave. Stimpy took this to mean the coke and drink had been too much. His hyena laugh implied she was a lightweight. Brooke was grateful for the misinterpretation. She'd rather have him believe that than the truth—that his entire presence, from his gelatinous shapelessness to his collapsed cocaine nose and train whistle voice reviled her.

Relieving her of the bottle, Stimpy headed to the couch, where he shoved aside stereo equipment and plopped down, patting the cushion beside him. Brooke sat on the arm of the couch, as far away as she could get, but it wasn't far enough. Stimpy reached over and placed his hand on her knee, kneading inside her thigh. Brooke couldn't recoil or appear scared, doing her best to act cool and casual. This Stimpy was like a dog—if he smelled fear on her, she was done for.

"So, Mike Rakowski," he said, air leaking out his nose like a perforated balloon. "What about him?"

Brooke couldn't answer fast enough.

"I know he ain't your boyfriend," Stimpy said, greasy smile curled as if he'd caught her in a naughty fib.

"No," Brooke admitted. "Not anymore. We used to date. We're just … friends … now." She'd intended to put Stimpy's mind at ease since he plainly didn't think much of Mike. Stimpy's lecherous smirk said he'd taken it the other way: she was available.

Stimpy's hand crept higher up her thigh.

Brooke hopped up, cradling her lower abdomen. "Sorry," she said. "Cramps." Before quickly adding, "Menstrual."

When men hear the words "menstrual cramps," an unappetizing picture plants in their mind, one that quashes sexual desire. Brooke had used those words to kill many erections. With Stimpy, however, it didn't work. His jacket fell open, parting to display a big, taut gut stretched too tight like sausage that had outgrown its casing.

"I should go," Brooke said, holding her lower abdomen, hoping the visual aid worked.

"What you really come here for?" Stimpy asked.

This was it, her in, her chance. He was asking. *You miss one hundred percent of the shots you don't take.* Brooke had to try. She recapped the night of the arrest, how she needed Mike to say the vials were his, her tone earnest but firm. This was a black mark against her, her first real one, and it would follow her for the rest of her life.

She'd said a lot in a short span. For a second, Stimpy's expression said she'd gotten through, request registering. He understood. Maybe Stimpy was remembering a time when he still had the chance to leave this life behind and the sincerity of her plea had touched him.

"Sure," he said. "I can help. I'll make it in Mike's best interest, if you know what I mean."

"Thank you," Brooke said.

Stimpy waved her off. "Nah, I get it. Mike knows how to play the game. You don't need to get caught up in this shit."

Outside a bus passed, slowed, grinding to a halt, drawing Brooke's attention to the window. The grueling workday over; honest men and women who slaved away at menial-paying jobs emptied into the street. Crooked Row was wretched, but Brooke liked to imagine these people and their pursuits as noble. Fighting against the tide, putting in the extra time to earn a better life for loved ones. Shifts completed, conquering heroes returning to their modest huts where appreciative families waited. Fathers and daughters, sons and mothers preparing to spend the evening huddled over homecooked meals, recapping the day, planning for the future, room filled with enough love and laughter to remind each other what this life is really all about.

When she turned back around, Stimpy had his soft stubby cock out, pumping up and down furiously, trying to stir his listless member to life, watching for her reaction.

Brooke stared. Stimpy kept jerking it, the slapping sound bouncing off cold cellar walls. His eyes never left hers, labored breathing growing heavier.

Brooke took a step closer. Stimpy smiled and parted his thighs. Clearing the way for an unblocked, hard kick to the balls. Stimpy shrieked. Covering his junk, he toppled over, screeching as his two boys burst through the door. Brooke had already been running that way, her timing perfect as she ducked their feeble swipes.

Catching stride, Brooke raced up the stairs, splitting the throng to burst free into the biting January night.

She never looked back.

CHAPTER TWENTY-EIGHT

NOW

Driving, I'm hit by a strange sensation, one I haven't felt in a while. *We could disappear forever.* I always hated the term "suicidal ideation." Too dramatic, clinical. I prefer the French version: *L'appel du vide.* The call of the void. Even when I was at my worst, I never wanted to die. When I was fourteen, sixteen, rock bottom, I longed to go to sleep and not wake up. It's a feeling you can't convey to most. Not without sounding crazy. During my time in the hospital, doctors explained I wasn't alone. Normal, regular people drive their cars every day, struck by a sudden impulse to veer off the bridge. Normal, regular people peer over the edge of a rooftop, feeling the compulsion to take a step. It's common, this inexplicable urge to snuff out a light forever. We don't crash head-on. We don't leap. The moment passes. We continue on.

I steer into the Holiday Inn, recalling my conversation with Nat Jones, the last man standing to speak with Brooke before she died.

She shared no secrets.

She had nothing with her.

It's over.

Parking my car in the lot, I walk beneath bleak gray skies, entering the lobby. I'm preparing for the elevators when the woman behind the check-in desk calls my name. At first, I'm startled she knows my name. Then again, how many people are staying longer than a night in a Mass Pike Holiday Inn?

"This came for you," she says as I approach, sliding along a white envelope. The only marking: *Bobby*, scrawled in sloppy penmanship. She waits for me to pick it up.

I don't.

In a lobby staged with showroom furniture and generic photographs of pastural scenery designed to make one feel safe and warm, I freeze.

The woman smiles as I am unable to fake the same.

Nobody knows I am here.

"Are you sure this is for me?" I ask.

"Robert Kirby?" She asks the question, already knowing the answer.

I pan around the lobby, searching out a stranger, as if he—or she— would be lurking in a trench coat in the corner.

"Did you see who dropped it off?" I ask.

She shakes her head. "Came with today's mail. Just a Post-it note: Deliver to 'Robert Kirby.' You're the only Robert Kirby staying here."

I look at the envelope, at that chicken-scratched, scrawled name I hate so much, pointing out the obvious. "There's no return address."

The desk clerk shrugs.

What am I going to do, chase down the mailman, demand to know where he received his parcel? I pick up the envelope, which is light with a slight bulge in the middle—square, an inch or so long. I say thank you as I run my finger over the irregularity.

Entering the elevators, I'm sweating bullets, jittery like I've had too much caffeine and not enough food, which is true. I haven't eaten a meaningful meal in days.

As soon as I'm in my room, I tear open the envelope and the flash drive falls out.

Retrieving my laptop, I sit at the desk and insert the drive. The file takes several minutes to load.

And when it does, I see my house, my bedroom, the bed I sleep in with my wife. The view is from the far wall. The picture frames a young woman from behind. Naked, she bounces up and down, writhing, black hair swaying as she gasps in ecstasy. Her face is never shown. The girl could be anyone, but I know who it's *meant* to be: Lily.

I slam the laptop closed, glancing around my hotel room—for what, I have no idea. A clandestine operative concealed in the drapes? I reopen the laptop. The video is just under ten minutes. I'm mesmerized. Her slim waist, ass grinding, the slapping sounds of high-octane sex. I fast forward. The view never changes—her spine, her ass, the back of her head. I turn up the volume. I hear her sultry voicing pleading, "Fuck me," in between the moans.

Until she says, louder and clear as day: "Fuck me, Bobby."

It obviously isn't me in that video. I don't even know if that *is* Lily. I spent fifteen minutes with the girl in a coffee shop last week. Her face is never shown. It's sure supposed to *look* like Lily though. And there's no doubt about one thing: that *is* my bedroom.

Fuck me, Bobby.

There is my bedside table—the books I am *currently* reading. This isn't a sound stage or elaborate reenactment. There's no CGI or green screen. That is *my* bedroom.

You're such a dirty boy. Give it to me...

How did someone get in my house? I now understand why someone would want to silence my dog. Someone was slinking around my home, scoping it out. They heard Bridget's yapping and knew it would derail plans to break and enter. Break and enter for what? To film this filth? I remember that rusted red car in the rain.

Come in me, Daddy...

I shove the laptop off the bed. It crashes to the floor. What the hell is happening? If this video clip found its way to me in a random roadside hotel, it could already be in Stephanie's inbox. *If there is one copy, there is a master.* Will my wife believe me? Will she take my word for it when I tell her that isn't me fucking some girl claiming to be *my niece* in *our* bedroom? That I've been set up as part of an elaborate con? Maybe. I don't know. Probably not. When do excuses transcend paranoia and creep into conspiracy theory?

We've never needed a fancy security system. Hadn't even considered it. Diemen is safe, crime rate zero. Steph is always home. That is no longer true. The police must be notified. Connecting dots, it's easy to see that whoever hurt Bridget must be the same person filming this video. Reaching for my cell, I stop. What am I going to tell the cops? If I'm unsure I can convince my own wife of my innocence, how do I expect to sway authorities, who already seem leery of me? How can I explain this video? A woman, having sexual intercourse in *my* bed, using *my* name.

Though I don't want to, I re-watch the video, turning down the volume, hoping for deep fake giveaways. The camera is not sitting immobile. Amateurish, it moves with the actress' gyrations, that shaky cam effect favored by late-'90s' cinema, cheesy TV shows, and found footage films. It makes me dizzy. Someone is operating that camera, panning, zooming, capturing the actress' cries of ecstasy, zeroing in on a man's hands holding her hips, hands that are meant to be mine.

Who could be doing this to me?

Several people dislike me, including Uniondale's own Ortho Warsh, but this goes beyond professional rivalry. Despite my feelings about Ortho, this is beneath him.

Only one man has ever hated me *this* much: Brooke's abusive ex, Mike Rakowski.

Why now? After all these years? I've been asking questions, poking around, making noise. I wouldn't know where to find him, even if I wanted to confront him. I've put his name in search engines over the years, praying to read he was dead. Nothing. Not a word about the man. No accident. No arrest. Instead, Mike Rakowski appears to have vanished as well.

I must be smart about this. Do I want to tell the cops about Mike? Because then they'd know about me—my role in all this, motivation betrayed by the guilt I still feel. *You were a bad brother, Bobby...*

"Shut up!" I scream to an empty room.

Be smart. Stay cool. *Think.* We are an esteemed professor at a prestigious university in full command of our faculties and in complete possession of critical-thinking skills.

Roommate. Yes, Vivi Pallotta mentioned a roommate. The woman who harassed Steph and me had claimed to be a roommate. She turned out to be nuts, but now that I thought about it, Brooke *had* been staying away from home more often... Right. Just before she left, Brooke, who had always been coming and going, went away and didn't come back. How long? A week? Two or three? Sure, that constitutes a roommate, from a certain point of view.

I call Vivi, who gave me her cell over coffee, which allows me to bypass pressing buttons at the FBI. As it rings, I tell myself this is standard operating procedure for agents to hand out personal cell numbers to men they just met inside a Dunkin' Donuts after discussing a twenty-year-old cold case.

"Hello, Robert." The warm familiarity of her voice excites me, rendering me conflicted and stymied. "Robert? What is it?"

She gave you her number. How does she know it's us calling?

A crazy thought pops in my head, fueled by delusions better suited for a crack fiend … *and now Vivi is in on it too…*

"How did you know it was me?" I ask.

She laughs. "Um, I work for the FBI. Are you okay?"

I can't answer that. I don't know. I don't feel okay. She isn't asking that though, is she? Like when someone inquires how your day's going. It's a greeting, a way to say hello, a meaningless salutation. Perfunctory. No one wants to listen to your list of grievances.

On the other end of the line, the wind picks up, as if Vivi has stepped outside. Her office? Her home? Is she alone? *What do you care? Why are we calling?*

"What's going on? Did you talk to Nat Jones?"

Do I tell her about the video? *No, you do not tell her about that video.* Do I trust her enough to mention Mike? *We already discussed that prick over coffee.* I listen to the two parts of me, Robert and Bobby, arguing over our next course of action, and it's insane. *This is not a dynamic of yourself you want to share with anyone.*

"Sorry," I say, cool and collected. "There's construction outside my room." I don't know why I say this. It's the first excuse that pops in my head. No noise bleeds from my end. In fact, it is stone silent.

"Room?"

I explain I'm at a hotel, that I still have "business" I need to attend to in the region. I do not expound upon what this "business" is.

Instead, I tell her I spoke with Nat Jones.

"Was he able to help?" she asks.

"You were right. Just an old drunk. Didn't remember anything." I feel my heart speed up. "This morning, over coffee, you mentioned a roommate? Torie something."

"Torie Dent."

"I'd like to speak with her as well. She called several years ago. I didn't give that call the attention it deserved."

"What's going on with you?" The concern is genuine. I can't be honest with her.

"Nothing. I'm fine. Like I said, Torie Dent contacted me, but I don't have her number anymore."

I can feel Vivi's confusion. I know my desperation isn't making sense, isn't rational. No one can understand unless I am willing to share everything. And I'm not going to do that. Not with Vivi. Not with Dr. Amy, not with Stephanie. No one. I can't get that sick video out of my head—perverted sexual images planted, infecting my brain.

"Please," I add. "I don't have Torie's number anymore. It was years ago—"

"I told you this morning what happened to your sister. I know this isn't easy to hear—"

"Y'know, after we spoke this morning," I say smoothly, calmly. Rationally. "I feel like I'm that much closer to closure. If Brooke was staying with Torie, maybe Torie can, y'know, help me say goodbye. To my … sister." I exhale and hope the cadence of my breath conveys my earnestness, my trustworthiness, my integrity.

"Hold on." I hear her rummage. "No number," she says. "Just a motel address." Vivi doesn't add anything else.

"I just want to talk to her."

"When I met with you this morning, I hoped to answer lingering questions. So you could stop running around, driving yourself crazy with uncertainty. I'm not sure I helped."

"You did. You really did. I can't tell you how much I appreciate it."

Don't blame yourself, Agent Vivi Pallotta. You can't answer the questions we have.

I'm losing faith anyone can.

CHAPTER TWENTY-NINE

January 7, 1998, 1:28 p.m.
One Day Before the Disappearance

New Year's is symbolic, an arbitrary marker. No magic occurs when that big ball touches down. We are the same people we were at 11:59 p.m., time itself a human invention, and these celestial bodies we use to dictate a new day or new year don't give a damn about our perceptions of personal growth. Logically, intellectually, we understand this. Human nature, however, craves hope. When Dick Clark ends his countdown, we have to believe this year will be better than the last, that this year will yield something special. It's why you can't find parking at the gym those first two weeks of January. December thirty-one, you get as fucked up as possible and try to make bad decisions. January first is when you pledge to quit smoking, drinking, and sleeping around. All these big plans hinge on a resolve, willpower, and dedication that, so far, have been lacking if not downright absent. New Year's is nothing but the starting point of another promise you won't be able to keep.

New Year's had come and gone for Brooke, and she didn't feel any different. Since her run-in at Stimpy's, Brooke had been crashing at Torie's one-bedroom dump in South Town. Although hiding out is more like it. Since their arrest, neither girl had been working at

Roseville Rest Home, both suspended without pay pending investigation, of which there was little hope of exoneration. Both women would be fired. And that was the best-case scenario. From there Brooke's options only got worse. Prison time. A pissed-off dealer hunting her down. A psycho ex who would never stop. For the moment, Torie's apartment seemed the safest place to be. Brooke's father didn't know any of her friends. Not that he'd tell Mike if he did. Her dad probably hadn't even noticed she was gone. Brooke often stayed away from home.

For a week, Brooke had been sequestered, isolation fueling paranoia. Fidgeting in Torie's downtown apartment, Brooke reassured herself that a dealer like Stimpy wasn't directing all resources toward capturing her. What had she done, really? Kicked him in the balls. Humiliated him. The fat prick had it coming. He also had enough hoodrats to clock her, waiting to put on the hurt. And *that* she'd brought on herself. Before she made the dumb decision to confront him, Brooke existed as an abstract to Stimpy. By showing up, she had put a face with the name. Now Stimpy might be worried Brooke would rat him out. She wouldn't. First rule of this game: don't talk to the cops. When facing prison time, however, people sometimes forget that. Brooke didn't believe she was in imminent danger. She also couldn't relax.

Traffic outside wheezed, buses caught between gears, exhausted. The deranged homeless screeched, hollered, and wailed at vengeful deities and other imaginary enemies. Community outreach vans drove around in the frigid cold, trying to lure the mentally ill inside to avoid hypothermia and enjoy free a cup of hot cocoa and maybe a cookie. Few took them up on the offer, too suspicious to trust or too obliterated to care.

South Town was a hardscrabble, working-class section south of Boston. Brooke was a middle-class girl. The two did not mix. All those badass badges they ascribed her in the suburbs exposed her as a fraud in the big city, where real criminals prowled, cornered, and killed. The way she'd been pushed around at Stimpy's served as a stark reminder that Brooke didn't belong there. Brooke had been outed as a pretender. For that she was grateful. Brooke didn't want to feel at home in Crooked Row.

Torie hadn't been back to the apartment for days. While Brooke relished the privacy, the time alone at Torie's also served as a wake-up call. Brooke knew Torie partied. She was also learning just how addicted and dependent her former coworker was. What someone did with their own body in their own home was nobody's business. Still, the drug use was alarming. The frequency of it, the need, a shock. Brooke wasn't a prude. The other day, she'd found a syringe in the bathroom, behind the toilet. Snorting, smoking, shooting—what difference did it make how drugs enter the bloodstream? But, yeah, it was jarring, seeing that orange-capped needle, knowing Torie was injecting drugs directly into her veins. Took shit to a whole new level. What scared Brooke most was how easily it could happen to her too. It wouldn't take much. One day she'd be hanging out, and they'd be drinking, partying, and someone would have a needle and Brooke would say, "Fuck it, why not?" That is how she'd lived her whole life up until then. *Fuck it, why not?* When she asked herself that question, she couldn't come up with a sufficient answer. She could feel that internal shrug, that defeatist part of herself giving in. What else was she doing with her life? *Fuck it, why not?* That question presents a slippery slope that slides straight to the bottom.

It was a little after noon when Brooke bundled up, forcing herself outside for a cup of coffee, maybe a bite to eat. She had to leave the apartment and her self-imposed imprisonment, if only for a short while.

The day was cold, blustery, raw. Each time the wind blew, it felt like a slap. She hadn't planned on it, at least not consciously, but as long as she was out, Brooke decided to get her money. She wanted cash on hand. She didn't know why this was important, or why the need hit the way it had. In times of distress, Brooke followed her gut. Right now instincts said to be ready for anything. Her bank had a branch up the block. Brooke went inside and withdrew two thousand dollars, almost all her money, leaving three hundred bucks to keep the account open.

Afterwards she went to a café across the street from Torie's. Patting the money in her purse, already feeling safer, she ordered a carrot, leek, and ginger soup, which arrived with a dollop of sweet cream on top. She sat by the window, watching all the ordinary people with their ordinary concerns. They all seemed so confident, assured, which exposed Brooke's need for a plan. She could leave. Like that. Two thousand dollars wouldn't go far, but it was a start. It would get her out of town, and that alone fixed a lot of problems. Her first court appearance was in two weeks. Brooke didn't plan on living life as a fugitive. She was hopeful her lawyer could plead down. Of course, she hadn't spoken with her lawyer in days—there could've been a new development— how would anyone let her know?

From the café window, Brooke studied Torie's apartment. What a dump. Rundown brown brick, sneakers on telephone wires, fire escapes that stopped halfway to nowhere. It was four walls and a roof. Not much else. Watching the bundled-up parade pass, faces wrapped three times in wool scarves, Brooke was grateful to have shelter. But she couldn't stay there forever.

Brooke had finished her soup and was pulling out change to leave a tip when she saw the two skinny men. At first, she wasn't sure. A lot of people in the city wore black hoodies and baggy jeans. Something about them... The longer she watched, the more certain Brooke became these were the same men from Stimpy's. The pair slinked around the corner. Every few minutes, they'd poke their heads out, peeping, smoking, lurking, waiting. How had they found her? *You're being paranoid. You're not that important. No one is following you.*

Then she saw Mike come up behind them.

CHAPTER THIRTY

NOW

The drive to Worcester doesn't take long. Like a lot of towns in Southern Mass, Worcester isn't a place you want to end up, and where Torie Dent is living sinks below that.

I already know Torie Dent didn't rise above. I was hoping it wasn't this bad. As I tour the seediest sections of town, with their liquor stores and crazies jabbering to themselves in Duct-taped, padded layers, I try and picture Torie. I know the name but can't get a face. If she and Brooke were friends, she must've been around our house at some point. I don't remember *any* girls visiting Brooke. Plenty of guys. Never girls.

I'm deep in it now, the narrows, the skids, the ghetto, the projects, hell, whatever you want to call it. It's a wasteland. There's no kindness in understanding here. Empathy is a trait we ascribe ourselves to feel superior. What good does it do these bums caked in their own filth that I feel bad about their plight? Tragic, homeless, hungry. Honest and true, it breaks my goddamn heart. Does it affect me, though? No. My mother and I weren't far from here. But for the grace of God, that could be me sleeping on that park bench, living under that bridge, diving in that dumpster for food. Do I do anything about it? No, I do not. Pity won't fill a belly or put a roof over anyone's head. And now I'm thinking about those church-going days with Connie, the phrases that still shine. Words without deeds are meaningless.

All these squalid streets look the same. Rundown duplexes, scarred tenements, and single-family, tract housing. It was Christmas a few weeks ago. There is nothing celebratory about this neighborhood. What gifts did these children receive? Socks, a new tube of toothpaste, some book they've read six times but it was on sale and their family didn't know what else to buy them? Or am I projecting? Maybe the money doesn't matter. My mother and I were happier penniless and alone.

I find the Summit Motel, so named because it crowns a nubbed, dirty knob above an auto body shop and fried chicken convenience mart. Splintered pallets litter the frozen tundra. Browned snow clumps around discarded appliances and old tire scraps. A plastic bag snags on a rusty spike, waving an impoverished flag.

There's a check-in office, which I bypass, lights off, moving toward the center of the court, where a pair of teenagers deal drugs, right in the open. I see amber powders in plasticine packages exchanged for cash. These are not gangsters or tough guys. These are children. Sad, broken boys with nothing to lose, their lives over before they had a chance to begin. I stand tall, back erect, striding forward with the assured posture of someone who belongs. Most of the motel's residents are outside, despite chilly temperatures. Beats being trapped inside personal prison cells, I suppose. Then I realize they are waiting their turn. No one will meet my eyes, these timid mole people huddled inside extra-large sweatshirts. When the next checkout lane opens up, they scurry to cashiers, grab their fix, rodents flitting to snatch crumbs of hard cheese, before scuttling back underground.

"What you need, man?"

He's a kid, far younger than the students I teach. He puffs out his skinny chest. This is someone's younger brother, out here on the front lines, trying to prove his meddle.

"I'm looking for someone."

"Try the internet."

The kid can't be more than fourteen, and if any of that empathy I claim to feel were real maybe I take the time out, try and explain there's a better life. I don't care what happens to this boy. Why pretend?

"Torie Dent," I say. "She lives here. Do you know which room is hers?" I've already surveilled the mole people and come up empty.

The kid swats a hand like I'm a bug and starts to turn away. I grab him by the arm.

"Don't touch me, mutherfucker." He swings a fist, intentionally missing me by two feet.

"Torie Dent," I repeat. "Which room is hers?"

"I don't got to tell you nothin."

"Maybe I tell the cops what you're doing up here. How you like that?"

The kid laughs and points over my shoulder, where two squad cars sit parked at the gas station across the road. The cops glance over, see what's happening, before returning to their coffee and conversation. Drugs are being dealt in broad daylight, and they can't be bothered.

I'm turning to the dark lobby to try my luck there, when the kid slaps the back of my arm.

"She in room two," he says.

At the side of the building, he drops on his butt, sliding down a patch of icy dirt to the sidewalk. The cops aren't fifteen yards away. They don't look up. The kid struts past them, around the corner, and out of sight.

The door to room number two opens.

There she is.

CHAPTER THIRTY-ONE

January 7, 1998, 2:51 p.m.
One Day Before the Disappearance

Concern for her safety gave way to feelings of betrayal. It was bad enough Brooke had to watch out for retribution from Stimpy, but she really believed, when push came to shove, even after all their troubles and all the bullshit, Mike would protect her. He loved her, in his own twisted way; he'd never give her up. How stupid could she be? He'd led them right to her.

Brooke didn't have much back at the apartment. When she'd gone to Torie's after Stimpy's, her plan, fueled by those better instincts, had been to sleep it off, return home in the morning. That was last week. She'd felt dramatic, hiding out at this hole in the wall, ducking drug dealing thugs on the hunt. Until she remembered something she'd once read: just 'cause you're paranoid doesn't mean they ain't out to get you.

In the café doorway, Brooke poked out her head. Keeping eyes peeled across the street, she waited to make her move. Then she saw Torie. Her friend stood at the complex's entry, fumbling with her keys, struggling to open the gate.

Brooke watched helplessly as Mike and the other two blindsided her. One grabbed her arm, another yanking open the door. Mike turned his stare across the street. Brooke ducked inside the café. She counted to ten and stole a glance. No one stared back.

They wouldn't hurt Torie, would they? They'd want to know if Brooke was staying there. And when Torie broke—and she'd break—they'd hang around until Brooke returned. Brooke couldn't go back to Torie's.

Hands in pockets, head down, Brooke beat a path in the opposite direction. A couple blocks later, she passed an ATM. She withdrew the last three hundred dollars she had in the account.

She found the car she'd parked half a mile away. For the rest of the afternoon, Brooke drove aimless, meandering in the drizzling rain with nowhere to go. The streets grew desolate. The freezing rain fell harder, before sleet turned to snow.

Now it was dark. Brooke was sick of going in circles. Too tired to fight anymore, she headed home. By the time she got there, it was late. If those men had found her at Torie's, they could find her here too. No doubt they'd been by already. They'd be back again. Brooke didn't plan to stick around long. She needed a couple hours' rest. The stress and strain had her seeing double. She wanted to sleep in her own bed one last time.

Unlocking the door, she entered the cold, empty house. She called out. Paul didn't answer. Neither did Bobby.

Climbing the stairs, one creaky step at a time, Brooke felt her energy drain, the life force being sucked out of her like a leak in the power line. There was no way around it: she needed to recharge. Despite her exhaustion, Brooke was too amped. Sleep would not come easy. Brooke grabbed a handful of benzos, planning on only taking one. She ended up taking all four.

In her bedroom, Brooke peeled off her jeans and crawled under the covers. The warmth and security enveloped her. Aided by the diazepam, Brooke slipped into a fast, deep slumber.

Nightfall descended. Thick fog encroached. Snow fell heavier. Buried somewhere within her subconscious, Brooke incorporated these elements into the vague periphery of a dream. She might've heard the downstairs door open and close when Bobby came home. Maybe she was aware, on some level, she wasn't alone in the house as the boy plodded around the kitchen, banging breadboxes and cutting boards, jangling silverware and slathering caloric bombs. Either way, Brooke never woke.

She dreamt. Pleasant, happy dreams at first. The benzos had her relaxed, floating on pillows of wind. No harbinger loomed, no signifier of the dangers yet to come. Neither conscious nor cognizant, no higher internal thought processes involved. Then something changed. Gone were the soft pinks and peaches and nonthreatening pastel hues. In their place: black erosion and murderous reds. The goofy narrative playing in her head, childhood games of double Dutch and run and hide surrendered to the nightmare-scape of the fire raging down below. Rounded corners were replaced by jagged edges; lilting serenades morphed into heavy metal shrieks. The rough beast emerged from the blood-dimmed tide…

Downstairs, Mike Rakowski opened the front door and stepped inside.

CHAPTER THIRTY-TWO

Have I seen Torie Dent before? I must have. Because I recognize the woman standing in the doorway of room number two immediately. I'm unsure what gives her away; she holds no special place in my memory. This woman is old, used up, with rat's nest hair, weather-worn hoodie, and Adidas shorts that reflect a poor fashion choice given body type and temperature. When Torie contacted me five years ago with the then-bizarre claim of having been Brooke's roommate, I didn't speak to her at length. She was just another caller in a long line of loons. I tell myself any familiarity owes to the mind filling in gaps. A passing glance. An old photograph. Maybe I saw her in a car with Brooke once. That doesn't feel right either. During moments like this I can't ignore how time overlaps, like projector transparency sheets laid atop a copy of a facsimile. I've never been to this hotel, never had this conversation—it's not déjà vu—but I know how every second is going to play out.

She recognizes me too. At least that is how I interpret the smile. I soon realize Torie's reaction is visceral, photosynthesis, a house plant responding to sunshine. I am smiling and being kind to a woman who is not used to either. No higher critical thinking skills involved.

I introduce myself, mentioning Brooke and the phone call Torie made to me.

Her face never changes its expression, as she stares past my shoulder.

"Do you remember me?" I ask.

"Mmm umm."

Up close, I see the facial abrasions and small cuts, the infected skin eruptions capped with shiny, orange-yellow crust. This is what happens when fat liquids ooze and harden to replace the epidermis that has been gouged with dirty fingernails. Still life with miniature active volcano.

The sun is a distant white dot smothered by blankets of silver cloud. I wait for more, a human response upon hearing Brooke's name, nostalgic reflection or lamentation. They were friends, after all. Roommates, right? Torie Dent gives me nothing, which leaves me standing at her front door, awkward and self-conscious.

I feel stares from motel guests, as if I'm another john, here to barter sexual favors in exchange for forty ounces of cheap malt liquor or half a sandwich. Why do I care what these people think of me?

"Do you mind if we talk inside?" I ask.

Without responding, Torie retreats into her room. I follow and close the door. I don't know if we are better off alone. Will she be more forthright? I'm beginning to suspect there is nothing to reveal, that Torie Dent is but a cauterized wound; the parts that could feel have been burned dead long ago. The woman carries all the charisma of a stump.

The room chokes with the stale scent of unwashed sex, an assortment of bodily odors, fluids, and lubricants, all nauseating. A smoky char lingers, phantoms of foil set aflame and inhaled deep into lungs to take the edge off and grant the mind a temporary reprieve from this never-ending misery. Clothes pile in separate mounds. Not laundry. More like rags scrimped from the trash, dumpster dived and retrieved, sorted to be sold. Or perhaps Torie is building a Richard Dreyfuss mashed potato monument to the aliens rattling around her skull.

Torie tells me I can sit if I "want to." I don't want to. Any exposed fabric is soiled or damp. So we stand. I've had plenty of awkward interactions—academia is not known for its social graces—but this transcends normal discomfort, broaching agony.

"You called me?" I say, helping her out. "About five years ago? You said you were my—you said you were Brooke's roommate."

"You got a smoke?"

"No," I tell her. "I don't smoke."

I hate being judgmental, but the woman stinks. With every twitch, a nauseous wave of BO funk and sexual residue wafts over.

Torie Dent bites her lip, grinds her jaw, quivers. She needs something to calm down. I am about to ask if she'd like me to run to the gas station for cigarettes when she reaches into a dresser drawer, its top cluttered with aluminum cans sawed in half. She fishes around inside, sifting through vending machine and condom wrappers to retrieve an unopened pack of cigarettes, which makes me wonder why she was asking if I had any cigarettes less than a minute ago. I already know the answer. The woman is like a woodland creature hoarding ground nuts and grubs for the long winter. I am the felled tree. Who knows the next time Torie is going to have access to what lies beneath the mulch?

"Brooke and I worked together," she finally says.

"The nursing home," I respond, confirming what I already know. "Roseville."

"Do you remember the night Brooke left?" Hearing the words aloud I appreciate the futility. I doubt the woman could answer which planet she is on.

"Her boyfriend was going to kill her." The lucidity of the response surprises me.

"Mike," I say.

"Mmm hmm. Came to our apartment. Night she went missing. Couple other guys were with him."

"Mike Rakowski came to … your apartment … when?"

"I told you. Night she disappeared. They were looking for her."

"Who are 'they'?"

Torie shrugs, before taking greedy drags off the smoke. "We got in trouble for stealing pills from the hospital. One of the dealers. Court case. I tol' the cops all this already. That wasn't why I called you."

"So you *do* remember calling me?" Progress. "You said you had new information. The police told me you didn't offer anything new."

"I gave them plenty. They didn't listen. Like *you* aren't listening." Torie grinds her teeth, grits her jaw, mangles her mouth twelve different directions. "The vials we stole!"

"You're talking about the arrest?"

"The dealer guy, Stumpy whatever. He wanted to kill her."

This is the first I've heard about any dealer.

Pushing aside an empty pizza box and concave two-liter bottle of Pepsi, Torie plops on the unmade bed. She pulls her knees to her chest, tight shorts pinching apple thighs. It's not a flattering position for a woman her age. From these stilted, disjoined fragments she's told me, I try to piece together the truth, or a version of it. Assuming she isn't hallucinating or flat-out lying, I think it's safe to say she's trying to tell me *some*thing.

Her eyes develop a sharpness to them—a sharpness that, to this point, has been lacking. "It all turned out fine for Mike though, didn't it?"

"Mike Rakowski?"

"Are you special or somethin'? Yeah. What other 'Mike' is there?"

"I'm sure he's in prison by now." The charges against Brooke may've been dismissed, but one way or another, Mike Rakowski is behind bars. If not six feet underground.

"Your sister was boy crazy." Torie giggles, the fond recollection of a joke I am not getting. The quick vacillation unsettles. I am happy to follow Torie's train of thought if it delivers us closer to a useful destination. I'm growing dizzy from the sudden stops and quick, jarring turns. Every second in her company is another chance to go off the rails.

"Yes," I say. "Brooke was popular with the opposite sex."

"He was needy, suffocating."

"Yes, I know. Mike Rakowski's always been an asshole."

"I mean the other one."

"Which other one?"

Torie points a plump finger at my face. "Yeah, right." She laughs again, this time less a chuckle and more a cackle. Torie Dent can't be *that* much older than Brooke would've been. The woman has skin like cracked leather, the distressed exterior of an old couch hauled to the curb and abandoned too long in the sun. "You funny, Bobby."

I don't correct her. I pity this large, misshapen woman with her bad skin, mossy teeth, and frizzy, split-ended hair. I will walk out of here in a few minutes, get in a nice car, and drive off knowing I will never go hungry, never have to compromise ethics or integrity for basic human needs. I don't know what Torie Dent's private life is like. Maybe I've seen too many movies about drug addicts, watched too many episodes of *Law & Order*, so I'm left to assume in half an hour she'll be on her knees sucking dick for three-fourths of a Kit-Kat bar.

Outside, trucks and buses deliver their goods. Ambulances and EMTs pick up the wounded. Factory workers and deadbeats scrounge their pay, securing whatever medications they'll need to survive the night. Police corral the guilty; the coroner collects the dead. And in between, you have Torie Dent, a barely breathing casualty who's slipped so far through the cracks, she might as well be invisible.

"Landscaping," Torie says, picking up a conversation we haven't been having.

"Landscaping?" *What the hell is she talking about?*

"All that money. Good company. Hot shit." She catches my eye. "I don't forget what he did to her."

"Who are you talking about?"

"Mike!"

"I don't un—"

"Rack."

"Rick?"

"Rack."

"Rock?"

"Huh?"

"What are you trying to say?"

She swipes a pudgy paw through the air, spitting a raspberry.

I want to understand—it is clearly important to her that I do. When she phoned five years ago, the woman sounded unhinged. Compared to this version, that one was downright lucid.

I give up. Talking to Torie Dent is tantamount to trying to discuss higher mathematics with a tuber.

As I'm turning to leave, I see her stick her little finger into a beer bottle and sift through the sludge for a waterlogged butt. There's a full pack of cigarettes on her dresser. The action makes as much sense to me as the conversation we just had.

Sitting in my car, I watch giant snow flurries tumble through slate-gray skies. I attempt to gather crumbs of reason and scraps of logic. I will rearrange them on my dashboard, chart a new path to the stars. This is how desperate I've become to erase the past.

My visit to Torie Dent yielded nothing but a colossal waste of time. And yet I can't move, stuck in this barren, inner-city wasteland. Surrounded by brown brick and drab concrete, I glance up and see a small, dead tree. They can't even be bothered to spruce up the place with a few shrubs, a bush or two, something living? Nope. Just a small, dead tree in a bed of empty beer cans and individual hard liquor shots.

The part I liked so much about my NEH proposal was the writing. Having spent my academic career penning dull scholastic reports, I was enticed by the opportunity to be creative for a change. I've found, much to my amazement, that when it comes to the creative process, most of the heavy lifting is done by our subconscious. My entire premise, that a city's vital, functioning components—from electrical to wastewater— mirror the human body, was the result of a dream. Or rather chewing on a concept as I was falling asleep, night after night, week after month, brain stirring the stew. My unconscious brewed the concoction. If the city is a living, breathing entity, the stark symbolism of this small, dead tree screams volumes. And I'd take the conceit further if another area of the circuit board wasn't lighting up, connections ablaze, demanding I redirect my full attention elsewhere, because as I stare at that small, dead tree there is no conscious effort on my part to tie anything Torie Dent said to me with what I already know. But now new words pop out: "landscaping," "good company," and "Rack."

I pull up my phone's internet and start typing. Sucked in like click bait, I am shocked by what I find.

CHAPTER THIRTY-THREE

January 7, 1998, 10:01 p.m.
The Night Before the Disappearance

The brain never sleeps, the subconscious always at work, always present, forever making connections. Brooke knew this because of her time at Midfield State. Her professor explained a study called "The Cocktail Party Problem." Basically, some scientist proved how we can focus on one conversation in a crowded venue, such as a noisy bar or busy store. To prove their theory, researchers recorded electrical brain activity with an EEG, which showed that even while sleeping, our minds can differentiate between imperative information and nonessential gibberish. Her favorite detail she learned that semester: when we die, our sense of hearing is the last to go, meaning when our loved ones are leaving this mortal plane—or even if they are just trapped in a coma or something—they can hear us. Brooke was thinking about this before the benzos took hold and pulled her under. Not "thinking" so much as a neuron flashing, a lightning bolt sparking. Zeroing in on this split-second of an infinitesimal blip, she lay upstairs in her room, transported back to Connie's hospital room, after they'd unplugged her life support system. It had been she—not Bobby—who was in the room when their mother passed. Brooke needed Connie to know she forgave her and, moreover, that she would not make the same mistakes.

Her mom had heard her.

When Bobby emerged from his bedroom, the house exhaled, as if it were alive. The pipes, the heater, the mechanisms that keep a home powered and functioning hummed with white noise. The incessant murmur was more comfortable than total silence. That's when Bobby's own thoughts could assault him, antagonize him, make him think things he didn't want to think.

Bobby went into the kitchen for a peanut butter sandwich. He didn't wonder where Paul was. His stepfather came and went, from work to the bar and back again, without a reliable schedule. It had been several days since Brooke had been home.

When the front door burst open, Bobby expected to turn around and see Paul. Or maybe Brooke. He didn't anticipate Mike Rakowski.

"Where's your fucking sister?" Mike said, drawing on a cigarette even though he knew you were not allowed to smoke in the house.

"She's not here."

"Fuck she's not." Mike pointed out the window. "That's her car, ain't it, numbnuts? She got home an hour ago. I got lookouts."

Bobby pushed the glasses up his nose.

"Fucking spaz." Mike climbed the stairs. Bobby returned to his peanut butter sandwich, spreading Skippy on white bread, cutting off the crust like his mom used to do.

A few minutes later, Mike came back down, smirking and pointing at the ceiling. "Yup. Told you. She's up there."

Bobby squinted.

Mike headed outside, letting the screen door slam. Bobby could hear him baying like a wolf in the night. When he returned, he carried a big brown paper sack, which he dropped beside him on the couch. Mike reached in, snapping a can free from plastic rings.

"Your sister is *out*." Mike shook his head. "Must've popped a couple Valium." He cracked a tab. "Some people want to talk to her. Won't be long now. And when they get here, she is *fucked*." Mike smirked as he draped his arm over the back of the couch, smoke rising in thin ribbons. "Have a seat, Bobby."

"I made a sandwich."

"You can bring your sandwich."

Mike never wanted Bobby around, never invited him to sit down or hang out. Bobby didn't feel comfortable saying no to Mike, who was older, tougher, cooler. Guys like Mike could make boys like Bobby do whatever they wanted.

When Bobby sat down, Mike reached in the paper bag and brought out another beer. Bobby stared at the red and white can dripping dew.

"Go on," Mike said. "Take it. You're a big boy."

Bobby remained rooted.

"Don't worry," Mike said. "I won't tell anyone. Jesus. It's just a beer. Don't be such a pussy."

Bobby didn't have many friends—Bobby didn't have *any* friends. He had bounced around with his mom for so long. Different towns. Just the two of them. They never stayed long in any one place. It was hard to get close to people.

Mike reached toward him. Bobby flinched. Mike mocked surprise, before clasping his shoulder. "You, my friend, need to relax." Mike pulled another bottle from the bag, this one bigger. It was black and white and filled with a burnt, golden liquid. Mike broke the seal, took a swig, and passed it along. "Go ahead, Bobby." He pointed at the big bottle with the black label. "Take a shot of that." Then at the beer: "Follow it with that."

Bobby didn't move.

"A shot with a chaser," Mike said. "Put some hair on your chest."

Bobby brought the bottle slowly to his lips, poised to take an apprehensive sip. Before Bobby could register how bad it smelled or tasted, Mike leaned over, grasped the bottom, and tilted it back. The alcohol flowed too fast into Bobby's throat for him not to swallow. He had to chug in order to breathe. His throat burned, like he'd drunk hot pepper sauce, and then he started coughing.

"Here." Mike thrust the beer in Bobby's hands. "Drink this. It'll help."

Bobby gulped the beer. Cool and refreshing, it tasted like soda at first. He liked the bubbles on his tongue. So he drank more, faster, trying to douse the heat. Then its bitter aftertaste caught up with him. Mixed with the gasoline he'd guzzled, it was all he could do not to throw up.

Mike bent over laughing, slapping his knee, like this was the funniest joke in the world. Bobby struggled to stop coughing and regain normal breathing, eyes burning, watering. The room felt like it was spinning.

"That's the first time you tasted booze, ain't it?" Mike leaned back. "Shit, my old man gave me my first beer when I was seven!" Mike scootched closer to Bobby, swinging an arm around his shoulder with newfound affection.

Bobby's face flooded with blood, heart thumping as his stomach churned. Then his pulse slowed, nausea subsided, as a warm, fuzzy glow took their place.

"It's all right, man," Mike said, passing back the bottle. "Try again. It gets easier. Promise." He winked. "Trick is to not give up, power through."

Bobby's eyes watered, but he did as Mike commanded, tipping back the bottle, and felt another pleasant wave douse the queasiness. For the first time since forever, his brain stopped talking to him and telling him how awful he was. Bobby wondered if this was how other, normal people felt.

"Take it easy, man," Mike said, snatching back the bottle. "You're pounding that whiskey like a wino!"

Bobby hadn't experienced many occasions when he felt cool. Sitting there with Mike, in the downstairs living room, drinking whiskey and beer, Bobby felt cool.

Mike's full attention was elsewhere. He kept checking out the window, glancing at the ceiling. Maybe this was why Mike wasn't being as nasty as usual. He was distracted and had forgotten how much he hated Bobby. Whatever the reason, Bobby liked this way better. He liked the crisp taste of the beer tingling on his tongue, how each swallow made him feel as if he were floating higher in the clouds, weightless. The beer didn't taste bitter anymore.

Kicking out a foot, Mike leaned back and cracked open another beer. Smoking a cigarette, he looked bad ass, like he couldn't care less if Paul came home, which might be any minute. Then again, Paul seldom came home after his shift ended. Closing time at the bar was later. Mike wasn't scared of anyone. Bobby was scared of everybody. When would the day come for Bobby to be more like Mike? A regular guy. A *tough* guy. A guy that girls couldn't say no to. Brooke claimed she didn't want to date Mike. She didn't say no or turn him away, though. When Mike came around, Brooke opened the door and let him in. She let him do whatever he wanted.

"As long as we're making a man of you..." Mike passed along his cigarettes, sliding one up. "Might as well go all the way."

Bobby didn't want to smoke a cigarette. His mom smoked cigarettes and she died of cancer.

"Bobby," Mike said, dipping his head until their foreheads butted.
"One cigarette won't kill you."

Bobby pinched the cigarette, Mike lit it for him, and Bobby
inhaled. Then he coughed a fit, prompting Mike to howl. He wasn't
mean about it or making fun of him. More like they were two pals,
goofing around, so Bobby didn't feel as self-conscious.

"You're all right, Bobby!" Mike slapped his shoulder and plucked
the lit cigarette. "Same thing happened to me my first time." He stubbed
out the extra smoke. "One vice at a time, eh?"

Bobby's throat felt like it was burning again. Mike passed him
the bottle. Bobby took a long swig. He wasn't worried about anything anymore.

"Y'know," Mike said. "Brooke likes you."

"No, she doesn't," Bobby said, before draining a healthy swallow.
Brooke hated him. Bobby knew why. Because their mom chose him.
He'd overheard her on the phone, talking to her friend Aaron how it
wasn't fair Bobby got to have a mother for ten years and she didn't.
Bobby felt bad about that. Bobby wanted to tell her what their life on
the road was really like, having nowhere to call home, never knowing if
they'd be sleeping in a car or anywhere indoors—wondering how they'd
eat, worried how they'd stay warm, if they'd survive the night. Bobby
couldn't tell Brooke any of this. She was a stranger.

Mike's face turned serious. He pointed his burning cigarette,
eyes flickering red. "She told me you like to watch her showering."
Mike smiled and passed the bottle. "Drink up. Tonight, we're partying, big man!"

Bobby was feeling fizzier, lighter, cozy like he was wrapped in a
toasty blanket. The alcohol didn't taste like anything anymore. No

burn. No stomachache. The beer he washed it down with was smooth and effervescent. He chugged extra hard this time.

"Whoa! Slow down, tiger!"

"Sorry, I didn't mean to—"

Mike jabbed his arm. "Naw, man, drink up. You're a bad mutherfucker, Bobby."

"No, I mean, watching—I had to ... use the bathroom."

"You talking about watching Brooke shower? Why wouldn't you? Man, Brooke is *hot*. And can I tell you a secret?" Mike leaned in, whispering. "She liked it." He pulled back, wriggling eyebrows.

Bobby didn't know if Mike was teasing him. He had to be. Bobby knew watching Brooke was wrong.

Mike sensed the guilt. "You feel bad because you think she's your sister? Man, she ain't your sister. You guys don't even know each other." Mike bent forward, clasping Bobby's shoulder, looking him in the eye, man to man, sincere expression softening his hard face. "You don't have anyone to talk to you about this stuff, do you? Not like Paul gives a shit."

Bobby pushed the glasses up his nose, blinking away the confusion. The whiskey and beer assaulted him in cascading swells, eyes growing blurry, sounds warbling.

"Man, there is nothing wrong with what you're feeling." Mike extinguished his cigarette in the empty beer can. "In fact, it's the most normal thing in the world."

"It is?"

"Of course! Brooke is a pretty girl. And boys are *supposed* to like pretty girls. How you think the human race got started?" Mike shook his head, sad and slow. "Brooke says your mom was religious? Then you know about the Garden of Eden." He spread his arms. "God made Adam and Eve. You read that in church, right?"

Bobby nodded. Everyone knew the story of Adam and Eve.

"Think about it. Adam and Eve had kids. And then *those* kids had kids. Who do you think they had kids with? Sisters, brothers—those are just words, man. We're *all* related."

Bobby's head flooded with conflicting thoughts; some of them didn't feel right, like how excited he'd get when he'd spy on Brooke without her clothes on. Sometimes he'd run away to his room, lock the door. Sometimes he'd rub between his legs. It felt wrong. But it also felt good. He didn't know why he was feeling hot, flush, why body parts responded the way they did. He'd see magazines with naked women and experience a rush. Boys at school talked about it all the time. He knew *that* part was natural, normal. But … what if it wasn't? What if his mom was right and even thinking this stuff was wicked? He remembered how many times Connie said God saw *everything*, and He didn't approve of earthly pleasures like lust and sex. She'd say, "Be *in* the world, Bobby. Not *of* this world." Bobby was never sure what she meant by that. He had to be part of this world. Didn't everyone? No one talked to him like Mike was now. The way he explained it, Bobby wasn't a bad kid. He was a regular kid, a normal teenager experiencing basic human biology. They taught that part in school. Yet when he was done, he always felt guilty and sad. Sometimes he'd cry. Bobby was always crying. He was glad no one saw how many times he cried.

"Want me to tell you another secret." Mike leaned in, nudging the bottle along. "Brooke? She wants it *all the time*. Gets her hot. I can't keep up, she wants it so much."

Bobby swallowed more whiskey, and that sexy feeling came back, which brought the same tinge of remorse, but it also felt exciting, dangerous in the best possible way. Bobby was hoping Mike would say what he said next, while at the same time wishing he wouldn't, and already feeling disappointed if he didn't.

"And Brooke *likes* likes you."

Bobby squinted up through his glasses.

"You worried because she's my girlfriend?" Mike laughed. "Man, it ain't like that. I think you're all right, Bobby. And Brooke..." Mike checked left, right, leaning in to whisper. "When I went upstairs before?" Mike inched closer, breath hot on Bobby's ear. "She wasn't wearing any clothes."

Bobby felt the blood rush.

"And she was telling me how much she wanted it. You know what I mean, Bobby?"

Bobby felt himself getting an erection. He didn't want to. Except he did.

"So, I fucked her, Bobby. Real hard and fast. And Brooke liked it. She liked it a lot. She was naked and moaning and fucking me right back. When we were done, she pouted, whimpering how she wanted more."

Bobby shifted in his jeans, averting his eyes.

Mike stared down at Bobby's crotch. "Don't, man. Sex is the most natural thing in the world. Your—Brooke loves to fuck. She fucks all the time. She can't get enough. And that's the thing, Bobby. Even after we were done, she wanted more. I'm all out, man. But you know what she told me?"

"What?"

"Send up Bobby." Mike fell back, pointing at the ceiling. "I'm not even kidding. Brooke is always horny. Total nympho. She knows you like looking at her. It gets her off. So guess what, man? Tonight is your lucky night." Mike pointed at Bobby's tightening pants. No matter how much Bobby tried to rearrange things, he couldn't hide what he was feeling. "Looks like you're ready, big boy. Brooke wants to show you how to do it. She's so horny, bro. You *have* to give it to her. She's like a bitch in heat."

The alcohol sloshed in Bobby's belly, his thoughts delivering him to alluring, forbidden places. He was overwhelmed, conflicted, drunk but aroused, every nerve ending tingling in anticipation.

Mike fed him another shot and a chaser, then helped him up, guiding an unsteady Bobby to the stairs, making sure he had both hands on the rails.

"Give it to her, stud." Mike sneered a laugh.

Bobby clutched the railing, focusing on each step, climbing steady. His heart pounded, blood gushing and ringing in his ears, Mike's words echoing…

She wants it.

CHAPTER THIRTY-FOUR

Vivi picks a Mexican restaurant in Back Bay called Lolita's. I am skeptical, the Northeast not known for its Mexican cuisine, but I agree because I need to talk to her. And if I'm being honest, I want to see her again, to be around her, which isn't the greatest feeling to come to terms with, my still being married, but it's important to be truthful with one's self. Stephanie hasn't returned a call in days.

I enter the cool, dark, underground eatery, which is slick and stylish, upscale like you'd expect to find in Back Bay, with an understated demonic theme. Not like devils or demons adorn every wall. This impression is left over from early religious years with Connie. The motif features bloody reds and nightmare colors. Plus, Mexican culture is more comfortable with the afterlife. For Americans, especially in the Northeast, death itself is taboo.

The maître d' delivers me to Vivi, who is already seated, enjoying what looks like a spicy margarita. An overhead spotlight shines on her. Hot jalapeños bob in a bright sunrise pool. She looks ravishing. This meeting feels more like a date than it does a desperate man seeking full disclosure from a federal agent. She smiles, twirls a finger through her hair, and I think I catch her blush. I tell myself I am imagining things. It wouldn't be the first time.

After perfunctory small talk about the weather and other inane topics I have no interest in discussing, I get to the reason for our visit. I was willing to have this conversation on the phone. When I mentioned the name "MK Rack," Vivi was the one who insisted on meeting over dinner and drinks.

I bring her up to speed, telling her about my drive to Worcester to see Torie Dent.

"So," I continue, "after Torie said that, I Googled that name—Rack—and that's when I found the landscaping chain. MK Rack. From there I was able to connect the company to Mike Rakowski." I fall back, proud of my discovery. I'm not expecting a standing ovation but, sure, acknowledgment for investigative prowess would be nice.

None of this information fazes Vivi.

"Yes, I know." Vivi dips a chip into the salsa sampler that has arrived, four tiny ceramic cups ranging from hot and tangy to chocolate and smoky. The subterranean candlelight flickers off her face, carving exotic features sharp, angular, and seductive.

"I had assumed Mike Rakowski would be in prison," I say.

"No, that's him," she replies, nonplussed. "I thought we talked about this over coffee?"

"About Mike?" I pull back. "We certainly did not. I *hate* that guy."

"Which you made perfectly clear. I believe you said something, to the effect, if you never saw him again it would be too soon."

"I may have. But I would like to know if he was involved in Brooke's disappearance."

"And," Vivi says, dragging out the word to respectfully disagree, "I recall telling you that he wasn't involved in your sister's disappearance."

"Stepsister. And maybe you did. But no one told me the guy was running a successful landscaping chain."

"Why would we?"

I throw up my hands. *Why would we?* I don't know, I want to say, because the man was a lunatic? Possessive and abusive? He'd been at the house the night Brooke vanished? He is the reason she left! Of course, I say none of these things. I mean, if Vivi can't see what's right in front of her face… Then again, how can anyone see anything in this place? It's black as hell down here.

"Are you okay, Robert?"

"It's … the dark. I don't like so much darkness."

Vivi glances toward the door. "We can go somewhere else?"

"No, no, it's fine."

A waitress delivers my drink just in time.

I smile. At least I think it's a smile. Earlier, my contacts were irritating me, so I took them out in the car. My eyes aren't *that* bad. If the lighting was halfway decent, I could make out borders better. But trying to focus is causing too much strain, instigating a headache. Pictures blur, nothing defined.

"I wouldn't worry about Mike Rakowski," she says. "He was investigated thoroughly. I promise, he was not involved. This was all Samuel Erskine. As you researched yourself, whatever Rakowski used to be, he turned it around. He's an upstanding member of the community these days."

Vivi then tries to change the subject, and it's not even about Brooke. She's talking about life and asking me questions about my work. I can't fathom how she'd think I'd want to discuss topics like my recent NEH grant or book proposal or anything other than Brooke's disappearance and Mike Rakowski, who has pulled the greatest trick since the devil if he has people believing he's a changed, decent man. Landscaping company? It has to be a front for the mob or something. I interrupt Vivi to voice this. And she laughs at me.

"No one calls it 'the mob,' Robert—"

"Call it whatever the fuck you want."

Now she sees how serious I am. I don't like cursing at a woman. I am flustered and irate. My eyes refuse to adjust, temples throbbing.

"I'm sorry," she says without knowing what she's sorry for.

"Mike Rakowski is a bad man. He did bad things. To Brooke." I wait. "To me."

"I know. Everything I've read about him was not flattering. He also did not have it easy growing up."

"I give a shit."

"I'm not trying to elicit sympathy."

"Good. Because I have none."

"His father was violent. The things he did to Mike—"

"I told you. I don't care. Some behaviors can *never* be forgiven."

"Forgiveness is up to you. But you should understand it's not uncommon for a boy with a tumultuous upbringing to have difficulty fitting into society. Sometimes, for someone like that, it takes longer to learn what is and is not appropriate behavior. That's the hallmark of trauma."

I don't know if Vivi is talking about Mike or me. I don't ask her to clarify. Instead, I pry into this landscaping business, hoping to poke holes in a ridiculous cover story.

Vivi doesn't add anything I couldn't find on the internet. A dozen or so years ago, Mike opened a landscaping store. MK Rack. It did well, blew up. One business morphed into a chain with hundreds of employees. With over a dozen outlets throughout Southern New

England, MK Rack is one-stop shopping for all your landscaping needs or some such horseshit. The truth is, I'm not listening to Vivi. I'm stewing in silence, recalling a bully who tormented the shit out of me. How was he able to escape paying back the hurt he owes? I've pounded my cocktail. *He is a bad person. He does not deserve forgiveness.* I hear this voice, clear as me to you. Again, I am left wondering who we are talking about.

A new server arrives with our food. In his tight black vest and crisp white collar, he deals our meals on oversized plates, arranging them in appetizing fashion. Exquisite fare consisting of Americanized versions of Mexican staples, enchiladas smothered in rich, claret sauces, topped with avocado, sour cream, and bubbling, melty cheeses. Fried duck and potato tacos. Roasted Brussels sprouts fragrant with sautéed chilis and garlic. I am in such a foul mood, I want to hate the offering. The presentation is splendid, however, and after the first bite I must admit the cuisine quite delicious. Eating affords a respite, a chance to calm down, and I'm grateful. I was getting too worked up. I could feel the old me teetering to the tipping point, fearful I'd lash out at Vivi, who has done nothing wrong.

The rest of the meal steers clear of Mike Rakowski. We don't discuss Brooke much, either. We talk about Vivi and what made her decide to get into law enforcement. It's a sad story that involves her parents being murdered. Her father, a justice crusader, made enemies with organized crime types. She's dedicated herself to continuing his work. Honorable. And a reminder that things are tough all over. I don't catch too many specifics because my mind, despite best efforts, insists on pulling me in myriad different directions. I'm listening enough to show compassion at the parts I'm supposed to, smile when levity is attempted, frown at the tragic. I try to bury my ire over Mike

Rakowski, stuffing it away with all the other monsters I don't let into the light.

When dinner is over, we climb the stairs into the cold Boston night. This section of the city teems cosmopolitan. We start walking together, no destination in mind. A spattering of holiday decorations remain, downtown twinkling merry. Bums camp outside the shops on Commonwealth Avenue. The light shines on them too.

"Would you like to grab a coffee?" Vivi asks.

I tell myself this beautiful woman is not hitting on me, that she has no interest in me. I also can't figure out why she wants to have coffee at this hour. We don't have more to talk about regarding the case. Moody and surly, I haven't been charismatic or remotely pleasant this evening. I decide to cut my losses, sensing the impending anger and depression.

"I think I'll call it a night," I say. "I can't keep living in a Holiday Inn." I feign a chuckle. "It's time I get back to my house and life in Diemen. To my son and family."

Vivi glances around. People stroll up and down Commonwealth. She doesn't say anything for a long time. I inhale that crisp, clean bite. The air tastes disinfected, like it is about to snow.

"I know how hard this has been on you," Vivi says. "I want to help."

"Why?" I ask. "You don't know me." It's an honest if unplanned response. I didn't mean to say it, but I meant what I said.

Her answer catches me off guard.

"You were a fourteen-year-old boy. That age is hard enough *with* parents. That's about the age I lost mine. And your start was far more traumatic. I went to live with my aunt and uncle, who were already active in my life. I wasn't coming from a nomadic existence of roadside motels, homelessness, and instability. We don't always make the best decisions when we're dealing with trauma."

I try to laugh, objecting to the term "trauma." Yes, my start was less than ideal. So were a lot of other's. I hate people who cling to hardship and use to it justify horrible behaviors. I don't want to be like that. I don't get the chance to raise an objection, Vivi inside my head.

"Yes," she says, taking my hand. "It *was* trauma. This is what I do, this work. It's more than investigating. I deal with people every day, people who never got a fair shake. Sometimes they make decisions so awful they have to pay a debt to society. Others deserve mercy and forgiveness." She squeezes my hand in a tender display that leaves me on the verge of tears. "You've turned your life around. I'm sorry you lost your sister, especially so soon after your mom. I am confident in what I told you over coffee. You saw the photographs. Brooke was in the wrong place at the wrong time. She's gone. Erskine is dead. But you, Robert, you are here. And you need to learn to live with the past and what was, and not dwell on all those things you wish could've been different." She lets go of me. "Otherwise, you'll miss out on what *is*."

With that Agent Vivi Pallotta smiles and turns up Commonwealth. I watch her walk away, wishing I could do what she said. Some sins cannot be forgiven.

A bum tugs on my sleeve, a gross invasion of personal space. I tear away my arm, continuing down the busy thoroughfare, in search of my car.

I've almost reached it when Aaron Reardon rings.

"Hey," he says, so chipper and enthused, I immediately slip into a miserable mood. "Great news!"

I have no interest in talking to Aaron right now. I'm still replaying what happened between Vivi and me. There was a definite connection…

"I found Lily," he says.

"Wh—where?"

"Amherst."

"The police said she wasn't enrolled."

"Not under 'Stillwater.' She's going by Brooke's real last name, 'Mulcahy.'"

How could the police miss that? How lazy and incompetent can you be? Did they even take my claims seriously? This is why I hated dealing with police in the first place.

"I thought you'd be more excited," Aaron says.

"I am." I can't explain what has me so distracted. "Did you get a working number?"

"Better," Aaron says. "I told you I work for a rehabilitation facility, right? I can get a blood test!"

"What?"

"Lily has agreed to come in for a blood test! This way we can prove whether she's Brooke's daughter."

"I'm not sure that's—I mean—Brooke's not here." No sample to compare it to. End of discussion.

"Right. And Paul's in the nursing home. We *could* get a sample from him but that would take longer. Then I was thinking—you're Brooke's *brother*! You pop by my hospital, give us a sample too."

I have no interest in getting poked, prodded, or participating in this production. I can't find an adequate excuse to recuse myself, so I agree, say sure, whatever. Aaron says terrific, he'll text the hospital address.

I can't get off the phone fast enough.

CHAPTER THIRTY-FIVE

January 7, 1998, 11:12 p.m.
The Night Before the Disappearance

Bobby's head was swimming. Emotions and urges flooded. Each step delivered him further into darker, muddier waters. On one level he knew what he was doing was wrong. The temptation too powerful, the desire to dive headfirst overwhelming, and the alcohol diluted any resolve to fight it off. He felt the black tide rising, certain he would drown unless he kept moving.

The stairs creaked.

Down below, music played and footsteps sounded. Or maybe it was the other way around, a separate order. Did a door open? Close? Whose breath did he hear? Where was he now? Not at home. This wasn't right. It was too cold. They were at another rest stop as he peered up from a backseat, choking on stale cigarette smoke. Faces appeared and receded. Bobby clutched the railing, trying to hold steady, keep his balance, climb. The stairwell wobbled, ground shaking beneath unsteady feet. His mom walked into another man's room...

The mixture of beer and whiskey was making him feel sedated and woozy. Every few seconds, his stomach would flipflop, and the walls would quake. Balance waning, Bobby dropped to his knees. The dehydration sapped moisture, his mouth cotton dry. He pushed himself up, extracting himself from the muck, motivated to continue his quest, this noble journey to return the ring, burn it forever in the lake of fire...

With each step, Bobby felt the flares blast, burn, smolder, his skin flush with a sick, perverted desire, but he couldn't snuff it out. Images kept popping in his head. Vile, disgusting, shameful images he vowed he would never share with anyone because if people ever knew the horrible things Bobby thought, they'd lock him away forever.

He had to push away the darkness, get back to his mission, the adventure, the fellowship he'd joined, the honorable quest that gave him purpose. Moving toward the watchful fiery eye was better than the other option, succumbing to the rising black tide that aimed to swell, cascade, and flush him out to sea.

In his mind, he saw her getting undressed, legs so long, so smooth. The thin silky fabric that covered her breasts and...

He recalled the shower splashing on her skin as he spied through the crack in the door, hands running over her body. He was hard. He began thinking about her mouth on his, how good it would feel with her hands on his hips as she guided him in.

In the dark room, Bobby listened to her sleep. Smelling warm vanilla sugar, he caressed soft skin, repeating the mantra over and over in his head.

She wants it. She wants it. She wants it.

He climbed on top of her.

CHAPTER THIRTY-SIX

Back home, I do not sleep well and find myself up before dawn.

I call my wife, who again does not answer. It infuriates me, how much power she holds over this situation, how inept I am. Emasculated. I have no say in what happens next in my own life. Like being whisked from one faceless town to another nameless city, jettisoned, a voiceless passenger strapped in the backseat of a car, a prisoner shackled, trapped, helpless. Held hostage.

This house is not a home. It's one, big cage.

I drink espresso, staring into the fields of dreary gray that span to the edges of a lightless horizon. There is no beginning, no end, no contrast to offer comparison. No resolution. It's just infinite, nondescript, colorless seas rolling over one another.

The Nest kicks on the heat, which has dipped as low as allowed before technology triggers, because I couldn't be bothered to get up and adjust the thermostat on the wall. The smart features override my poor decision-making because they know more than I do. A slow heat rises from the vents in the floor, descends from the ceiling, thawing me out before I can die.

I wait till nine a.m. and call the main office of MK Rack. I am not surprised that reaching Mike Rakowski proves difficult. There are several regional offices, Mike an important person, the big cheese. I try not to laugh, thinking of all the hoops one must jump though just to speak with the great Mike Rakowski. After the fifth or sixth transfer, I leave a message with a secretary.

I have no choice but to wait.

Unable to work or do research, I sit in my cold kitchen surrounded by all these elegant designs that don't mean a damn thing. Regency tables, Zline stove. The scene changes but the story remains the same. No different than driving around the Northeast with Connie, fishing cold, hard French fries from between the seat cushions, not knowing when my next meal would be. I am still that fat clueless boy being taken for a ride.

A little while later, my cell rings.

"Robert?" my wife says when I pick up.

I do not answer.

"Are you there?"

No, we're not. We are back in the car with Connie, listening to the ghosts of AM radio. The wind in the wires makes a tattle-tale sound...

"Robert?"

"Yes," I say. "I'm here."

"You called?"

No shit, I want to tell her. You're my fucking wife, of course I called. Is it so fucking crazy for a fucking husband to call his goddamn wife? Don't I have a say in this marriage too? When you cut me, do I not bleed? Feel pain? But I don't. I don't have a say. My opinion does not matter. So I say nothing.

We remain on the line, silent.

How could someone I've been married to for this long be rendered a stranger?

"Did you want to talk to Peter?" she asks.

"I have his cell." Then: "Are you having an affair?" The question just comes out. It hadn't been formulated or dwelled upon. I know it's been on my mind by the way I blurt it. Just as I know what her answer will be.

The confirmation doesn't come via words. It carries across the line without response, evidenced by the lack of denial. It's in the winds that beat against the exterior, in the cold gray that colors my world these days. It's in the anchor that slams against my hollow gut.

"Who is it?" I ask.

"Robert—"

"Who is it?!"

"It's not important."

"Oh, I'd say it's pretty fucking important."

My wife exhales, a burdensome reply, as if my line of questioning is an inconvenience. So sorry, darling, for putting you out.

"Do I know him?"

"This isn't the time," she says.

"When will it be the time?"

"I'm at my sister's. There's no ... privacy—"

"Then fucking walk outside."

"Do *not* speak to me that way. I need space. Time." She grows flustered. "We'll talk about it later—"

"Space? Where's that? Fucking Mars? Time? When's that? When you get back from fucking Pittsburgh? Are you coming back from Pittsburgh?"

"Don't be ridiculous."

"Ridiculous? *I'm* being … ridiculous? That's great, Steph. Fucking gaslighting bit—"

"I have to go."

"Yeah, you do that." I end the call before she can, exercising what little power I still hold.

Almost immediately my cell buzzes back. I want to ignore it. Let her know how it feels to be the one left wanting.

I'm not that strong.

I take the call without checking the ID.

"Bobby?" a man asks. "It's Mike." Then after a long pause: "Mike Rakowski. My assistant gave me your message. Sorry. I've been running over half of New England this morning…" He gathers himself. "It's good to hear from you, Bobby."

When I tell him I want to talk about Brooke, Mike suggests meeting in person. I say that's not necessary. He presses.

I do not want to see Mike Rakowski. Not now. Not ever. The man is my bane. I can ask my questions over the phone, and then be happy to forget I reached out in the first place. What's he going to tell me? My heart is rattling around my rib cage, making it harder to breathe. There's nothing he can say to get me to forget or forgive or move on. Even if I know holding onto resentment is like drinking poison and expecting the other person to die. I'm willing to swallow that pill if it ends us both.

A part of me knows I must face him.

I don't know where Mike considers home base—according to the internet, MK Rack has locations all over the Northeast. He must be close by because when I tell him I'm in Upstate New York, he says he'll come to me. I don't want Mike Rakowski knowing where I live, so I pick a random pop-up coffee shop in nearby Reine, another suburb outside Troy, albeit a less affluent one with too many chain restaurants.

The coffee shop is a tin trailer off the interstate, a total hipster hotspot that is always crowded. I don't want to be off the beaten path with the guy. I want well populated with plenty of witnesses. I don't know whose benefit this is for.

Java the Hutt sits off Interstate 90. I've been here many times meeting students, the university not far up the road. They always pick the coffeehouse when given the choice. It's cool, I guess. Reine is a funky little town with its own sordid history. Years ago, a young woman was brutally murdered by a mentally handicapped handyman. I don't want to be thinking about this. I should've picked another coffee shop in another town. Where though? Is any place free of sin? The thoughts start racing, planting bad images in my head. I dry swallow a pill to make them go away.

I sit in my car as snow softly falls, watching college kids line up at the tin shack to grab their overpriced fancy blends, laughing and joking, a sea of North Face, Patagonia, and Eddie Bauer. They all seem so young. I'm not even forty yet. I feel so old.

Pulling my collar, I wrap my scarf and lock up the Porsche, blowing on my hands. There are no seats at Java the Hutt, no interior. The café is a long tin car with railroad ties to sit on out front. All along the railroad ties, college students perch in flexible positions, legs up, arms draped, an after-class rap session. I'm staring up at the slate sky, thinking I've made a terrible mistake, when I hear the familiar voice.

"Bobby?"

CHAPTER THIRTY-SEVEN

NOW

Mike Rakowski heads my way, coffee already in hand, pleasant smile plastered on his plump face, leaving me to wonder how he got here before me. Then again, I don't know where he's coming from. I don't know anything about this man. I try to maintain the upper hand. I am not that fat fourteen-year-old weirdo anymore. When I stride to greet him, I let him know that.

"It's Robert," I say. I want the declaration to come out bold and strong. Instead, the words sound meek and apprehensive, like a little boy who makes up his own nickname.

He apologizes, and I feel stupid for insisting on the correction. He doesn't look like the guy remember. Why should he? It's been close to a quarter century. He's heavier, older, softer, less ... intimidating. His hair is trimmed short, styled in a way that mitigates the fact he's balding.

Mike peels off his Scully & Scully leather gloves, extending his hand, taking mine in a warm, hearty shake. "It's good to see you, Robert."

Ordering while he waits, I pretend to be focused on the menu. College students converse in line. Last night's rager. So and so's getting so fucked up. Normally, I eschew notoriety. Today, I am hoping one of them recognizes me, interrupts with a respectful, subservient, "Dr. Kirby," so I can show how tall and important I am. I long to showcase the self-assurance I lacked when Mike Rakowski knew me. Of course, as is often the case, such interruptions only present themselves when they are inconvenient.

After I collect my macchiato, we walk the length of the railroad ties to the nearest vacant spot at the other end, the one closest to the parking lot. Tall stalks of frozen grass poke up from the gravel, dirt, and ice. Overcast, the afternoon bogs foreboding, one of those frigid Northeastern days with its biting winds and murmuring trees, the kind where you feel like you've stepped out of a Grimms' fairy tale and straight into a witch's clutches. Maintaining that pleasant smile, Mike sits and cracks the lid of his plain black coffee. Steam rises, plumes of smoke merging with leaden skies. I can't get over how much older he looks. It's been twenty-something years—of course he looks older—but his expression conveys more than that. Instead of appearing worn down or used up, the years have been kind to him. There are more wrinkles and gray hairs, which is to be expected, but these details don't sap vitality; instead, they appear to have invigorated. When he glances over, I see what's different: the eyes. No longer whittled and intense, they crinkle with kindness, creased crow's feet adding an air of joviality, a word I never thought I'd use to describe Mike Rakowski. His burden has been lightened. I want to believe this is all an act. I tell myself not to be fooled. I remind myself that tigers don't change stripes.

"I am glad you called, Robert."

I long to snap back a witty, biting retort, like, "The feeling is *not* mutual." The man who sits beside me is not the same one I've spent the past twenty years hating.

I don't know what I was expecting. Not this.

"Landscaping, eh?" I don't know why I ask the question. I don't care about his stupid company. What I want to do—scream in his face and let Mike Rakowski know how big a sonofabitch I think he is—feels misplaced. Any hostility at this point would be entirely one-sided.

The question provides a respite, allowing Mike to talk about his business. At some point, I will cut him off to boast about my doctorate and revered position at Uniondale, my recent grant and the rich, privileged lifestyle I enjoy. It will be petty, showing off. But this man killed Brooke, one way or the other. I don't cut him off, however. I let him talk, and my silence renders me enamored.

"I've wanted to reach out to you for a while," Mike says, and I don't know where we are in the conversation, how long my thoughts have held me hostage, casting me adrift.

"What for?" It's a snarky response on my part, childish, forcing him to say it.

"To apologize."

This man has no shortage of transgressions to apologize for. He owns a laundry list of unfettered cruelty.

Instead of citing his sins, Mike says, "It's part of why I call my company 'MK Rack.'"

I tilt my head, curious.

"You go by Robert now, right?"

"I hate Bobby."

"Yeah, well, I hate Mike Rakowski." He glances at the roadway. Truckers blow past, big wheels kicking up ice, drawing dust in their drift. "Mike Rakowski was not a nice guy."

That's an understatement. *He was a fucking asshole, a vicious prick ... a killer.* I say nothing. These are jabs. I want the knockout blow.

"There's no excuse for how I behaved." He pauses. "How I treated Brooke." Another pause. "You."

I shrug, as if to say it's no big deal. We both know that is a lie.

"When you're a kid," Mike says, unbuttoning the heavy coat, releasing his pot belly, "a house needs love. Growing up, my house didn't have any to spare. What little there was, we fought over, my brothers and me." He holds up a hand, shaking off his explanation. "There is no excuse for the things I did. I hurt a lot of people. Nothing I do will ever change that."

"It was a long time ago," I say. I don't know why I say this, offering absolution to my abuser. I came here to rake this sonofabitch over coals, put boot to neck, make him confess. Instead of making him squirm, I'm letting him off the hook.

Mike doesn't take the easy way out.

"It took me a long time to grow up," he says. "To learn my place in this world. Losing your sister—"

"My sister," I repeat, weighing down the words.

"It was a wake-up call," he says.

"Yeah," I respond. "You already apologized." *We won't grant him the absolution he seeks. Stay strong, make him hurt like he hurt us.*

"You have every right to be angry."

"Thank you. I'm not angry." I sip my macchiato, gazing at meaningless scenery. "And I don't need your permission." My response comes across as juvenile.

"The police cleared me of any wrongdoing regarding your sister's disappearance—"

"I'm aware—"

"But I'm not innocent," he says. "I helped drive her away. I felt she betrayed me and I wanted to hurt her. I used you to do that. That's something I have to live with." Mike reaches into his long coat, returns a shiny leather wallet. He slips out a picture of a little girl, maybe five, seven?

He taps the picture, beaming.

"My daughter, Emma." Mike runs a hand over his balding crew cut, wrinkles his mouth. "When Emma gets older, if someone like me comes along..." He doesn't have to finish the sentence.

I hate how sincere he's being, and worse how much I believe his remorse is real. All semester I have students who underachieve and are flunking. They come into my office at the last minute, begging for extra credit with sob stories about another grandparent who has died, a computer that suddenly crashed and ate all their homework. I've gotten adept at sniffing out the act. Mike's regret is genuine.

"Let's hope you do a better job than Paul," I say. It's the best come-back I have.

Mike asks me questions about my life. Though I don't want to talk about my life, I share intimate details. With each of these details, he seems to listen and care about my response. He meets my gaze, doesn't stare past my shoulder, waiting till my mouth stops moving so he can speak again. He is invested. My defenses erode, which gets me talking more. About the school, the challenges and upcoming projects. I even touch on the trouble Stephanie and I have been having, including the recent rift I feel with my son. If I didn't know better, I'd say it's a helpful, cathartic conversation. What Mike did is unconscionable, unforgivable. Thinking about the horrible things he's done only brings me around to the horrible things I've done. Am I any better? Because if I believe I am different—if I believe I am a better man—how can I deny another the same consideration to change and evolve? I hate thinking this.

"I was jealous of you," he says.

I must do a double take because he laughs and doubles down.

"No, I'm serious. Once you figured this place out, I knew you'd do great. The world is made for guys like you."

"Guys like me?"

"Smart, savvy, a survivor. You had so much self-confidence." He laughs again. "Didn't give a damn what anyone thought about you."

I wish I could laugh with him. I don't recall *ever* being confident. I was a warbling ball of doubt, as far from self-assured as self-assured gets. Back then, I didn't have any friends, didn't know how to communicate. I was a messed-up kid with his nose stuck in a book who ate too many peanut butter sandwiches and smelled funny. Strange how we appear to others. No one is privy to our internal monologues.

"Maybe in the end," he says, "we're not that different."

It's a bold statement, one I'd like to take offense to. With the serenity I'm feeling in my heart, however, I back off for agreement's sake. "I suppose we both ended up with good careers—"

"No. Back then, too. We were both coming from a rough place. I think I recognized that then, even if I didn't *know* it. I didn't believe I'd ever pull it together. That terrified me." He looks me in the eye. "It wasn't you I hated. It was me."

Across the snowy fields, a deer and a doe dart out of the forest. No one calls attention to the chase, though we both see it, the elegance and grace of their long strides, before the pair dive back into the thicket. The ordinary moment feels more profound than it should, and I know I am ascribing weight that doesn't exist. It doesn't take long to identify the strange sensation I am experiencing: acceptance and peace. I struggle to reclaim the righteous anger I need. Until twenty minutes ago, I'd have bet everything I own on Mike's being responsible for Brooke's disappearance. I am not so sure anymore.

Now is not the time to share Vivi Pallotta's serial killer theory or any of the terrible things she told me about Samuel Erskine. Even if Vivi is wrong and Brooke escaped that particular fate, freezing to death alone on a mountain offers little consolation. I don't know why I wish to spare Mike more agony.

"The night ... she disappeared." Mike looks pained as he strives to pluck perfect words. "I don't want to call it an epiphany. It would take a lot longer for that to click." Mike tries to smile but this time the gesture can't cut through the shame. "We were drinking downstairs, you and me, and I was busting your balls pretty hard, taking a lot of shit out on you. When you left, I thought, 'Who are you, Mike? Is this who you want to be?'"

I could correct his version of events. We weren't "drinking downstairs"—he'd been plying me with booze, and what he'd done to me landed a long way from playful ribbing. Instead, I say nothing, hoping he will locate the right words to allow me to give up the ghost too.

"I didn't want to be like my father," he says. "I know that's cheesy and sentimental. That's how it hit me, though. I didn't have the vocabulary to think of it as 'breaking the cycle' or whatever the modern terminology is. I knew my old man was a violent, drunken asshole who treated people like shit. And there I was doing the same thing." I think I catch him dabbing his eye. "You did me a favor. More than you know." We are surrounded by fluffy balls of white. He stares into the mounting accumulation and flicks a finger in the vague direction of downtown Troy over the horizon. "All that I have now, a wonderful wife and family, wouldn't have been possible. I'd have kept on being a bully, a drunk in one of those bars, pushing people around. I owe you more than an apology. I owe you a thank you."

What can I say to that? Neither of us speaks for a while. After a few beats, he steers conversation into more genial territory. I'm happy to abandon the heavy and existential if only to get rid of the lump in my throat. Conversation winding down, we talk about the people we used to know. Outside of Brooke, Mike and I don't have much of a shared history. A few names overlap. He mentions neighbors on our street. I'm surprised I remember as much as I do.

"Sandy Anderson," I say with a laugh. The neighborhood gossip, the old woman's blinds forever bent. You couldn't leave your garbage cans out too long without Mrs. Anderson's mentioning it.

"Whenever I needed updates on your sister, I'd ring ol' Sandy. She was like a browser history nowadays."

We do this for a while, going back and forth about the less painful wounds that don't sting as much.

What he says next catches my attention.

"Such a shame about Aaron."

"Aaron Reardon?"

"He took Brooke's disappearance hard."

I can't think of why Mike would care. I don't recall he and Aaron being friends. In fact, it was the opposite. Aaron hated Mike for having Brooke's body, and Mike hated Aaron for having her heart.

"I didn't know you guys were close," I say.

"We weren't." Mike then reiterates everything I'm thinking, the rivalry, the jealousy, making it even tougher to understand why he's brought up the guy.

"It's sad that anyone with such a bright future would end up the way he did."

I am about to tell Mike I actually just spoke with Aaron, who is doing quite well.

"You remember Torie Dent?" he says.

I am wondering if he knows what I've been up to. I recall that battered red car in the rain, the one parked on my street, watching my house. This version of Mike Rakowski wouldn't be caught dead in such a lowlife vehicle.

"After Brooke left, Aaron and Torie got together. Torie had a drug problem. The hard stuff. Heroin. She got Aaron started on that shit."

"Aaron?" I spit an incredulous chuckle. "Aaron Reardon, the guy voted most likely to join Doctors Without Borders? *That* Aaron Reardon? Junkie?"

"That's the other reason I changed my name for the business. He used to call me, nonstop, threatening me, saying he knew what I did, before breaking down in tears, begging for twenty dollars. The first few times, I paid him off, trying to alleviate my own guilt. I knew where the money was going—Rocky Cove is a small town."

"I thought he worked for a rehab?"

"Worked for? More like he was *in* rehab. I have a friend employed by the state. Aaron's what they call a frequent flyer. A permanent fixture. One of those people who gets their money on the first and fifteenth, splitting their time between cheap motels, state institutions, and the street."

I know how much Mike—at least the old Mike—hated Aaron. I try to convince myself he's confused, or at least exaggerating. Maybe he's conflating times and places. I am having difficulty picturing goofy, goody-goody Aaron shooting up hardcore narcotics. Those people, the ones with drug dependency issues, *can* end up in the field, helping others. When they clean up—*if* they clean up. Perhaps that's what's happened?

Mike points east, where a town could be. "I still have business in Rocky Cove. Last time I saw Aaron, he was outside Burger King, rattling an empty soda cup, panhandling for change. I wanted to stop, say something, *do* something. I didn't think seeing me would make him feel better."

I do the math, trying to recalibrate, add and subtract, deduce when a man who had been begging for spare change could get his life together enough to kick drugs, secure a good-paying job, and be able to afford a cell phone plan.

"How long ago was this?" I ask. "The last time you saw Aaron?"

"Summer? Maybe the one before?"

"Are you sure?"

"It was warm out. Which is how I was able to walk away. Not sure I could've done that that in the dead of a New England winter."

Soon afterward, we say our goodbyes. Mike climbs into his big, black truck with MK Rack stenciled in crisp, defined white. I let my gray Porsche idle and start to pull up Aaron's number but change my mind.

I punch in the address for the hospital he texted, the one where he claimed to work, afraid of what I am going to find.

CHAPTER THIRTY-EIGHT

January 7, 1998, 11:20 p.m.
The Night Before the Disappearance

Sleeping pills and alcohol don't mix. Brooke knew this. Well, she didn't know this at this particular moment, because she was still asleep, trapped in dreamland.

In the beginning, she was resting, calm, billowing on breezes. Like most dreams, the narrative played out in snippets, an episodic collage, satisfaction both tenable and forever out of reach. There were rooms and faces and people she thought she once knew but whose names she couldn't remember. Same for towns she'd visited, stores she'd frequented, men she'd fucked. None of this was bad. Nor was it good. It just was. Because this was a dream, there was no sequential order to these events. One moment she was mesmerized by fireworks on the pier with her mom and dad. The next she was at a carnival snacking on buttered popcorn with Aaron. Dreams aren't supposed to make sense. She was lucid enough to know that.

Then something changed, the dream no longer peaceful. Brooke could still smell, taste, sense something was wrong in the real world. This was evil. It was real and it was coming for her. Shapeless entities swarmed above, wayward angels flying in figure eights having tasted free will, incensed for having been denied so long, resolved never to miss out again; to make up for lost time. She'd returned to the tactile and could feel the weight pressing down, like stones crushing her bones. Roots reached up from the bowels, ensnaring her wrists and ankles. Incapacitated. Smothered. Suffocating, choking, violated. Brooke clawed at the earth and tried to scream but dirt clogged her airways. The weight—it was too much, splitting apart her ribs. Shovelfuls of heavy earth dumped on a coffin. She was being buried alive.

Brooke opened her eyes to find her brother Bobby on top of her.

CHAPTER THIRTY-NINE

NOW

Stonybrook Rehabilitation is a tall brick building that towers many stories high in the bitter part of the city without bars and restaurants. It belongs to a larger complex and seems to rise forever into the clouds. Nothing about the residence screams upscale. In fact, the opposite rings true: this is a facility that caters to the lower echelon of society insured by the state.

Entering the lobby, I expect a hospital dedicated solely to the addicted. Rehabilitation, however, appears to be only one facet offered. I see signs for an oncology ward and pediatric wing. According to the site map, the rehab is divided into two parts, a detox center on the sixth floor, with long-term, in-patient housing on the ninth.

A security guard approaches holding a clipboard. I explain who I am and whom I'm here to see. At the word "rehab," his face sours.

"Those floors are confidential." He starts flipping pages. "You have to be on the visitor's list. What's the name again?"

"Aaron Reardon."

"That's your name? Or the patient's name?"

"My name is Robert Kirby. And he's not a patient. He works here—"

"I don't see your name."

I look around. People are coming and going, many of whom are not well dressed. Here I stand, a regular, normal person getting harassed for trying to visit a friend.

"If you're not on the list, you need to leave." The guard places his hand on my shoulder, an invasion of personal space. I respond accordingly—you are not allowed to put your hands on other people without consent. Next thing I know, two more guards approach, each securing an arm, dragging me to the front door like bouncers tossing an aggressive patron from a strip club. I am stammering objections, leaving gawking onlookers to think I've been caught stealing from the gift shop.

Now I'm standing outside as a cold rain falls. Tiny pins prick my flesh. I stare up at the windows and their streaked black glass.

"Hey."

I turn to the voice. A man, scarecrow gaunt, leans against the side of the building in a too-big tee, his bare arms exposed to the elements and scratched with cheap-looking tattoos. He smokes a cigarette under the awning, which connects via side door.

"Don't worry about them," he says when I'm within earshot. "They dicks." He points up at the vents atop the glass wall. "Hear everything out here. Name's Jamie."

Jamie reaches over for what I think is a handshake. He looks ill. I don't want to touch that. He doesn't want to shake hands. It's some ridiculous, choreographed fist bump routine that I half ass.

"I'm long term," he says. "I get to smoke outside." He rolls his eyes like we're in this together. "You lookin' for Aaron?"

"Yes," I say. "Aaron Reardon. He's a counselor."

At this, Jamie busts up. "Aaron tol' you he a counselor? He ain't no counselor, man. He a patient same as me. Or was until last month."

Jamie flicks his nubbed cigarette and instantly lights another. "He'll be back. Everyone comes back."

I look over his clothes. Ratty shirt, baggy jeans, untied sneakers. No hospital gown. No plastic bracelet. I don't know if this guy is full of it or what.

"Are you sure we're talking about the same person?" It's a stupid question. How many guys named "Aaron Reardon" could there be associated with Stonybrook Rehab?

"Aaron Reardon." Jamie holds his smoke high to illustrate a man about six feet, which doesn't help. I don't remember how tall Aaron was. "Pasty-ass? Forty-something? Rocky Cove?"

The specifics match. "You wouldn't know where I could find Aaron?"

Jamie doesn't answer, eyes fixed, expressionless. I get it. Nothing is free. I extract my wallet, slip what remains, and pass along all the cash I have on me. Twenty-three dollars.

He stuffs the bills into the pocket of his baggy jeans.

"Aaron got money. Family did anyway. You do this shit long enough, ain't got no money no more. Ain't got no family. Ripped 'em off too many times." Jamie bobs into the distance. "There's an abandoned warehouse on the south side. Stays there sometimes. If he's not with his girlfriend."

"Girlfriend?"

"Running partner. Young girl, cute."

"Raven-black hair?"

"Her hair is black, yeah. Don't know about no raven. You wouldn't know she's a junkie. Cleans up nice."

"What's her name?"

Jamie shrugs.

I'm not sure it would matter. I doubt "Lily" used her real name. If they've gone through this much hassle, slapping together a fake ID isn't out of the question. They've been playing me from the start.

"Girls like that love guys like Aaron."

"Guys like Aaron?"

"Bad boys."

"Do you have an address?"

Jamie laughs. "For the girl? Nah."

"How am I supposed to find them then?"

"Tol' you. Abandoned warehouse. Tremont Street. Boarded up, broken glass. A squat. Trust me, you'll know it when you see it."

He's right.

The cracked-out, concrete warehouse is swallowed by unruly timberland. It's the kind of abandoned factory that plagues the darkness of many an East Coast town, a hopeless hole where dreams went to die long before anyone knew the condition was fatal. Most of the windows are broken from where cross-eyed, teenaged townies hurled rocks and bottles, frustrated by a life that hasn't gone their way, unaware it only gets worse. Chunks of wall have been excavated, worn down by geology, time and pressure. A tall chain link runs the length of a ruptured lot. The fence ripples, sags, like falling drunks trying to do the wave at a football stadium.

It's easy to find a hole to crawl through. I'm not the first. Every twenty feet or so, someone has wrenched apart line posts and fork latches, snapping tension wires. I peel back the interlocking links and step onto the property. There are footprints in the snow. Several sets. A strong wind rustles bare branches, bowing weaker limbs.

How do I know anyone stays here? Let alone preppy, popped-collared Aaron? That man at the hospital, Jamie, could have been lying.

Drug addicts are born grifters. Doesn't matter what made-up level they assign themselves, how many gold stars they stick on an activity board to buoy self-esteem. I don't understand how the police wouldn't have evicted trespassers. I stare up at the windows and think I hear music. Grating noise, metal-on-metal screeching. Then it's gone. I stand in the middle of what used to be someone's livelihood, a former parking lot where good, hard-working men rose before the sun came up to join their unwashed brethren on the assembly line of this old, ravaged warehouse before proprietors deemed them expendable, cast them aside, tapping a fresher lifeforce for greater profit.

Jamie did not tell me how to get inside. Options appear limited. It's not like I can stroll up and ring a bell. Back when my mother and I were on the road, we often encountered condemned buildings like this one, four walls and a roof to provide shelter for people who couldn't afford rent. My mother was a rundown wreck who belonged. I am out of my element. This old warehouse feels like it has eyes. I sense someone watching me. I'm wearing a fifteen-hundred-dollar Lucas Spanish Merino sheepskin coat. I worry I've been set-up, lamb-led prey.

Far away, small, disfigured houses rear ugly heads between the skeletal bones of a fruitless season, cheap, single-story dwellings too distant to be relevant, as if they too know this neighborhood is bad news and wish to steer clear. Each step crunches more snow, crushes more broken glass, as I feel myself drawn further into my anguish.

Doors are threaded with heavy chains. I shake, rattle, and hope the steel is for show. I try several doors, all the same, locked and forti-fied. Giant metal signs plastered everywhere: *Private Property. Do Not Enter.* Might as well read, *Abandon All Hope Ye Who Enter Here.*

Around back, I find torn selvage that grants access to a shipping dock where delivery trucks used to back up to collect commerce, before setting out on the great American highway. I climb the concrete steps to a back door, which I find suspiciously ajar.

Questions assault my mind, too fast for me to sort out, let alone address. *What am I doing here? Looking for? What will I do if I find it?* I've spent years in therapy pushing dark memories into a black corner where, without light, I thought the wild things could not grow. I was wrong. Left alone and ignored, I've provided ideal conditions for them to flourish.

The space is vacuous, unlit, dark. Musty odors choke the air. I detect the fetid stink of human excrement. Urine and feces deposited without working plumbing. It's too late to turn back. I keep moving forward till weak gray light penetrates. Water drips from the ceiling. I can see well enough now to maneuver around the sharp metal machine parts scattered in the dirt. A light fixture dangles. I trip a switch on the wall, already knowing the answer. There's no heat. The condemned factory has long been without such luxuries. Echoes taunt, the methodical madness of that dripping water getting the best of me. I pull out my phone and activate its flashlight. I shiver in the concrete icebox.

Broken pallets and dented barrels scatter the floor, chains and ropes, assorted plastic pans, nozzles, the odd screwdriver. Hunks of metal, belonging to the machines that used to serve a purpose, sit like boulders, too rusted for me, a civil engineer, to identify. I can name a few individual components—fragments of feed chutes and troughed conveyor belts—but I can't tell you what they made inside this plant.

"Aaron?" I call out. My voice travels, bouncing off the hard surfaces, concrete floor to ceiling grates. I survey the main frame rafters, eave struts, and side wall girts. Even with the phone's light, it's hard to establish a sense of place. I feel like a goldfish drowning in its own bowl. Beside the odor of shit and piss, I search for signs of recent human occupancy. I discover a few dingy sleeping bags, soaked from the elements, waterlogged beds in putrid pools of mildew and mold and God knows what else.

I descend further into the bowels of whatever this place used to be, whatever it has become. At the bottom of a well, a shadowy figure emerges from the darkness.

"What took you so long?" he says.

CHAPTER FORTY

NOW

Aaron Reardon holds a battery-powered lamp, the glass lit darkly. The man I see is cadaverous, eviscerated, a specter who bears zero resemblance to the Aaron Reardon I recall, the young urban professional with nice clothes and white teeth. The thing that slouches before me is a filthy creature with dirty pants and a mouth full of rot. Yet, I know it is him. He retains an essence of the man he used to be. I can smell him ten feet away. It's so cold in here. He wears a tee shirt, no coat. I step closer and see the scabs and sores, the infected bumps, railroad tracks up and down his arms. I've seen enough movies to know what injection sites look like. His hair is long and stringy. His ratty clothes slag off his torso, a living coat hanger.

"Why are you doing this, Aaron?"

Without responding, he turns, drawing me deeper into his world. Through a basement arch, we descend into the catacombs. I feel like I've been drugged. The well reeks like a subway. At the end, we enter another room, a storage closet. With this entire giant factory to himself, Aaron has chosen to exile himself to its remotest reaches. In the corner, candles burn. Images of Jesus Christ and the Virgin Mary, cheap ninety-nine-cent ones you can pick up at the Spanish markets where they sell discounted milk and benzodiazepine wrapped in balls of cellophane. In the center of the encampment lie syringes, burnt spoons, and cigarettes with the filters torn off. A tourniquet, a rubber band nurses use to draw blood, snakes the soot. Giant water jugs sit on the floor filled with a dark yellow liquid. The pungent scent hits my nasal membranes. My eyes water, and I pinch my nose and try not to breathe any more than I have to.

"What's the matter, Bobby?" Aaron leans against the concrete wall spray-painted with graffiti. "You don't like my home?"

Whatever they produced in this factory, this is where they dragged the machinery after it broke down and died. Scraps of belt sheaves, wheels and impellers, shafts and bearings. Couplings. Funnels. Motor drives. One big junkyard of worthlessness. Anything down here worth a dime has long been sold and shot up. Exhaust pipes poke out from walls and dip from the sky, silver accordion ducts, unconnected. The floor is uneven, ruptured, tilted in the way a building will settle.

The smell is too much. My eyes won't stop burning. Though the candles aren't near me, I can feel the fire, the heat. I've gone from freezing to suffocating in the swelter.

Aaron draws on a cigarette, its hot cherry tip sizzling. "I know what you are, Bobby." He sucks long and hard. "I know what you did."

I let the accusation drift by. I still retain enough internal fortitude to do that, deflect. Who is this junkie to criticize me? I am a valued professor at an exalted university. I'm not the lowlife who maimed a dog or filmed a blackmail porno. I don't have enough moral reserve left to take the high ground. Somewhere, deep in the recesses, where our most painful secrets reside, I am split down the middle: the part anxious to wage war; the other that begs to die.

"You burned my dog," I say, shaking my head for added effect. "Who hurts a helpless creature?"

"Who rapes his own sister?"

I will not dignify that with a response. *We didn't do that.* I know we didn't. *We wouldn't do that.* I'm a good man! A good father and husband, a good teacher. *We help people! We matter!* I can't get these words out.

"Your sister told me what you did. You and Mike. Sick fucks."

Worn down, I don't have enough left to defend myself against these perverted, baseless allegations. That's how he gets in my head, forcing me to succumb to shame and regret. I feel the tears welling. *Don't cry! Not now.* I did not do these things. *Yes, we did.* No, I did not. I'm a good person. *No, we are the reason she left. We are the reason she died.*

Aaron jabs the lit cigarette toward my face, his scornful eyes etched by the ghastly flicker of candlelight flame. "Admit it!"

The glow from the burning ember further illumines his emaciated face. I can see behind his pockmarked skin, right down to the white ivory of his brittle milk bones. Or maybe it's he who can see through me.

"I didn't ... do that." I begin to weep.

"Admit it!" he screams again. "You rapist piece of shit!"

I sob. Broken, I start convulsing. I'm fourteen again. I can't stop. I can't breathe. I try to push out words. "I was just a b-boy... I don't ... I d-don't remember." Now I'm hyperventilating, bent over, heart beating spastic in my chest. The tears won't stop. *We are a monster.* "I'm so sorry, Brooke," I whisper. "Please forgive me." I'm not sure the words are audible through the wailing and snot running out of my nose like a freshly tapped spigot.

"On her way out of town," Aaron says, basking with delight over my suffering, "she stopped to say goodbye. She gave me her necklace as a promise she'd be back, but I never heard from her again." Howling laughter turns to hacking cough.

I stare at the industrial ceiling. White flakes, which I am certain are asbestos or some other hazardous material, float down like snowflakes, poisoning my lungs and brain.

"I kept waiting for a letter, but none came," he says softly. "She died somewhere in those cold, snowy hills, afraid and alone." Aaron glares at me. "Because of *you*."

Twenty years, the mind plays tricks. These are implanted memories. He's somehow tapped into my worst fears and is manipulating me. None of that happened. I dreamt it. This junkie fuck has gotten inside my head, found *it*, stolen it. He's brought it out into the world and made it real and now thinks he can use it against me. I will not live with his truth.

I want to call Aaron a sonofabitch and a liar. I reach down deep, scouring for proof, reminded that no such evidence exists, because after all these years, I've managed to convince myself it was a bad dream.

"I loved her," he says.

I crouch down, screaming in silence. The tiny veins in my brain threaten to burst. He pulls so hard on his cigarette that half of it instantly turns to ash. I take a knee.

"When I saw your fucking name in the paper. That goddamn award, I thought, Why should he be so blessed when so many of us are hurting? My life is shit! I have nothing! And there you are, celebrated and adored. I don't care if you were a kid. You conned the house from Paul, sold it, got to keep all that money. All Brooke got was dead."

I gesture weakly at the drug addict wares on the floor. "Go pump more poison into your body." I get to my feet, make for the door. "I'm going to the cops. I'm going to t-tell them about what you did to my dog, trespassing, breaking and entering, about the video you sent. *You're* the sick one—"

"No, you won't," he says, so calm, so self-assured.

I stop and turn back. I want to grab one of these jagged metal machine parts and thrust the sharp point into his cerebral cortex, pick up one of these bricks scattered about the dirty floor and smash in his skull.

"Lily," he says. Through the gloam, I can see his wolfish yellow teeth snarl, so smug and satisfied. "You go to the cops, and Lily will have them draw blood. And then they'll draw *your* blood." He smirks. "And when the results come back, everyone will know *you're* her father. Everyone will know *you fucked your own sister*, and there's the proof. Blood never lies."

We either die, here and now, or we fight.

"Lily?" I say. "Yeah, your buddy Jamie told me all about her. More junkie scum, like you. It's a scam."

"You sure about that?" The bastard winks at me. "You want to take the chance?"

"What do you want? Money? I don't have m-much money of my own. It's all my wife's. I'm a teacher, for Christ's sake. That grant was f-fifty-thousand dollars! It won't last me h-half a year. Our monthly bills alone—"

"It was never about the money. I wanted to see you hurt."

I think back to the day he invited me for lunch. "Remember w-when I was on my way to Boston?" I hate the needy urgency in my voice. "You wanted to m-meet for coffee. We're f-f-friends."

Aaron howls, Adam's apple poking through the thin epidermis of his pencil neck. "Like you'd agree? I've known assholes like you my whole life. You shit on people you don't need. You're a user, Bobby." He starts laughing, snickering, mocking my pain. "The best part? You didn't need my help. You fucked it up all on your own.

Your wife and son already figured out what a loser you are. You've lost everything." Cackling, he flashes his snaggled, tobacco-stained teeth. "They ain't coming back. You're gonna die all alone, Bobby—"

I charge at him with everything I have left inside me. Flying through the air, I drive all my weight into his wispy frame. His bones are delicate, like a tiny bird's. I feel them crack when we smack against the concrete. I listen to his ulna and radius splinter. He screams. I hope I've broken his spine.

I am not a violent man. I keep telling myself this as my fists tighten and I rain blows on his face, neck, sternum, and ribs, a furious barrage of punches. I wind up and bring down everything I have. The wet sound of bloodied knuckles smacks lax skin, like tenderizing veal with a mallet. I don't stop. Aaron doesn't put up a fight. He's already defeated, caught between crying, laughing, sobbing, and wailing. A gurgling sound escapes his throat. Blood gushes from his mouth, nose, ears. Even then I can't quit. I hit him harder, the flesh around his orbital sockets swelling, bone cracking like eggshells. He lies there, taking it, defenseless.

"Liar!" I scream. "You're a fucking liar!"

I hear my own voice, but it doesn't sound like me. I'm floating high above it all, watching that fat fourteen-year-old, drunken freak creep up the stairs to do such an unspeakable thing.

My hand finds something hard, a machine part, a brick, a chunk of concrete rock. I grasp it, cock it high, and slam it into his bloodied face. I do this again and again and again. Until the gurgling sounds stop. Until all I hear is my own heavy breathing, which overpowers the radio waves in my head.

I don't know how long I beat him. If it's ten seconds or ten minutes. I only know when I am done, I'm staring down at my shaking hands, and I am no longer in an abandoned warehouse. I am sitting in my

Porsche, covered in blood and crying. My car is parked on the side of the road, and the snow has turned into rain.

I want to go home. I don't know where that is. I see my phone, stained crimson and slick, screen cracked. I can't stop crying or shaking long enough to slide it on and see where I am. I can't plug in my address. I can't find my way home.

CHAPTER FORTY-ONE

January 7, 1998, 11:21 p.m.
The Night Before the Disappearance

"What the fuck?!"

Brooke emerged from a deep slumber to find her half-brother Bobby humping her knee like a pound mutt. Eyes rolled back in his skull, muttering indecipherable, he stank like a brewery.

"Get off me!"

She shoved his shoulders to try and pry free. A big boy, Bobby was not easily moved. Breathing heavily through his mouth, he'd affixed his pudgy arms around her leg, snug as a koala pencil topper. Using his girth to hold her in place, he was too drunk to locate what he was looking for. No matter how many times Brooke punched his back and told him to fuck off, the fat, horny thing kept pumping away at her shin.

Ripping off her necklace, Brooke swiped at Bobby, cutting his neck with the long end of the crucifix. When he let go of her knee to reach for his bleeding collar, Brooke tilted her shoulder, gaining leverage, and with a final shove managed to push Bobby off, his chubby hips slow to stop gyrating.

"What the fuck is wrong with you?"

Bobby pushed his glasses up his nose. Their eyes met, fury in hers, horror overtaking his. For a split-second, he recognized what'd he'd done. Twelve different expressions of remorse flashed in that instant. Then all comprehension was gone, eyes glassing over. Bobby turned his head, opened his mouth wide, and threw up on her bedspread.

She jumped back. "Fucking fecto!" Brooke patted down her body, like a gunslinger in the aftermath of a shootout searching for bullet holes, relieved to find everything intact and her underwear still on. What a way to wake up, roused from a benzo stupor, unsettled by a disturbing dream she'd already forgotten, to find her weirdo half-brother dry humping her leg. Bobby continued to retch. The foul stench evoked peanut butter and soft, chewed breads. Fire blazing in her belly and outrage flowing through her veins, Brooke reached for the words to eviscerate. *That little shit, who does he think he is? Comes into her life, home, her room, and tries to* what? *Cop a feel? Get off?* Staring at the pathetic thing, in his oversized rumpled pajamas, covered in stringy pieces of gamey vomit, Brooke felt the anger wane, recede, and before she could get anything out, Bobby heaved one last time and fell face first, passed out in his own sick.

Brooke poked him. The kid wouldn't wake. He was snoring, gulping for air. She tipped him on his side so he wouldn't choke to death on his own vomit.

Her heart rate slowing, she wasn't mad, even though she should be pissed. Looking at the chubby dope conked out on her bed, covered in puke, Brooke didn't see evil. She didn't even see a bad kid. The boy was just lost, messed up in the head. He wasn't stupid—far from it—and if he could find a way to deal with the damage, get help…

Not her problem. Not anymore.

Brooke pulled on her jeans, found a heavy coat in the scrapheap, and stuffed her bag.

At the bottom of the stairs, she discovered the house empty. She was pretty sure she'd dreamt of Mike, which had her expecting to find him waiting downstairs. But there was no one. The empty beer cans Bobby had drained lay scattered on the coffee table. Paul didn't drink Budweiser. When she saw the crumpled Marlboro Reds, she knew. That fucker...

She needed to get out of here. Now. She thought about leaving her dad a note. What could she say? How could she bridge a twenty-year gap? They weren't father and daughter, not the way they needed to be. No words could suffice. *Hope you get to keep the house when I skip bail?* Yeah, it was shitty to leave her dad holding the bag. Wasn't he the one who said to live her life?

Brooke raced out the door, urgency propelling her to keep moving. She tossed her bag into the backseat of her car, hopped in the driver's seat, revved the engine, and floored it in reverse. Later she'd realize she'd forgotten something in the house. Then she'd remind herself she didn't leave behind anything that couldn't be forgotten.

Where would she go? North. Yes, higher up. Brooke had always liked the snow.

First, she had one last stop to make. There was one person who deserved to know the truth. Aaron had been there from the start. He was the one person she could count on. Would she tell him everything? If Aaron knew she was leaving, he'd want a plan—Aaron, so pragmatic and practical. It's good to have a plan. She didn't have one yet. For now, she only needed to see as far as her headlights to keep going.

CHAPTER FORTY-TWO

NOW

I wake the next morning in my own bed. For a brief second there is no division, no Bobby, no Robert. There's just me. A sentient being with a clean mind who opens his eyes to face a new day. There is no dread or regret. A state of calm exists without turmoil. The world is perfectly still.

It can't last.

The center cannot hold.

Orange sunlight bleeds through the blinds and onto my stained bedsheets. Streaks of blood scratch up the linens, claw marks from what rough beast I do not know. The skin around my knuckles is raw, exposed, infected and oozing pus. At first, I don't feel the pain, and then it radiates, sharp and agonizing, every naked nerve ending activated, agitated, aggravated. I hold up my right hand to better inspect. Misaligned, crooked. I read about this. Boxer's knuckle. The radial sagittal band creates a grotesque dorsal bump. I try to make a fist but can't. My hand is broken.

In the bathroom, I tend to my wounds. Placing my shaking, swollen hands under hot water, I try to pick out the bits of hair and filth with tweezers. I can't see well enough to get it all. I let the hot water run until the outer layer of skin is loose enough to peel and expose what lies beneath. I douse my trembling knuckles with hydrogen peroxide, coat them in antibacterial ointment, and cover them in gauze. I'm planning to put in my contacts and better stabilize the right hand, the broken one, when I hear the front door open.

Descending the stairs, I don't know what I expect to find. The police. Lily. A reanimated Aaron…

Instead, I find my wife, Stephanie.

"Where's Peter?"

"My sister's."

I step from the shadows into the brighter kitchen light, shielding my eyes from the harsh glare reflecting off too much metal. Espresso maker, stovetop, refrigerator—it's blinding.

"My God, Robert, what happened?"

I stare at my bandaged hands, turning them over to study each. They are foreign, alien entities. These belong to someone else. Blood has seeped through the gauze, pale pink blood like raw, frozen chicken dethawing in a plastic bag. Holding them higher still, I inspect the phalanges, twiddling each. They move somewhat on my left, but on my right… My hand appears to be worse than I originally thought, leading me to speculate it's not just broken. I've severed a ligament or torn tendons. I can't rotate the wrist, the Synovial lining impaired.

"Robert," my wife repeats, maternal and stern. "What did you do?"

My stare is vacant, glazed. What *did* I do? I grab my spare glasses, the ugly ones I keep in the giant junk mug on the counter. I want to replay yesterday's events, but someone has erased the tape. *It's okay. How do any of us know what we do?* Everything we think we remember is open to interpretation, filtered through the lens of personal history, blending with countless other stimuli, books, films, observations. You think we met at the beach. I say a park. How do you know it wasn't a concert? Neither of us is insane. Only one of us can be right. *We will forget about this too.*

"Your … hands," she says. "Robert … did you get in a fight? Have an … altercation?" She covers her mouth in melodramatic fashion, and I loathe her for the theatrics.

I catch my wife's eye and can't help but smile. All the times she thought me weak. There was that one weekend where the man whistled at her outside the bar, said something lewd, and she was angry I didn't "do something about it." I eschew physical violence. *Who's weak now?* It's clear I've been in a fight, and for a moment I am like a regular man, one of those bristled, beer-bellied, rowdy types. This thought makes me laugh, because it is so not who I am. It's fun to pretend though, isn't it? How we conflate movies we've seen or books we've read, adding their adventures to our own. *Die Hard* was on TV the other day. Last month, maybe. It's a Christmas movie so Peter and I watched it together. For Christmas. He'd never seen it. Steph doesn't like him watching R-rated movies—she doesn't allow it—I made an exception. There's nothing but a few curse words and the flash of a breast. I checked it out on a parental database first. I'm a responsible parent. John McClane kicking ass for two hours is a fun movie for a teenage boy. I didn't leave a man for dead in a warehouse. My hands aren't bloody and raw from pummeling another man's face into pulpy hamburger. It was a movie. I've watched plenty of violent movies, read countless books with gratuitous sex. I've lived thirty-six years, experiencing much depravity. I've confused real world and fantasy. *Yet again.* I need to believe this but discover it was easier to lie to myself when I was fourteen.

"Robert," Stephanie says, stepping closer. "This isn't about… you didn't…"

My disassociated gaze will not focus as I try not to laugh at her sanctimonious sincerity. If she cares so goddamn much, where has she been for the past week? Which has been, hyperbole aside, among the worst of my life.

Nowhere to be found, that's where. We're on our own again. Like before. Like always.

She takes my hands, by the wrists, expression dripping concern. For the first time, I abhor this woman I call my wife.

"Did you..." She drops my hands to return one of hers to her mouth. "Is Ortho okay?"

I tilt my head, smile overtaking my face. She thinks this has to do with the NEH grant? I start laughing and can't stop. How ignorant can she be? Like I'd beat a man to death over a stupid academic award? Hilarious.

Stephanie sits at the kitchen table and doesn't speak. My laughter subsides as I grow distracted by encroaching clouds blotting the sun, watching shadows slip off the wall.

"How did you find out?" she says.

It takes a moment to come around. I am stumped, confused, befuddled, perplexed, flummoxed. Find out what? About the grant? She knows when I received the award—she was there! My mind is slow today, though. I didn't sleep well, my hands are throbbing, and I may have killed a man, leaving me to wonder if police will show up at my door any moment. I don't want to, but my mind's eye returns to the look on his face when he knew it was over, that his life was being extinguished, eyes growing wide as he fired bullets into the sky, and now I *know* I am confused. That wasn't me! That was Hans Gruber falling from Nakatomi Plaza. *We didn't push Hans Gruber from a window!* What a great character. Easily a top-ten, all-time villain. Such a shame the actor who portrayed him, Alan Rickman, passed away. I enjoyed that night with my son, just the two of us. I want to see my boy.

Then I understand.

The smile doesn't leave, though. It morphs, from absurdity to whatever lies beyond preposterous. Like Encyclopedia Brown and those cheap paperbacks I'd read in the backseat of the car while my mom visited strange men in motels, promising she'd be back in five or six minutes but staying gone a lot longer than that. I've solved the mystery.

"The affair," I say with mild amusement. "That's who you're having the affair with. Ortho." I don't pose this as a question. "Ortho Warsh." I laugh.

Stephanie averts her eyes and doesn't answer. I remember that old movie *Barfly*, the one about Charles Bukowski, whose writing I've always found self-indulgent and sophomoric, save for the occasional poignant turn of phrase, though I know I am prejudiced, having grown up the way I did, with Connie and the bars and the men—it's difficult to divorce ourselves from art; and I'll leave it to others to find romance in the squalor. But that movie. *Barfly*. The part where Mickey Rourke says to Faye Dunaway, after she fucks Frank Stallone, Sly's brother, something like, "Why did it have to be Eddie? He symbolizes everything I find sick and wrong in this world." I could Google the exact phrase but I'm smack dab in the middle of having solved the mystery of my wife's infidelity, knowing she didn't just allow another man's cock to penetrate her, sucking it with the same mouth I kiss, swallowing his ejaculate, but that it was Ortho Warsh, my sworn mortal enemy, a man who stands for everything I find sick and wrong in this world.

"Are you going to say anything, Robert?"

We'd love to, dear. But we can't. We're laughing too hard. We can't stop. And it's not manufactured or affected or for show. It's a deep belly laugh, our entire body in on the joke. We are erupting. We can't catch our breath to stop it.

Unable to stand, I am doubled over, the howl escaping my lips trapped between shrill and deafening, or maybe it's Stephanie who's screaming. Maybe she's the one who is crying now.

Am I Robert or Bobby?

Does it matter anymore?

CHAPTER FORTY-THREE

A LITTLE LATER

On a crisp, early spring morning, a woman enters a niche boutique shop outside Buffalo, New York, a nowhere town hidden among countless others like it. The woman is ordinary but only because she wants to be. If you looked closer, you'd see in this tall, fit woman something radiant, amazing. Instead, she chooses to blend in, a superstar undercover. She dresses like the other locals here, with bulky coats and heavy boots, hiding a body that's remarkable for its forties. She doesn't fuss much with makeup or bother painting on a face. The woman has been living here for most of her life. At least since her early twenties. She pretends she doesn't know the exact date she got here. In a way it's true. She was a different person back then. God, she had nothing. No car. Barely any belongings. She'd just escaped a near-death experience, which isn't overselling the drama. Looking back, in a weird way, it all helped, being anonymous without possessions. She was able to reinvent herself. It's the lies we tell ourselves that keep us living.

The specialty shop sells trinkets, do-dads, souvenirs for tourists who stop on this little road of this little town as they return from Niagara Falls or one of the other regional attractions, Fire Hall or Drummond Hill—the Neto Hatinakwe Onkwehowe Native Arts

Gallery. These people, middle-class families on their annual two-week vacation, don't pay close attention to the locals. Anyone could disappear here if they tried hard enough.

The woman picks up and inspects items. Random homemade arts and crafts. The bell above the door dings. It's a dad and his daughter. The little one clutches a teddy bear from the Niagara Children's Museum. The woman thinks about her decision not to have children. When she was younger, she figured one day she'd be a mom. She doesn't regret that decision, even if she can, at times such as these, wonder what a different life would look like. For the most part, it was a healthy decision, prudent. Her lifestyle choices didn't leave room for a child. Having grown up the way she did, under the instability of a mother who abandoned her (more than once), a father better suited for another line of work, the history of depression and substance abuse, traits and qualities she worried about passing along—no, it was the right call not to have children. Plus, you can't miss what you never had.

Many of the gifts in the store are designed to appeal to kids. Smart marketing strategy, since families passing through often have little ones in tow, tugging sleeves like this daughter does now. Her dad says, "Maybe." But the knowing grin says otherwise. Why else would he have brought the girl in here? It's all pink ponies and blue cowboys. Stuffies and figurines. It makes her smile, watching the father with his daughter, who selects a toy boat. The woman catches the dad's eye, and he shrugs as if to say, *What can you do?* It's sweet.

The pair heads to the register. The woman continues perusing wares. She has no intention of buying anything. This is research. The woman is a well-respected artist in this town. Sculpting, pottery, crafts she commissions in shops like this one. It doesn't earn her much money. She's not going to grow wealthy from it. But she's made enough to buy the small house by the water. It keeps a roof over her head. Food in the belly. Doing what you love for a living. Like rhythm and music, who could ask for anything more? Last month, the Oh Canada, Eh! Theatre did a production of *Girl Crazy*, which the woman caught. Uproariously funny. That's what the *Gazette* called it. They weren't wrong. Laughter doesn't seem like a big deal to ordinary people. If you grew up in a home without much of it, the joyous expression is more valuable than millions.

The father has paid for his daughter's boat and they've left the store. Now it's just the woman and the owner, an elderly lady, who reconfigures the small book selection, straightening out titles of the regional history of the Falls. It's a slow morning. It will pick up. It always does.

"Hey, Jill," the proprietor says, over her shoulder. "Stuck on the next project?"

"A little." The woman, Jill, smiles. In front of the checkout counter there are teeny figurines of trains and steamers, assorted miniature modes of transportation that fuel young imaginations, the adventures and journeys that await us all should we be bold enough to undertake them.

"I wouldn't worry," the older lady says. "You'll figure it out. You're half the reason people stop in here."

The woman known as Jill brushes off the praise.

It's true though. For whatever reason, her art seems to resonate. An entire section of this store is, in fact, dedicated to her work. Word of mouth delivers customers, who will often remark these creations come highly recommended. Jill can't imagine how this little town generates "word of mouth." She's never advertised or pursued making her business grow. One time the local paper wanted to do a story on her, with a big photograph of the artist working in her studio. Jill declined.

Jill dabbles in several mediums. This store showcases her glassware and pottery, which isn't the usual collection of cups, plates, mugs, saucers, and bowls. Jill's work infuses absurd realism, so her pieces function on more than one level, serviceable *and* decorative. The career she fell into lands a long way from the one she'd gone to school for. Seems like a lifetime ago when she was studying to be a nurse. God, what a mess she was back then. She'd just lost her mom, her father was checked out, and that weirdo bastard half-brother of hers... Sometimes she wonders what happened to him. What kind of man he turned into. It's funny because she never much liked the kid. She feels horrible recalling the derogatory names she used to call him. Cruel, vicious. But when we come from homes where love is hard to find, we fight for what little of it there is. We pass along our slights, the injustices we feel have been committed against us. He was hurting too. At twenty it's not easy to see beyond *your* world and how the pain affects *you*. Like one of her favorite songs goes, *How can you explain personal pain?*

"You okay?" the older lady behind the counter asks. "You seem lost in a daze."

"Sorry." Jill shakes her head. "Thinking about stuff."

"You are always creating, aren't you?"

No, it's not like that, she wants to say, *just a random memory*.

Jill wouldn't be lying. Memories of her past life flitter in and out, like soft breezes on idle summer days.

Back at her house on the water, Jill makes herself dinner, soup and a sandwich. Maybe it's the stillness, the silence, something she smells, the sense most associated with memory. Whatever causes it, she recalls the night of the accident. That's what she calls it: an accident, never the crash. A happy accident. No one would get the private joke, which goes back to this old painting show she liked when she was a kid. Bob Ross. This mellow hippy on public access with a boxed hairdo you only find in the 1980s. When Ross would make a mistake while painting, he'd call them "happy accidents." The stormy night Jill drove her car into a ditch turned out to be a happy accident.

Of course, she read about her old life, the one she buried after she went "missing." Papers had all kinds of crazy theories about what had happened. Most of these were outlandish, off the wall. They'd give her a perverse chuckle. There was one though that was much more bone-chilling.

This particular theory referenced an opportunistic serial killer. Jill wouldn't have given it a second thought, except for the man who picked her up walking down the snowy rural road that night. The irony was, before that man, another kinder, older gentleman had offered a ride first. And Jill had said no, not wanting to get in a car with a stranger. When she started walking, she found her resolve eroding in the debilitating cold. The first vehicle that passed was straight out of a horror movie—a plain white van. She didn't look at the man driving it because she was scared it would give her pause to say no, and at that moment, if she didn't get into something warm, Jill was going to die of hypothermia.

They'd been driving a few minutes when she caught his eyes in the mirror. You can tell everything you need to know about someone from their eyes. And this man's eyes confirmed her worst fears. Jill couldn't help but smile. Not because she wasn't terrified—she was. It was the twist. Just her luck. Turn down the nice guy. Take a ride with the bastard.

The man introduced himself as "Sam" and asked where she was going. Jill said the highway would be great. From there she could hitch-hike north. She wanted out of that van as fast as possible. When Sam started taking wrong turns, delivering them deeper into the dark wood, Jill knew they were not headed toward the highway. You don't need to be from somewhere to understand when you are going the wrong way.

Light started to fade. The night turned blacker and she could feel his malicious intent. Normally—meaning any night before tonight—Jill keeps her mouth shut long enough for something bad to happen. Tonight was different. She'll never know what made her speak up, and not only speak up but scream with a timbre and tenor that evoked her unstable, alcoholic father at his most unhinged. Like a spark ignited, a switch tripped, and she was ablaze.

Jill doesn't remember what she said, not word for word. It was a variation of not to fuck with her, that it had been a long goddamn night, and she'd gouge a mutherfucker's eyes out, demanding Sam pull over right fucking now unless he wanted to see what crazy was.

Sam ended up driving her all to the way to the highway, dropping her off at a truck stop. Whatever Sam had planned to do wasn't worth attempting with this crazy bitch.

For a long time, Jill felt bad, as if she'd overreacted. Then many years later she saw a story online with a photo of a man named "Samuel Erskine" who was accused of murdering two women and suspected of more. He'd been living just up the road from where she had her happy accident. Jill knew, as sure as she was still living and breathing, that he was the man in the van who picked her up that night.

Jill never told anyone. Who could she tell? What difference would it make? Erskine was dead, and she was someone new.

After dinner, Jill heads out to her studio. She often works late. She loves these small hours, when everyone else is asleep. It's here she finds her peace, her comfort, her being.

The studio has a little cottage in the back that came with the property, which she bought in 2010, when regular people with regular jobs could still buy houses here. It was also when the housing market was at its nadir, interest rates ridiculously low. Turned out to be a shrewd investment. Because of the booming tourism, the property keeps appreciating. Not that she plans on ever selling or moving. Like her business, it just worked out. Her whole life has been that way since that night. Fortuitous. Good breaks. Sometimes all it takes to change our fate is to make the jump. A flyer. A leap in the dark.

You get one life. Make the most of it. Don't give it away.

Jill has taken those words to heart, incorporating them into everything she does.

Firing the kiln, she rolls up her sleeves. Her eyes linger on the tiny, yellow, washed-out tattoo inside her wrist. So long ago. Might as well be someone else's life.

The moon shines high and bright. Setting her music library to shuffle, Jill grabs the clay and takes her place at the wheel, accepting the call to be inspired once again.

ACKNOWLEDGEMENTS

Thank you to my lovely wife Justine and my two boys, Holden and Jackson Kerouac.

Thank you to my agent Jill Marsal, publicist Lisa Daily, and designer Christian Storm.

Also, in no particular order, thank you to Brian Panowich, Tom Pitts, Jennifer Hillier, Riley Sager, Josh Mohr, David Corbett, Wendy Walker, Shannon Kirk, Mary Kubica, Michael Thompson, Rob Pierce, Joel Landmine, Renee Pickup, and other members of the crime-writing community I call ... friend.

A shoutout to the rest of my family: Melissa Greco, Kid Sofia, Anthony, Celeste Bancroft, all my Upstate New York cousins (especially Jason), and Lucky Dog, the greatest toy poodle a man has ever had the privilege to know.

This work of pure fiction (and a warped, twisted imagination) is probably my most original book, in that I draw on nothing but the darkness of the world I see around me and the worst humanity has to offer. But, y'know, hopefully, in a fun, entertaining way. I don't know any of these people, and apologies if the dog scene was upsetting. I should also thank Chris Walter since I borrow a page (literally, or literarily) from his book *East Van*, at least in terms of character arc.

And, lastly, a huge thank you to all my readers. You're why I do what I do. I appreciate all the love and support.

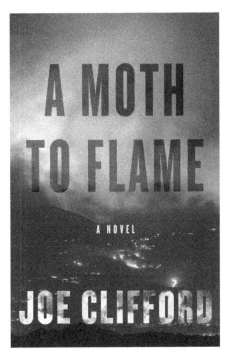

Keep reading for an exciting
follow-up to *All Who Wander*

nyc·to·pho·bi·a   / nïktə fōbēə /

noun *Extreme or irrational fear of the night or of darkness.*

THE NIGHT OF THE PROTEST

The Rider on the Plain, Broadcast Excerpt, Thursday, March 14, 1991, 11:49 p.m.

Lies. Bullshit. Spin. You know it. I know it. And trust me, the school board knows it. Brad Pearce was the best teacher we ever had. And they fired him. For what? For telling the truth, pushing us to challenge authority's self-serving deceptions, and encouraging the student body to open its eyes to the gross inequities of a system built to exploit us. But this is what they do, isn't it? Divide and conquer. Control. It's always about control. Get brother to hate brother, sister to hate sister. Misinformation. Don't trust your own eyes and ears. Believe what they tell you is the truth. They want you to travel down the road they've paved, the one that leads to profits for them, and ends in subjugation for us. They want to keep us caged like rats spinning wheels, fueling their power trip. The machination of oppression. The ones in control have been pulling this crap since the dawn of civilization. They isolate, subjugate, legislate. An economic divide favoring the ruling class, rendering a few royalty, the rest of us servants. And they keep us down by force feeding propaganda, fattening us up like ducks so they can extract our engorged livers to spread on their gold-dusted bread. Work us to the bone, break our backs, bleed us dry, throw away the carcass. There's plenty more waiting to take their turn. Mr. Pearce confronted our perceptions, challenging us to look behind the curtain and uncover the master's puppet strings. We are meant for more than punching clocks, wasting our best years in boxes or factories. We are meant to live.

Right now, if they have their way, we're gonna die. Look at what's going on in the world half a globe away. Iraq, man. Dropping bombs to keep the price of oil down and their stock options up. I'm telling you, this war, this war isn't over. It's going to rage on and on—it's our generation's Vietnam. How long before we get sent overseas, left in the desert to risk our lives to protect their interests?

This school doesn't foster independent thinking. They choose the curriculum, pick the books, redacted and chockful of revisionist history. Like Mr. Pearce said: you can't sell out if you never buy in. And what did he get for dropping that knowledge? Fired, that's what.

But I'm telling you, man, we've got them scared. We've started a movement! The Pasa Ardo Police Department—the FCC and FBI—are listening in on this right now—hello, you bastards!—they're closing in, trying to identify me. And they will catch me.

Because I'm gonna let them.

Sometimes winning means surrender. We only have a few minutes. Tonight, I'm sorry to say, our time together comes to an end. Right now, the pigs are triangulating this roving signal, ready to slap on the cuffs. Then what? No clue. What's the prison sentence in this country for telling the truth? Ask Leonard Peltier. Ask Mumia Abu Jamal. Ask Brad Pearce.

Brad Pearce was more than a twelfth-grade English teacher. He was an inspiration, the one person who had the balls to rage against the machine, *to tell it like it is and not regurgitate homogenized agendas. Thanksgiving and the Fourth of July are myths. We didn't eat turkey with the Indians. We slaughtered them. This land isn't our land. It's their land. No one told me about Wounded Knee until Mr. Pearce. Fourth of July? More blood and bullshit. When fascism comes, Brad said, it will be wrapped in the flag and carrying a cross. God? The only god they worship is the almighty dollar. Brad didn't lie to us. He talked to us like regular people and not little kids. But he's gone now. This is our fight. We will not sit down. We will not shut up. We will rise up and tell Principal Sheinbaum and the rest of the school board that no, we will not respect their decision to fall in line and salute their flag. They had their time. Now it's ours.*

It's almost midnight. The Feds are en route. This radio broadcast was never about me. It was never about Mr. Pearce. It was about all of us, a unified scene, fighting together.

You hear that, man? The sirens? Right on cue. They got me surrounded. They want me to come out with my hands up. Like a goddamn movie.

I'm pulling over.

It's been an honor to be your captain on this voyage and I am proud to go down with this ship. Let this be our reminder that we can all be something bigger.

Rider out!

THE MORNING OF THE DISAPPEARANCE

Friday, March 15, 1991, 1:12 a.m.

It had been over an hour since the Pasa Ardo PD and Feds arrived in Soledad Gorge, squad cars screeching, followed by several unmarked sedans, men in dark suits and darker sunglasses at night, all to take down ... the Rider. Jess Barrett never got to see who the Rider was, the mystery man behind the garbled, disguised voice, the one who helped start a revolution. The scene pure chaos, everyone running in different directions, screaming, bullhorn blasting, shouting for the riot crowd to disperse, stop where they were. *Every one of you punks is in trouble! You are going to jail!* Yeah, right. Like they were piling a hundred students from the privileged valley into the back of the prison bus. The Class of '91 should've stood their ground, fought back like Rider had rallied them to do, but seeing those flashing blue and red lights was scary. Talking tough is no problem until you're staring down a gun.

Jess had drunk more than she'd intended. She wasn't much of a drinker. Add a few pills... This night was a big deal, a celebration. No, a coming out party. A declaration. A creed.

Hearts were also broken.

Jess had been more optimistic before the fight with Cam. She and Cam never really dated. They'd hooked up a few times. Okay, it was more than that. They had feelings for each other. Strong feelings. She was downplaying their relationship because she didn't want to be the bad guy. She loved him. It's not you, it's me. Empty excuses.

She hadn't been totally blotto, but after their fight, she'd wanted to be numb, obliterated. Mixing meds and hard liquor was never a good idea. Turned out worse than that.

Can you love more than one person? Jess was pretty sure she did. Cam was special. He was also a boy—a cute, interesting boy. That didn't compare to a man. Cam was more mature than any other person her age. Being the chief of police's son—as well as the only black student at Pasa Ardo high—Cam had to deal with shit Jess couldn't imagine. Nothing seemed to rattle Cam. He was smart, strong, self-secure, and now Jess was thinking maybe she'd made the wrong choice. Or maybe she didn't love anyone, and recent decisions had been a chain reaction of chemical interaction, sexual attraction. Longing. Desire. Pure wanton, animalistic lust.

What did it matter now? Neither one was here. She missed him so much. How he smelled. How intelligent and sophisticated he could be. Society said it was wrong. The protest felt like a call to arms, a trial by fire, and she'd been exposed, center stage on the witch's stake. She'd heard the whispers. In the hall. Tonight on the hillside. Saw the greasy smirk Geremia flashed when he palmed her the pills. In a way, she was relieved. She wanted people to know the truth. The weight of secrets drags you down and broken hearts are as heavy as stone.

What had she hoped to accomplish tonight? What had any of them hoped to accomplish? She had time to mull this over now as the sounds of law and chaos faded behind her. Jess walked in the darkness, unsteady on shaky legs, the crunch of dry brush and dead twigs beneath her feet, echoing throughout the valley. The night dipped colder, her skin clammy. She didn't stop running.

Why had she run in the opposite direction from everyone else? Because Jess Barrett always went against the grain. And she always would.

Jess swigged the rest of the bourbon, washing down the remaining pills Geremia had given her. She'd planned on taking one. She ended up taking all four. The slug of bourbon mixed with the meds, and the rush hit her at once. And it was beautiful. She could smell the far-off citrus orchards, the air piquant with spritzed orange and lemons. A kiss of sunshine in the dark valley in the dead of night. The hillsides blazed with yellow mustards and red brome juxtaposed against blacks so black they appeared blue. The shrubs on the prairie. The wild grasses of the valley.

Jess's run slowed to a walk. She walked a long way.

When Jess heard crunching twigs, she thought the cracks came from her steps. Time was playing with her, like a recording on a half-second delay, the opening to a Pink Floyd song. Until she looked down and realized she hadn't moved. Must be a rabbit or other woodland creature. A squirrel skittering around a tree. No, whatever was out there was bigger, heavier, deadlier; a disruption of ground cover unearthed a slinking beast stalking its prey, the movement too methodical. A coyote, bobcat, mountain lion. The valley was filled with terrifying creatures that hunted at night. She waited for yellow eyes piercing the dark, the sharp claws that would tear her limb to limb.

Could she outrun it? Fight it off? Jess was tall but slim. She didn't like her chances against jagged incisors. Through wobbly eyes, Jess scanned the forest floor, trying to focus enough to find a sharp stick. She reached in her pocket, extracted her house keys, slipping metal spikes between her knuckled fist.

Then the sounds stopped. The beast had changed its mind, didn't want the hassle, had retreated.

Or whatever was clocking her had its timing down and was ready to pounce...

Jess spun and locked eyes.

It wasn't a wild animal.

The thing that stared back was far deadlier.

ABOUT THE AUTHOR

Joe Clifford is the author of several acclaimed novels, including *Junkie Love* and the Jay Porter thriller series. He lives in the San Francisco Bay Area with his wife and two sons. Joe's writing can be found at www.joeclifford.com.